❖ ❖ ❖

To Carly, my co-pilot.

❖ ❖ ❖

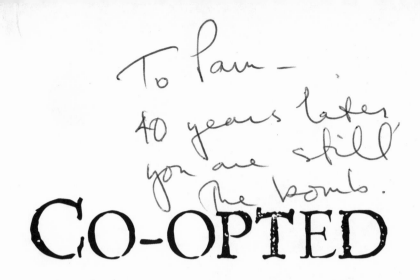

To Pam —
40 years later
you are still
the bomb.

CO-OPTED

A mother and a daughter. All in one.

A Novel by

Joan Bigwood

ISBN: 1-4392-5668-3

ISBN-13: 9781439256688

Chapter 1

*W*henever she takes the train out to Connecticut to see her parents, which isn't all that often, now that she is an established single woman in New York City with adult friends and a mad social life, she says a little prayer that she will meet someone on the train who will change her life forever. It's not that she is suffering, exactly, in the current iteration. Living her life is like reading a new hardback. It is hefty and new, but cumbersome and sometimes quite dull, and she is not even a third of the way through. She expects a lot more is going to happen, but she can hardly imagine what and it drives her crazy. She looks for signs everywhere. Who, or what is important enough to remember for later on? Maybe some chance encounter has already changed the course of her life, and she doesn't yet know it. Maybe she stood back to let an old lady on the train first, or took a seat that someone else was eyeing, and that set off a chain of events that will ultimately lead her to something transformative. Sometimes, just to be sure, she will stand on the platform and let more than their fair share of passengers board the train first, then maybe just a few more, to shake up the fates a bit. When she finally takes her seat, she wants to believe that the very matter that makes up her destiny has been cosmically rearranged and a new chapter is about to begin.

Today, the train leaves Grand Central Station packed with commuters hurtling home for the weekend, crammed in every available seat, balancing laptops, books, flimsy food trays, anything to make the journey go by faster. She is seated next to a window, across from a harried mother and her two young children, the younger of which wriggles perpetually in his mother's lap. His older sister sits in her own seat, eating a bag of popcorn one kernel at a time. Her chubby baby brother keeps reaching for the bag, but she wordlessly body blocks his attempts. Mother looks hot and tired, perhaps a little resentful.

"Sorry if we're a little rambunctious here. He wants to get down. Buddy's very busy," declares the young mother in a tired sing-song as she hoists the fat toddler, and points out the window at the grimy cityscape.

"Say *bye-bye New York!*"

Sister reaches for Buddy's leg and gives it a loud kiss, then goes back to her popcorn.

"Baa baa!" bleats Buddy.

"How old?" she asks, wondering what it must be like to be a mother of two.

"Twenty months."

"I'm four," adds the little girl with the popcorn hulls in her split ends. Buddy arches his back and slides down his mother's knees, nearly touching the floor with his scuffed white shoes. She heaves him up onto her lap again.

"Wow, you sure have your work cut out for you," remarks the twenty-something traveler with nothing more than an aging suitcase in the overhead rack to worry about. She waves tentatively at Buddy, working out how old twenty months is, and wondering what babies can do at that age. Her older sister Pat would know. She was always the babysitter in the family."We went to my Grammy's," announces the four-year old.

"That must have been fun," faking enthusiasm.

"Fun," sighs the exhausted mother, adding "Buddy, don't, dirty," as he reaches for the overflowing little wastebasket under the window.

"We call Daddy's mommy Grammy. Daddy's in Paris France," the little girl chats on. "Mommy's mommy died. We call her Nana."

"I'm sorry," murmurs the traveler.

"Thanks," whispers Mom.

She turns to the window and watches a blur of dark warehouses through the grime. She is ashamed to have it so easy, for she feels so incomplete. Yet this poor woman, strapped with two little kids, her husband away, orphaned, or at least no mom to talk to, back from a long day visiting her mother-in-law with an out-of-control toddler...the loose-limbed traveler seizes up, her eyes bug at her faint reflection in the window, as the drone of the train on tracks pounds in her head. Is THIS is the sign she has been praying for? She has always secretly hoped it would come in the form of a bachelor stockbroker looking for someone to love and spoil...not a strung-out housewife crawling with toddlers. That woman is a billboard come alive: DON'T DO IT. *Marriage is not what little girls imagine when they slip on the make-believe veil and Mommy's high-heeled shoes!* But in the next instant, that sweet little diamond solitaire on her ring finger winks at the young woman like a commercial and she thinks, *love comes at a price,* and *it's no bargain.* But all of this is pure theory because no one has yet to bend a knee in her direction; she doesn't even have a boyfriend. What she has is a ringside seat to the afterparty and it is not pretty. But the diamond is. She goes back to her book while Buddy whimpers on and his sister polishes off her popcorn.

They pull into the station at *NOO* Haven, as the conductor mispronounces it, right on time at 6:32. She bids the drowsy little family of three fare thee well and drags her gimpy luggage down the platform, a college graduation gift on its last legs. Back then, she wanted something bold that announced *here comes Francesca Wilson and she means business*, in a stylish sort of way, hence the hunter green canvas with the pink monogram. This evening, one wheel scrapes and squeals while the other does all the steering down the tunnels to the Sistine interior of the recently renovated, nearly empty main concourse. The rows of cherry sleigh-shaped benches and massive clock three stories up and one story high recall a more bustling era of rail travel. Then, New Haven's Union Station, a formidable brick edifice with its mansard roofing and wall-to-wall windows, was one of the main portals to Yale University. The station went to seed during her childhood, when rail travel went the way of the Greyhound bus. You couldn't even resurrect it in an oil crisis. Back then, she went to New York a couple of times a year with school or family and the station was increasingly dirty and smelly and liberally sprinkled with what were known as bums.

Her father's Subaru idles in the drop-off zone, so as to save her a wobbly walk to the parking lots. He is standing at attention next to the open trunk.

"Are you staying a week?" he groans, as he lifts her bag into the back. Francesca plays along, even though there is nothing outrageous about her weekend's supply of clothing and accessories. She needs a nice outfit for Muth's debut in The Importance of Being Ernest at The Red Barn tonight, which she will re-use on Sunday for church, grubbies to help Dad in the yard tomorrow, pj's and a robe...

"I couldn't decide what to wear!" She says despairingly, almost as fine an actress as her mother, and he chuckles.

"Thanks, Dad."

"Not at all, not at all, not at all." He always says it in threes. School friends thought he was saying *not a tall, not a tall, not a tall,* as in *not a tall order.* That's what it sounds like when he says it. It means you're welcome, in British.

"Come give me a kiss!" It's Muth in the passenger seat. Francesca hadn't seen her there. When they hug, Francesca is treated to a much too loud *MWAAH*, too near her left ear. Ouch.

"So, are you ready for opening night?" Muth is playing Lady Bracknell, a role that neatly draws on her imperious side. Is it type-casting when all you ever play are character parts? Because Muth is certainly a character.

"She has been in the bathroom most of the week," says Dad as they buckle themselves in for the ride to the theater, where Muth has a make-up call.

"I always get the runs before a run." Slick, lighthearted Muth; Francesca knows she is actually overcome with nerves. She was raised in this *primadonna*'s wake, after all. Muth takes her amateur acting career very seriously, always has. It could be because she started out believing she could be a professional, and never quite shook the notion.

"When I heard Vivian Pinkes audition, I knew I had it in the bag—no pun intended! You should have heard her! *A hondbog?*" Of course, it should be *A hendbeg?*" Muth does accents exceptionally well. Her grasp of humility is less certain.

Dad chuckles all the way to the stage door, as Francesca describes the latest triumphs and pratfalls of her job at the magazine where she finally has a smidge of seniority, her zany roommate issues (she lives with a gay man, which is mostly workable, but can get awkward of a Saturday night. She doesn't talk about that part), cockroaches, New York's latest mayor…it's open mic, and she has the stage, but only because Muth is in her pre-performance zone. Quiet, pensive, nervous, she rallies briefly with an old standard:

"How's your love life?"

"Well...I love my friends."

"I love your friends, too. But I don't see why they don't introduce you to more eligible young men. That's how it was always done when I was a gull."

When Muth clambers on her high horse, she sounds like early Katharine Hepburn. She has described time and again the tea dances her mother hosted at the rectory of St. Stephen's Episcopal Church in Madison, Wisconsin. Grandpa, a popular parish priest, lent just the right amount of propriety to attract the crème of bachelor society, but the truth was, dear Muth in her teenage years risked becoming what her faintly Victorian Mother would call "a chubby little petter." It was in those days of dancing close that Muth was in her element, clutching dashing men, many of them soldiers, and playing role upon debutante role in the local theater. But apparently men dance with one kind of woman, and marry another. At 25, Muth was still single, an old maid. Thank God for the letter from the State Department, offering her a clerical position at the US Embassy in Brussels. She barely remembered filling out the application form, but it was as good as a proposal because it meant she could leave town with her head held high, despite the bare fourth finger. And boy, could she type.

Francesca's father was like so much low-hanging fruit when Muth stepped off the S.S. Rotterdam in her cunning tweed suit. A dashing, but "totally unsophisticated" civil engineer, he was working at his first job since returning to Belgium from London, since the sudden evacuation as a teenager to England, on May 10, 1940, when the Germans invaded Belgium, then France. Muth found him within weeks of her arrival and Francesca came along eight years and two other kids later. Girl, boy, girl, stop. They had returned to the States by then. It was surely hard for Dad to leave his beloved hometown for a second time, this time for the American invasion that was his saucy fiancée, and in fact he attempted one final return when the kids were small and he had an opportunity with an international engineering firm. Twelve months into the strangest year of their lives, immersed in French and even some Flemish in school, eating strange foods like sea snails and marzipan, drinking sterilized milk and watching people pee against public buildings on a regular basis, Muth met someone at a cocktail party who offered them a way back home, in the form of another job opportunity for her charming British husband. This time they left Brussels for good. He had so wanted them to love it as he had. But he was destined to leave against his will yet again.

Muth is convinced that if her youngest doesn't find a spouse, she simply won't rest in peace. Francesca is reminded of Dante's Inferno, with souls sorted into levels. A vast expanse of cubic yards is reserved for mothers whose daughters never married. They float around wringing their hands for the rest of eternity. Francesca often wishes someone could have simply arranged a marriage for her. She can make the best of pretty much any situation. But alas, Episcopalians don't go in for arranged marriages. It's pretty much every soul for itself in the Anglican Church, tea dances notwithstanding. It probably has to do with the fact that Henry VIII, the founding father of the Anglican Church, separated from the Roman Catholics because he wanted to divorce Catherine of Aragon. That set the tone for a rather self-serving attitude toward marriage you don't see so much in other religions.

Francesca attempts to steer the talk to safe topics such as work and art exhibits to distract Muth from the mirage of eligible bachelors lining up the length of Madison Avenue to date her daughter. Muth never fully recovered from a virulent case of acne that struck Francesca at puberty. Nineteen year-old Francesca overheard her on the phone with her sister one evening, declaring that Francesca's teenage acne had "ruined a gorgeous face." Apparently, Francesca had been the beauty of the family, cousins included, but at the age of fifteen, her pores revolted and held siege. She still has the identifying scars to prove it.

Francesca does actually have one date coming up, but she doesn't want to tip her hand this early on in the weekend. They still have five more meals to share. She announces instead that a friend has asked her to write some sample articles for a new style magazine he hopes to launch; she has been working in the field for six years now and she is starting to feel she has some talent.

"Is he married?" A standard response.

"No, Mother, not the marrying kind."

"Harumph."

"That should be interesting!" Her father loves to hear about new ventures. He is an entrepreneur with no formal business education, save what he has learned over thirty years of trial and error. There have been more successes than setbacks, but it has nonetheless been a wild ride for Dear Old Dad.

"I don't know how you manage to have time for all that writing and still stay in circulation." This is her parting shot. Francesca doesn't have the energy to defend her passion for things unrelated to marriage. They leave Muth at the curb and head home for a quick supper before show time. On the drive home, she and Dad trade opinions on the marketing opportunities of the new style magazine. Neither of them has any clue what is involved in launching a magazine but they have always shared a blind optimism that all roads lead to limitless possibilities. They carry on the conversation as they put together a cold supper of chicken parts and salad. Then they change and head back downtown.

Growing up, Francesca used to go to Muth's plays with her best friend Terry, but she lives in Grand Rapids now with three children under the age of six. So tonight Francesca will be her dad's date. It's the first date she has had in ages where the guy actually wants to hear what she has to say.

Dad cuts a dashing silhouette in his navy blue suit. His weight hasn't changed since he got out of the army in 1945. Francesca suspects that nothing about Dad has changed much. He is just so... unaltered. Muth, on the other hand, is as changeable as cable TV. But she is a great actress, no denying it. Tonight, she delivers the famous line, "A handbag?" with just the right touch of horror and she gets a standing ovation at the curtain call.

On the ride home, they talk about the other thing they always talk about, each other, or at least those who aren't present. Apparently her brother Henry the dentist is in over his head with the bigger house they recently bought, because his wife Margaret 'fell in love with it.'

"If she loved Henry half as much as the house, she would have stayed in the other one on Edgewood. They were perfectly fine there."

"Henry doesn't do anything he doesn't want to do, Muth."

"He just needs a few more root canals on the calendar!" chips in Dad.

"He needs to stand up to that wife of his."

"As long as you don't."

"I never said a word." Muth is quoting her own mother here, who was unusually meddlesome—unusual, at least, according to Muth. By mocking her mother, Muth steers clear of any similar judgments by her children. Or so she thinks.

Francesca's sister Pat has a prolapsed bladder. She is increasingly incontinent, but refuses to wear anything to catch the slips. She says it would be admitting defeat. Her doctor thinks it's related to a fall from a ladder when she was picking apples in their backyard—very sour apples, she's always bringing everyone bags of them as hostess gifts and they end up getting tossed out—when she tweaked her back. 36 years old and she already needs adult diapers? Francesca wouldn't want to give in either.

"I told her just to invest in some of those heavy flow pads." Even Dad doesn't have a cheery quip.

Chapter 2

S ome people get bouquets of flowers after a performance but Muth gets something better: news of Francesca's lunch date with Steve Mackris, a media buyer from a Madison Avenue advertising agency. It's 10 a.m. as the Wilsons breakfast around the Swedish table with its folding mechanism that adds the equivalent of two leaves with a flick of a lever. Dad imported these for a couple of years, before China started making them much cheaper and no one stayed married long enough to wear them out. With the leaves tucked away, Francesca sits very near her parents. It is warm in the breakfast nook. When Steve Mackris comes up, Muth visibly brightens. For a devout Christian, she is surprisingly superstitious. She tries halfheartedly to paint a bleak picture.

"He probably drinks too much. Don't those advertising executives all have three martini lunches?"

"Muth, that was thirty years ago. No one drinks at lunch."

"Well, if he offers you a drink, don't accept. Women who drink at lunch are considered loose."

"Or at least they will be after three martinis!" adds Dad.

"Anyway, it's just a lunch date, guys. He's probably not my type, anyway. They never are."

"Darling, life is not a buffet where we slide our tray along only taking what we like, or what we think we want."

Muth's similes can be downright ridiculous. Francesca can't wait to see where this one is headed.

"It's more like a sit-down feast, where you must eat what has been prepared, beautifully prepared, and you must try everything because that is the polite thing to do...and you may find you like—"

"Could someone pass me the marmalade?" Dad is not swept away.

"We make an impression whether we intend to or not, with every breath we take." Muth's accent has gone all Hepburn again.

Toward eleven, they clear the breakfast dishes and Dad and Francesca head out to the yard.

He is as at home in his garden as the plants and shrubs. His ancient gardening hat, frayed around the brim and stained permanently around the crown, his "wellies" that come up just below his bony knees, the slight incline of his otherwise ramrod straight back, they are so much a part of the scenery that he ought to have his own Latin name. *Pater Familiaris.*

"What's this stuff again?" Francesca points to the ground cover that blooms in three different shades. Edged in a tangerine color, it fades to pink, then darkens to a maroon at the center.

"That's portulacas. It's a marvelous succulent. They don't come any heartier. They'll survive all weathers." Just like their keeper. He goes back to his weeding with a wince as he bends to the task.

After a couple of hours of pinching innocuous green shoots from God's good earth, mostly for the pleasure of communing with her old man, Francesca stretches, feeling the ache of middle age whispering to her from across the decades. She is ready to transition to a more sedentary afternoon and calls out to her father who is fiddling with his favorite lawnmower.

"Dad?"

"Hmmmm?"

"Wanna grilled cheese?"

"Oh, I wouldn't say no." He always says that. "But what I really need is a flanged bearing to get this old war horse moving again."

"Oh." She pauses, for effect, heading at hom with comedic purpose. "Well, I might have just what you need. Let me get my bearings!" Reaching in her pocket, she waits for his laugh, but then remembers this is Dad. He is not quite as quick as the rest of the family.

"Not to worry! I'll make a trip to the hardware store." He straightens up at half the speed of yesteryear and she instinctively grabs him for the last little bit of effort. She notices he accepts her help.

"What we need is some lemonade." He always says that at the end of a hot day of work in the garden. Inside, they peel open a frozen can of his finest pink and add a little less water than is called for, then lots of ice. They stand in the kitchen waiting for their sandwich cheese to melt and drain two tall glasses each. His drink reappears in rivulets of sweat down his neck, which he mops up with his ubiquitous monogrammed handkerchief. He has four unopened packs in his underwear drawer, and eight in constant use.

She takes a hot bath while he drops Muth off at the theater for back-to-back performances. Saturday night dinner is leftovers, then a few rounds of Declaration, a simple bidding card game. During a ginger ale and popcorn break, she sighs audibly.

"What's that about?"

"What's what?"

"That world-weary sigh. You could hear it in the next county."

"Me? Oh, I dunno."

"You sound a mite burdened, dear girl."

"Aw, no…I mean, not really burdened. I guess sometimes I just wish something would happen to me." This is a true enough statement, though she has never actually expressed it out loud, and now she is not at all sure what she means.

"Things are happening to you all the time!"

"Something big, I mean." That's what she means.

"I think you'll find that big things are not always all they're cracked up to be!"

"Nothing ever happens." Pouting.

"What about the new magazine?"

"It's not a definite."

"Very little is definite, my love. You'll see. When things start happening, as you put it, you will be good and ready. But I don't suppose that helps."

"No, not really." The popcorn stops popping and starts burning. She lunges for the microwave before the carbon spreads. Dad puts the "ginger pop" back in the fridge and carries their clinking glasses into the living room, calling over his shoulder:

"There! Something's happened now. The popcorn's burned!" They resume their card game and Francesca forgets all about the hole in her life she longs to fill. When her father heads out to get Muth, she goes off to bed. Snuggled in the single sheet set under the eiderdown she has had since childhood, she is drowsy and content. There is no room in here for anyone else. It suits her tonight.

When she leaves on Sunday, Muth is in front of the TV, watching Joan Fontaine in *Rebecca* to help her "get in character." Dad takes the suitcase to the car while Francesca says good-bye. Muth hugs her from a seated position, employing her very loudest *MWAAAH* to compensate for not getting up. She nearly bursts her daughter's eardrum.

"You were amazing, Muth."

"Kind of you to say!" she flirts, ever the coquette.

Her mother is so charming, but charm is only inviting when the door is open, and with Francesca's mother, the door, with its faded star, is firmly shut for now. She must rest for her next performance.

"Talk to strangers!" she screams down the stairs as Francesca disappears.

Chapter 3

*M*onday morning. A restless creature stirs awake deep inside, a yearning that cries to be fed. It's her biological clock again. She had rather hoped that her encounter with the over-burdened mother on the train would have yanked that clock's cord right out of the uterine wall once and for all, but apparently it's a portable clock. When at last she uncoils herself, and her room-mate Paul has cleared out of the teeny bathroom with the murky fish tank and the radio that starts up with the light switch, she stares at the self-conscious young woman that she must once again doll up and bring to work. The too-large earlobes frame a hope-ful face, one she back-lights as often as possible to downplay the ruts and crevices left over from her adolescence. Her forehead and the hollows of her cheeks were once crowded with acne. Like so many border refugees, these raw, angry sores multiplied on the fringe. No one invited them, no one wanted them there, yet they wouldn't leave, for they had nowhere else to go, except to her back, where there grew another settlement across her shoulders. Those refugees left their footprints behind when they finally moved on sometime after her twentieth birthday. She practices flashing her green eyes, to keep people from noticing the pockmarks. People like Steve Mackris, her lunch date.

Francesca met Steve at a launch for a new perfume from Maison de Roquemaurel, his client. He is tall, and at this point, that is enough. When he asked for her email address, she assumed it was to send her press releases, to get free publicity. When the email arrived asking her to lunch, she was still under the impression that this liaison was strictly business-related. But when the electronic bouquet arrived, with the petals spelling out Have a Nice Day, she finally got a clue. Still, she is glad they are only having lunch, in case they have absolutely nothing in common. So far, they have ascertained that they both have dealings with a certain M. Vin, the investor relations man at de Roque, and neither of them can stand him. Steve laughed hard when Francesca quipped,

"Just because Monsieur Vin wears a de Roquemaurel necktie doesn't make him the owner of anything more than the tie." The old girl still has a few laps left in her.

Lunch is at a corner bistro near her building. That was very thoughtful of Steve. He gets another point in the yes column. Steve appears passionate about his work, which is refreshing, considering Francesca just saw a headline stating *Americans Hate Their Jobs More Than Ever*, so he gets another point in the yes column, right? Not exactly. It turns out he talks of nothing else.

"I mean, the way people go on about their pass-along readership, you'd think no one actually buys their periodicals!" The pass-along readership is the number of hands that actually touch an issue, once the original owner is through with it. The pass-along readership of *Twenty-one* magazine is not all that high, because young women who read *Twenty-one* want their very own copy so they can fill out the self-discovery quizzes in private, adjusting their answers for better scores.

"Do you have any idea what the pass-along readership is of say, a *People*?" He keeps putting the article in front of magazine titles. She could never marry this guy.

"It's probably pretty high, since *People* is in every waiting room in Manhattan."

"Just guess."

She hates guessing on demand. You never know whether the person wants you to guess right, or wrong. She figures this guy probably wants her to be wrong, but to make a very good guess. She pauses, acting like she is doing some kind of algorithm in her head.

"Seventeen?"

"Ha! Are you serious? A *Fish and Game,* or a *Golf Today* would be seventeen! Try fifty-three!"

"You're kidding!!" She gushes. *Are you for real?*

Steve spends the next hour talking about the media plan for Maison de Roquemaurel. He tells Francesca tales of TV spots that fell through due to bidding wars, a double page spread that was placed in the center of the biggest issue of *Cosmo*, so that the magazine literally fell open to it.

"An incredible piece of luck. I have to admit, I kind of suggested to my boss that I had fought hard for it. Don't tell anyone." He winks exaggeratedly. She gives him the OK sign and whispers,

"I'll go to my grave." Sooner than she ever thought.

"Oh, and Francesca?" he brushes her hand with his knuckles, which are hairy. "If you have any say at all about ad placement..."

"I really don't."

He nods mock seriously, and winks again.

"Well if you DID, we love the table of contents. Who doesn't?" he adds, waggishly.

"Agony." She says when Muth asks about her "hot date."

"So I take it you're still not betrothed? Just kidding!" trills Muth.

Bring on Girlsday, is all Francesca has to say. That's the day of the week that falls between Fried Day and Someday. It is the best day of the week.

Chapter 4

*W*hen Francesca started as a summer intern at *Twenty-one*, she was still healing from her adolescence. Her face still smarted, but at least it wasn't in a constant state of near eruption. She felt sure she was hired to help make up the ugly quotient; the majority of the girls around her were in the prime of loveliness—blooming cheeks, dewy skin, glossy hair. She has always been above average from the neck down, and that does tend to compensate. But such a painful face. Her job in the early days was conducted primarily over the phone, and later, via fax and email. She struck up lots of chummy relationships that never required meeting face-to-face, and that pulled her through.

Once she had spent some time on photo shoots, however, she started to see how the professionals work with raw material, and she came to understand that it's the body that you need to have right. Bones and balance are what is required. The rest can be achieved with make-up and lighting. Francesca had been an athlete all the way through college. She never saw its application in the mating game before, except maybe for a tennis date with someone's fixer upper. She took mental notes on make-up application at every opportunity. If applied correctly, you actually can use a trowel to cover up imperfections. She mastered the art of facial decoupage and the results were promising.

Next, she hit the bars, the clubs, the lounges, you name it. She danced and kissed and rolled around with anybody who looked her way. Thank God she always packed condoms; these were the eighties and a friend of her parents had already died of fast living by the time Francesca was taking all comers. The last time she saw him was when he came through New York and her parents came down from Connecticut and they all had lunch together. His face was dotted with dime-sized black scabs and none of them knew what was wrong with him, though he did. They only found out from the gay guests at his memorial service that he had died of complications from AIDS. Francesca never forgot those scabs and she never went out without a few condoms in her purse again.

But all those mornings waking up with smelly, hairy strangers, in someone else's ghastly little hovel, with no clean underwear, is enough to make you want your acne back. She was headed straight for a breakdown of some kind, when Mac cornered her one afternoon in the ladies' room at work.

"Hey, Francesca, if you don't have plans, Lisa P. and I are going to raise a little hell tonight at Wham Bam. Wanna come along?" It felt so good to be asked to do something that was not an indirect pitch for another roll in the hay, and she rose to the occasion.

"Lemme check my calendar." She didn't yet know a good thing when she met one in the restroom.

Well it turned out she was free, and she kept being free, and then she was pretty much booked solid, all of it with Mac and Lee. They made her feel sane again. Partly because Mac in particular is such a lunatic, and partly because Francesca stopped giving away huge chunks of herself every time she stepped out on the town, this is when the real healing began.

They worked all over the building, an old warehouse with lots of cool loft spaces. Before the company introduced universal loft décor, when the lofts were theirs to design and drape, Rose Remendelli (that would be Mac, before she married Hugh McEntee), of Montclair, New Jersey, was a cut above. Her homemade mobiles were extraordinary feats of engineering and political moxy. The company finally had to intervene when her chef d'oeuvre, a collection of dolls' heads smeared in garish make-up hanging from tiny dog leashes caught the attention of the preppy fashion editor, Liz Whittle. Either the mobiles came down or Ms. Remendelli packed her things, was the subtle message the all-staff memo conveyed about disruptive loft decorations. Up came the spider plants and Laura Ashley prints and down came Mac's morale, until she began planning her wedding to Hugh, a flight attendant whom everyone assumes is gay, and became the sophisticated newlywed Rose McEntee, and she put down her whimsical form of agitprop once and for all. Hugh is a metrosexual. A decade ago, he would have been just another flamer marrying for convenience. But today he is an icon of the personal as political and he wears his flamboyance proudly. He likes to keep himself bronzed and bulked, plus he highlights his hair, so women passengers admire him, but are little threat to his wife. Flights to San Francisco can get tricky, but he handles any advances with good grace. Mac and Hugh have been together since college, and they have a very deep friendship. They sound like collaborators when they're together. Lots of word play, punch lines, nudges and winks. Mac is a creative genius. She can write, paint, draw, sew, sing, dance, act, and even play the banjo. It's just hard for her to start and finish any of her projects. Hugh just applauds madly from the sidelines whatever she does and that is why they go together so well. Maybe he is gay, who knows.

Lisa Poehailos is the last gorgeous single woman in New York. Lee is a pouty-lipped C-cup and those parts are original. With her copper-colored hair, her round, high rump, Lee is a walking, talking freak of nature. She is a stunning dresser on a limited budget (she gets the majority of her wardrobe 70 percent off). She is part Lithuanian and part cowgirl. Her mother was Homecoming Queen at South High, in Boise, Idaho. At a banquet at the mayor's house in 1965, Lisa's mother, a bright-eyed teen beauty, was serving hors d'oeuvres for extra pocket money. She passed a date rolled in bacon to Prince Darius, a direct descendant of the ancient kings of the Kingdom of Lithuania. He was accompanying his father, Darius the twelfth, on a speaking tour. The date wrapped in bacon reminded Darius XIII of the orchards in the walled garden of his father's ancestral home, and within a year he had courted and married the serving wench, producing their only child, Lisa.

If there really are multiple intelligences, then there ought to be a special category called "Lisa smart." Lisa smart is when you are highly organized, and always ready for anything, except love. Lee could have been married six times over already but she is waiting for that special someone who will take her to a different astral plane. When you are as ravishing as Lee is, you scare off most of your best prospects and instead you attract a lot of presumptuous losers. Men who are attracted to Lee tend to be shallow solipsists.

But the ones who get away don't realize that Lee is even more beautiful on the inside. Maybe it has to do with the fact that she was sexually abused for two years by a cousin who lived with her family when she was growing up in Boise. Mac and Franny are the only people in the whole world who know about it and they haven't told anyone which is certainly one of Mac's greatest achievements. Lee just wants to forget about it, yet it comes up every time they tie one on at the One-Eyed Jack, which they frequent regularly for drinks and onion rings, and inevitably they get waterworks from Lee. *In vino lacrimae.* She simply can't let herself forget. And without a nice rich husband to supplement her journalists' salary, there won't be any intensive therapy forthcoming, so for now she just keeps a lid on the whole mess and this lends her an air of standoffishness, which isn't a bad thing, given her looks and vulnerabilities. She still sees the cousin occasionally at family reunions and the only thing that brings her any closure is that he has lost all of his hair and a couple of rotten teeth and he looks like the bum she knows him to be.

As PAs for senior editors, they got to try their hands at copy-editing. Months would go by before they'd see an information box they'd authored, untouched by anyone but the managing editor. Their efforts were painstakingly paying off. *You can't rush genius* they used to say, roaring at their humorous take on a collectively feeble career trajectory in magazine journalism.

The stock market crash of '87 took the wind out of everyone's sails, but at least the three of them kept their jobs. People assume women's magazines are something of a luxury item, and when the economy tanks, sales should follow. But it's not the case at all. When the economy tanks, there is nothing a woman wants more than to spend most of five bucks on a one-way ticket to that far-away land Mac calls *Femalia*, *The Land of Random Tips*. It is a journey of self-discovery, and all of it in a horizontal position, in your fat jeans. Just add ice cream from the carton.

A few years later, as they approach thirty, they have attained some seniority but they don't know what it's like to be twenty-one anymore. In fact, they're clinging to the last little bit of their twenties like Titanic survivors.

They call themselves The Three Graces. These are *Joy, Beauty* and *Charm*. Lee is *Beauty*, that goes without saying, Mac is *Joy* (the other two wonder if she isn't undiagnosed manic, but she's a helluva lot of fun, especially after a couple of fingers of Tanqueray—never mind a whole hand), and that makes Franny *Charm*, which fits. For the most part, she gets what she needs in life by making people want to give it to her, whether it's a promotion or "just a warning" from a traffic cop. This makes her sound like a guileful shrew, but the fact is she is positively allergic to confrontation. In her first loud argument with a grade- school classmate in the girls' bathroom, she literally developed hives. The whole thing stressed her out so much the hives developed into shingles, and she has avoided confrontation ever since. Mac and Lee say she is extremely passive aggressive (they hear of things she has done to men and colleagues or both, who have wronged her) but she just answers that she is a Taoist, which is stretching the truth enormously. She doesn't know much of anything about Taoism, except that the *Tao is the Way*, likened to a river, and she tends to float along as best she can without getting snagged on any rocks.

It is Girlsday night at the 92nd Street Y. The Three Graces are listening to the feminist poet Liz O'Claire shout out a poem about female circumcision. It is a stirring piece, weaving imagery of the African landscape with a sensual, florid description of the female anatomy. But it is the sixth poet tonight and The Three Graces are getting restless. This could explain why, when Ms. O'Claire starts ululating and gyrating on the stage, Mac snorts with laughter. When Mac snorts, Franny is in trouble, because it means Mac has lost control and she is next. Mac is shaking like a bobblehead and Franny starts heaving silently in her chair. Lee shoots them a look, *cut it out you two* and Mac tries to pull herself together but she snorts again, a really long one. This gets Lee going and now all three of them are bent over double, shaking uncontrollably. Liz O'Claire slows her monologue down to a low, bass moan, and begins thumping on an African drum, rolling her eyes back into her head. Fran has attempted to straighten up for appearance sake, but Ms. O'Claire's eyes make her start up again. People are starting to notice this private little commotion. Then Mac snorts again and that makes her whoop. Franny looks like she has been stabbed. Lee gets up, and takes Mac's hand, Mac who is crying, she is laughing so hard. Franny pretends she is not with them. She turns toward the other aisle and cakewalks out of their row, ready to burst.

They meet up outside, in the muggy night air. Mac ululates, Lee gyrates and Franny chimes in with some extemporaneous feminist verse:

You are the patriarch of a house of cards
Yet one whisper of dissent will tumble your castle keep
Mr. Man with your flashing blade and
Your traditions
I am the black queen

"I need a martoony!" yells Mac.
"Me toony!" Lee echoes.

We'll soak our souls in gin
Mr. Man
To numb the pain of your slicing blade
Your ancient rituals

"Gee, Franny, that's terrible!" says Mac.
"Thanks, I wrote it myself!"
"I think she's a genius," says Lee, hooking arms with the poet.
"I think you're a genius, too, Lee." They start doing the Yellowbrick Road dance down the sidewalk.
"Wait for me!" cries Mac.

"Nope, only misunderstood geniuses allowed!" Francesca yells over her shoulder.

"<u>I'm</u> misunderstood!"

And it's true, she is. Mac takes Franny's other arm and they continue on their way.

"We're off to drink martoonies! Martoonies with gin and vermouth!" booms Mac.

They settle in at the Jack for drinks and fat grams. Lee pulls the onions out of their casings and eats them like worms, straight down her throat. Mac eats the casings.

"Lee, I know why you only eat the onions."

"Shut up Mac." Mac turns to Franny, engaging her.

"She eats them to make herself poop." Franny doesn't encourage her, but covers her smile with a salty margarita glass.

Lee sticks her tongue out at Mac and throws an onion at her, which catches on the rim of Mac's drink.

"Waiter, there's an onion ring doing the backstroke in my drink!" cries Mac. "It's the onion diet!" she adds, returning to her previous point.

"When is Hugh going to send you to obedience school?"

"We should share it with our readers. Onions and tic-tacs."

"She is so obnoxious after she's had eight drinks."

"Four. Five, if you count the one I am about to *dwink*."

Then Lee farts audibly, which to many would be like seeing a statue of the Madonna shed real tears, but to the Two remaining Graces, it is a pretty regular occurrence at the Jack.

"I rest my case!" crows Mac.

These days, Mac is contributing to cosmetics and spa, Lee does surveys and research and Franny cranks out East Coast perspectives in all kinds of features. But that's not all they do. They define themselves more by their sidelines: a common practice in young

New York. Mac is writing a musical comedy about a hat shoppe in London where the hats sing and dance. Lee is writing a romance novel that she describes as totally formulaic, but you know she longs to live and breathe every word of it. Franny has been working on a screenplay about a young out-of-work actress who pretends to be a clothing designer on a dare and ends up getting her own line with a major house. She has taken a couple of screenwriting classes and dated a very arrogant interior designer of hot, new restaurants on both coasts (he is how she got the idea) but it still needs a lot of work. And she has other, more pressing business.

Muth will not let Francesca forget for a moment that she is not a little behind in the matrimarathon. She doesn't have much in the pipeline—not that she has circulation problems; there are launch parties for every imaginable product and service, and she has invitations to all of them. It's just that you don't tend to meet eligible men at these things, or they are few and far between, and at least fifty percent of them are out of the running. The remaining are dating or married, or, if the planets are aligned just so, *in between* relationships. It is easy to spot the straight men—they usually have a shiny cluster of women barnacled to them. Beautiful, very young women. Often the women are models. The few times Francesca gets her licks in, they have a little repartee, maybe trade a winning smile or a lingering glance...but since her unofficial vow of celibacy, no real follow-up.

Muth keeps a dog-eared photo in her wallet of herself on her wedding day, flanked by eight bridesmaids swathed in floor-length satin. Her groom is conspicuously absent from the grouping, because this photo was the best of the bunch, catching as it does an ephemeral radiance to Muth's ecstatic expression, her collarbones cupping just the right amount of shadow. Tucked in with dated school photos of her children, and a frayed head and shoulders shot of a much younger husband, this photo of Muth as major-general of a troop of willowy lieutenants has been pulled out over the years, in lines at the grocery store, the post office, and airports, serving as a constant reminder to her youngest daughter that she is falling short of her matriotic duty.

Chapter 5

*O*ver the next few weeks, Francesca has on her personal social calendar two wedding showers, three baby showers and a volleyball tournament with a lesbian friend she knows from improv class. The class is supposed to help Francesca prepare for the unexpected, but five showers and a gay volleyball tournament is sadly not all that unexpected these days. Her clock ticks on.

The volleyball tournament is at NYU; a round-robin, elimination tournament in which she expects to play for a fraction of the morning before she makes her team lose. She has never been good at volleyball because it hurts her hands so much. Wrists, knuckles, fingertips, knees, it hurts!

At the gym, she meets her friend Rachel, who steers her to the organizer where she is assigned to a team, though not with Rachel. Together, they find her court, high-five, and Rachel jogs off. Francesca has that first-day-of-camp frozen smile and clammy palms. She introduces herself to her four teammates and promptly forgets all of their names. Her heart is racing and they haven't even started warming up.

There are two men on the team, both tall enough, and neither seems to be gay, or at least they play volleyball as if they aren't, yelling at their teammates and grunting on every play. The two women are definitely gay. They play more like the men than the men. Then along comes another guy, and he stands on the sidelines. Francesca assumes he is someone's boyfriend, lover, whatever, come to watch. He is too cute to be single, or straight. It turns out he is just late, and needs a spot. One of the men offers him his place, so disgusted is he with the level of play. They are pretty spotty, mostly because of Francesca who has perfected the flinch and cower. For once being a crappy player has paid off.

"Hi everybody! I'm Alec!"

Alec is not ostensibly gay. He is a little too disheveled to be gay, his shorts and top don't go, and he doesn't seem at all interested in the young lads parading around the place in too-short shorts and stiffened hair-dos. No ring. No earrings. Yet he is not all that aware of the women either, except as teammates and opponents. He's somehow too forgiving for a straight man. Then he takes off his shirt. He doesn't have any fat on any part of his torso, better to view his long obliques and the subtle rise of his pecs. He has that naturally born insouciant physicality that makes you want to walk right up to him, grab him by the gym shorts and drag him over to the gymnastics mats in the corner for a make-out session. Alec is simply too good to be true. Fit, agile, with plenty of auburn hair, though not too much of it on his chest (Francesca hadn't realized how much she likes auburn chest hair, and not too much of it), tall but not too tall, that warm smile...

He is very focused. He has a way of taking charge of the team, without yelling, except encouragement, at any of his teammates. Before too long, Francesca is one smitten teammate. By the third game, her wrists are red and raw, but she will play until the last whistle to be on the same half court with this gentle man. He reminds her of someone she can't put her finger on. Could it be someone she has dreamed about? She often plays steamy love scenes in her sleep with faceless Casanovas, waking up with a longing in her heart that could sell platinum. But Alec...he is <u>too</u> familiar. Then it hits her.

That three-letter word that begins and ends with D. This must have been what Dad was like in 1952 when Muth found him. Pleasant to look at, pleasant to be with, pleasant enough to take home for dinner and later, to wed. Sighting a single man in Manhattan in the 1990's with even a passing resemblance to her dear, unassuming British father is like finding an endangered Amazonian butterfly in a subway car. She realizes then and there that Alec with the dark blue gym shorts and the forest green t-shirt is her destiny. She is also struck by another, all-too familiar feeling. Struck down, might be more descriptive. It's the same feeling that makes her sigh audibly and unknowingly, the same sensation in her gut that makes getting up some mornings such an act of faith. It is the overwhelming sense that she is not at all in control of her destiny. It's the deep intake of breath that comes before you blow out the candles, wishing mightily for something you barely have time to articulate before the wish is over.

But this time is different. The wish has taken shape, torn off its shirt, and stands within an arm's length of her. It glistens with sweat and pulses with youthful vitality. It is messy and smelly and beautiful. Never before has she felt so sure that this is what Muth has been so desperately wanting for her. Like a savant doing a calendar calculation, she can see in her mind's eye with great clarity Alec in a tux standing next to her in a perfect portrait of their entire wedding party, then throwing her baby in the air on a cool spring morning, and draping his arm around her at the beach at sunset. And she understands, for what may be the first time, that you cannot wait for great things to happen. You must make them happen. Just then, a ball that Alec has set spins across her field of vision, virtually dangling three feet above her. As she throws back her head, she springs off the balls of her feet, and swings her right arm in a perfect arc to execute a flawless spike that lands squarely in her opponent's right eye socket. They win the point, the poor guy with the eye injury has to step off the court for a minute, and while she rushes off to find him an ice pack, she is flushed with glory, with a sense of purpose that she has never known.

The change is not momentary. She could not shake off the mantle of responsibility she now wears, even if she wanted to. Her mission is clear. She has only a few hours to coax this rare specimen into her net. Like a skilled entomologist, she must tread oh-so-lightly.

With her newfound intention, Francesca recruits a group of players to head out for pizza, and sweeps Alec along. When he emerges from the changing room, he is in blue jeans and a T-shirt with a large diagram of a fly's eye on it. She can't hold this against him, since his day began trotting into a gym for a volleyball tournament, but it does cross her mind that he might never have graduated from college, that he works in a movie house tearing tickets.

She grabs the seat next to Alec in the overcrowded pizza restaurant with the battle scarred booths of solid oak. For the next thirty minutes, while the pizzas are being prepared, they talk. And talk. She can't seem to stop talking.

"Your job sounds like a lot more fun than mine!" he says self-deprecatingly. It turns out he doesn't work in a box office at all. He is an investment banker. And such a sweet, unassuming banker with beautiful brown eyes and the most beguiling grin. She feels like a celebrity sitting next to the oversized fly eye. By the time she staggers out of the cab and up to her apartment at three in the morning the next day (she corralled a smaller group, Alec included, to go dancing in one of the black-box clubs in Greenwich Village), she does not even have Alec's phone number, nor he, hers. But she feels she might have succeeded in intriguing him. At one point, he asked her what her lineage was. She sort of tossed off the part about being descended from one of the mistresses of Mad King George. It's not every day you meet a descendant of the House of Hanover playing volleyball. He seemed impressed when she mentioned that George had been baptized on the 4th of July in 1738, and how ironic that that date would become significant later, during his reign. As a magazine journalist, she trades in obscure facts. Men love obscure facts, though most prefer to be the one spouting them. Alec is different. He has a way of looking at you while you talk that suggests he would be quite content to listen for a long time. Either that, or he is a very skilled daydreamer.

Much of Sunday is spent in a feverish haze. Francesca thinks back to that marathon conversation with Alec in the pizza parlor and methodically combs through the tangles of her Cosmo-infused memory to recall any clues that might help her plan her next move. She cannot, must not call him, even though she knows exactly where he works and what department he is in. It would be a simple matter of cooking up some excuse about needing to make up a team for a thing in the park...but then she would have to coordinate a thing in the park...and besides, whoever said he was looking to date a cruise director? She needs to get very sneaky. At around four in the afternoon, a fact filters up through the ether that will ultimately launch her assault.

They had both encountered a cocktail years before at a well-known eatery in New Haven; *Daddy I Don't Want to Drink This* combined orange juice, champagne, cointreau, and vermouth. He said he'd had the same drink, a direct rip-off, called a *Five Car Pile-Up* at a cocktail bar on 50-somethingth. He said he didn't normally drink cocktails, but his buddy owns the bar, and a group of guys usually go there before dinner on Fridays. You don't say "a group of guys" if you're gay. You say "some friends." And she is sure he said Fridays with an s. That makes it a standing date. A pattern of behavior. This isn't going to be so hard after all. Conjuring up her newfound chutzpah, she figures it's only stalking if you do it more than once. She has one shot.

At work, she lets her fingers do the walking through the yellow pages until she finds a couple of likely bars in the 50s that might sell fancy drinks. She makes a few personal calls asking after *Five Car Pile-Ups*. She might make it sound a teensy bit like she is doing research for an article, because one owner starts reciting his drinks menu and then moves on to opening hours before she can shut him down. Another bartender is obviously lonely at that time of day, suggesting she might like the *Sloe Gin Screw with Cream*.

She takes the long way home everyday that week, trawling for cocktail bars in the 50's. On Thursday evening, after work and before aerobics class, she winds up in front of an upscale fire-grilled burger place called the Pie Hole, with a packed bar adjacent. She chooses the restaurant entrance and appears to breeze in. She might be giving off the slightest impression of being a food editor. Minutes later, she is staring at a description of the *Five Car Pile-Up* with its splash of grenadine.

She calls Mac and Lee who are up for anything. Girlsday is never the same day of the week but they have to make a major adjustment to their lack of routine if she is ever going to dig herself out of her rut of passivity. For the next four Fridays, they will stake out the Pie Hole for signs of her *objet de désir*. As it turns out, they don't need the remaining three weeks, which again indicates to her that this relationship was destined from the start.

The next night, they walk into the restaurant entrance, and a cocktail waitress who has wandered out of her territory takes their order.

"I'll have the Five-Car-Pile-Up," announces Franny, the way a private eye might announce a solved case. Mac orders a G&T and Lee orders sparkling water. She is on a water and cabbage diet to give her skin a youthful glow. She got the idea from the nutrition editor at the magazine.

Mac has dressed incognito, for laughs. She looks frightful in her push-up bra and bustier, teamed with a satin mini skirt. Lee is perfect in a black crepe blouse over a lacy camisole and velvet leggings. Francesca wears a brick red dress and matching suede shoes, which demand attention while she tries to remain demure. They move around the establishment as one. She leads them from the restaurant into the bar, expertly navigating the imperceptible movements of the herd. Twenty minutes later, she is staring at the backside of Alec. From the many hours she spent crouched by him on the volleyball court the previous Sunday, she recognizes the jut of his hip and his thumbnail, planted near the small of his back. In his stiff cotton dress shirt, his broad shoulders fan out before her.

The idea is to melt into the background, track their plans to leave, then ambush them outside. She sends out an advance party.

"You go flirt. Just leave the tall guy alone," she instructs Lee.

"Got it," Lee says, eyeing his thick-haired friend.

"Find out their plans, then meet us out front. I might have to cut you loose after that."

"I wanna be cut loose!" shouts Mac, who is very much married but likes some fun. With Hugh traveling a lot, he is grateful for Girlsday because they keep Mac out of trouble.

"No, I'll need you when we go in for the kill. We can all hook up later." They head outside. On the way, Mac grabs a to-go cup from behind the bar, near the olives, onions and cherries. She dumps her second glass of wine in the cup and leaves a dollar under the empty glass. Francesca hasn't dared order another drink for fear of losing her composure outside, but she loses it nevertheless, laughing so hard with Mac she nearly wets herself. Mac is very funny when she pretends to talk to people who aren't there. Mac takes all the parts and it gets quite out of hand. It is a balmy August night and they couldn't be in a better mood. When Lee finally emerges from the bar, Mac is being Franny, talking to Alec. "Franny" is measuring his large frontal lobe and quizzing him with trivia questions.

"They're leaving <u>now</u>!" Lee hisses and darts for the restaurant entrance. They had hoped for a little more warning, but at least all the laughing has warmed Franny up for the next phase of operation.

"Run!" She grabs Mac by the purse and they both take off at a gallop. If Alec were to have come out a moment sooner, it would look like he had just interrupted a purse-snatching. They run down East 56th Street on their tough little high-heeled shoes, stopping once in a doorway to check their position. Thanks to Lee, they have put enough distance between them to circle back nonchalantly and stroll toward their target. Lee will be decorated for this. Unfortunately, she can never meet Alec, or he'll know he was set up.

They walk unnaturally slowly toward the group of guys who are gathering themselves together, and while one of their party looks for a cab, the others jape and jive. Alec stands somewhat apart, stretching his long spine. Franny is still trying to regulate her breathing as they draw nearer. The guy on the curb tenses, as if he has spotted a cab. Fran has to think fast.

"Mac, hail that cab!" she murmurs, then shoves her cohort toward the street. Mac whirls around and sticks out her hand.

"Hey," shouts Alec's friend. "We had that!"

The cab slides up to the curb, passes the women, and like a well-trained dog, stops in front of the restaurant. Franny had hoped for more of a confrontation, but clearly fate has played a different card. The men will all climb into the cab and leave the Three Graces in their dust. Just then, Alec strides up to his friend and has a quick word with him.

"It's OK, you take it!" he calls out to the girls, who are now close enough to be illuminated by the street lighting outside the restaurant.

"Thanks so much!" Franny calls out cheerily.

"Francesca?" Alec looks suitably surprised. And he remembers her name!

"Ummm…hi!" she says, feigning confusion, her head cocked to one side, revealing her good side. Back-lit, of course.

"It's Alec, from volleyball." He looks genuinely pleased to see her.

"Alec, hi! Sorry about the cab. You guys take it, honestly. We're still trying to decide on dinner."

"Yeah," says Mac helpfully.

Just then, in a fit of pique, the cabby drives off.

"Oops," squeaks Mac.

"You should join us!" offers Alec. We're going for Shabu-Shabu at Yukari."

"Sure!" pipes up Mac.

At that moment, which she will savor for the next six months, knowing as she does with every fiber that Alec wants HER to have Shabu–Shabu with him, that her plan has worked, that the ocean liner of love can safely leave port because she has made the sailing, and Muth can wave tearfully from the dock, just then, the door of the bar swings open and out flies Lee. She sees Franny before she notices the group of guys standing just past her line of sight, and is about to say what she later explains was going to be "Did you catch them?" when Mac cries out:

"Lisa, is that you?" That is when Lee notices the guys.

"Rose, hi!"

One of Alec's group turns to Lee.

"You know her?" He must be the one she flirted with, because he has a lecherous gleam in his eye.

"We're all going for Japanese." Mac is trying to convey something with her eyes, that even Franny can't get, and Lee looks stumped.

The wolfish guy says to Lee, "I thought you were meeting someone."

"I was. Her." Says Lee, gambling it all.

Mac hooks arms with Lee. "I left you two messages." As if that explains everything. And it does seem to satisfy the group.

"I brought Francesca. Cess, this is Lisa."

"How do you do, Lisa," Fran gushes.

"This is Alec," she adds, with a flourish.

Lee lowers her eyes demurely. "We've met."

About bagging Big Game like Alec Carlton, you can't just stuff him and hang him on the wall. You have to raise him in captivity. It takes Franny fourteen months to coax a proposal out of him. Fourteen months of being understanding when he is late or a no-show, of laughing at those disaster jokes she loathes, of never, ever, persuading him to talk about anyone they have met or know, other than to say, *yeah, they seem nice enough* and thirteen months of some seriously challenging calisthenics in the sack. Alec has a penchant for variety. You've got to show willing, after all. It's the fourteen months of seeing a lot less of Mac and Lee, which is the hardest part, but when your mother is cooing down the phone like a love-sick teenager, asking for blow-by-blow details of your whirlwind romance, there is an overriding sense of urgency that cannot be ignored. You just hang on for dear life. The entire affair has become a recreational drug. She recalls snippets of their love life to relate to her mother. Snatches of pillow talk:

"Have you ever stolen anything?" He thinks about it for a minute while she snuggles deeper into his shoulder.

"Well, I did, yes, once, I did, when I was around eight."

"What did you steal?"

"I stole coins from my father's collection. A couple of handfuls of silver half dollars. I hitched a ride to the station with Mother and Ernestine the maid, and while Mother escorted her up to the platform, I ran off to give my coins to the bums on the benches."

"Did you get away with it?" She runs her finger over his sincere brow, and traces a line along the one frown line.

He aims a kiss at her hairline.

"No. I had to go around and get all the coins back, but first Mother gave me a roll of nickels from the glove compartment to swap. It was pretty awkward when the guys were awake. I wasn't allowed to touch anything when I got back in the car. Do we have any more of that Dutch coffee?" Pillow talk is over and she has learned something else about her lovely boyfriend. He might be a little too perfect.

When she tells Mac and Lee this story, Mac points out the similarities between Alec and St. Francis of Assisi. Mac's Irish grandma lived with her growing up and she is consequently well-versed in the saints, ordinary and obscure. The coin caper is the kind of thing St. Francis would have done in his early life as the son of a successful cloth merchant.

St. Alec is tied up with work quite a lot, and Franny uses that time to rest her limbs and throw together the occasional Girlsday. Mac and Lee are very understanding about her demanding schedule. When Alec takes her to Hilton Head one weekend, Mac and Lee throw her a pre-bachelorette party, so sure are they that THIS IS IT. They are right.

Chapter 6

*T*he wedding takes place in New Haven, at St. Thomas', the church of her childhood, presided over by a new priest only a couple of years older than the bride and groom. They have included communion in the service, even though Alec could care less about religious tradition—the Wilsons, on the other hand, care a great deal. Ma Wilson, that is. Even the kiss has been scripted—they incorporate it into the Passing of the Peace. The reception is held at the Courtside Club in downtown New Haven, rated one of the top tennis clubs in the nation in 1980 by *Serve and Volley*. It is where Francesca spent most every summer of her childhood swimming on the swim team, and working her way up and down the tennis ladder. Otherwise, the main clubhouse is a great space for wedding receptions, deeply discounted for members. To this day, there is a running joke at the club about the elimination of baby boys among members to make way for daughters and their low-overhead wedding celebrations.

The family is all here—Muth, who is uncharacteristically poised, as if she is playing a leading role and Dad, the perfect Prince Consort, big brother Henry and his wife Margaret and their kids, Mindy and Tom, and Francesca's older sister Pat, a public defender, and her husband Ted. Alec's parents, who are older, have invited many of their friends from Mainline Philadelphia, making the whole affair very staid.

The chicken *à l'orange* splayed on wild rice was more tender when it was sampled a month ago, and the *haricots verts* are a tiny bit limp, but the raspberry chiffon wedding cake is perfect. The band is exactly what you would expect: toe-tapping seniors with perfunctory talent and a repertoire of schmaltz as long as your train. The grand ballroom, where the crowd of 150 enjoys a sit-down dinner at twenty round tables piled with flamboyant floral centerpieces, twenty years ago held about half as many seventh and eighth graders lining the walls, learning the finer points of ballroom dancing. This went on for two academic years and none of it stuck, judging by how Francesca staggers through the first dance with her hapless husband, both of them concentrating so much on counting and stepping correctly that Muth whispers "Smile!" as they lumber past her, looking for all the world like the losers of a three-legged race.

Much later that evening, the sight of Francesca's niece, the cherubic Mindy Wilson throwing up magenta wedding cake all over her organza gown reminds Francesca that it is time to change into her going-away outfit. The time has come to begin a new phase of life, the one she took charge of planning back on the volleyball court two years ago. Alec has been an excellent subject for her longitudinal study in manipulating outcomes. The results to date are impressive. Above all, Alec wants to please his lady love, and Francesca attributes that to her unwavering commitment to personal goal-setting. Nowadays, when Lee moans about being single, Francesca reminds her that if she really wanted to be married, she would be: a very simple dictum for a once baffling human condition. Francesca could teach seminars on keeping your eye on the prize.

She will keep her name and a few other treasures, like her stuffed bear, Panda. They will move into a boxy one-bedroom apartment on East 89th Street, and when the first baby comes, they can put up a dividing wall in the living room for a very small second bedroom. She wishes Alec and she could have lived together for a while first but both had decent rent-stabilized apartment shares and neither one could accommodate the other. Francesca has not had the confidence to discuss how they will divide up their respective incomes, but she secretly hopes to keep hers.

On her way in a hurry, but suddenly forgetting where she is headed, she sees her sister Pat, who grabs her by the forearm and they skate momentarily along the ballroom floor. Before she can retire the wedding gown, Pat reminds her, she must toss the bouquet. They round up all the single women and position Francesca on the fourth step leading up to the club's stuffy second floor. Aiming for Lee, Francesca throws the bouquet into a reef of grasping bare arms. Lee bobbles it, drops it and a mad scramble for possession ensues. Lee prevails but only after quite a scrum.

The band starts back up and everyone returns to the dance floor. Alec is bantering with his groomsmen, as his new bride makes her way through the crowd to change. Francesca hunts around for one of her bridesmaids. Mac is dancing in Hugh's arms with her bare feet up on his shoes (she probably couldn't stand otherwise). Amidst the roar of animated conversation mingled with Madonna, she tracks down Lee, who is resting near a window, staring at the bouquet in her lap.

"Come unhook me!" she screams.

They sneak off to the hushed, powder-scented inner sanctum of the Ladies' Lounge. The silence that greets them is a far cry from the pre-ceremony mayhem of four hours ago. Alterations, make-up and hair disasters, a Coke spill, some tears, some laughs, a pounding headache…it was not relaxing to be the bride on the bar stool that served as Francesca's pedestal. Now she turns away from Lee and faces herself in the wall-to-wall mirror, her golden tresses threatening to unravel from their braided crown, a not-so-young bride with the beginnings of bags under her eyes, the telltale signs of ravaged skin more or less erased by the skillfully applied foundation, a certain bravery in the regard… she edges backwards toward Lee for her to unbutton all the little pearls down the back of the formal wedding gown. It is then that she realizes Lee is smashed. She can't even get hold of one single button. She had chosen Lee to help her change because she is the only bridesmaid who did not bring a date today, but she overlooked the fact that when Lee gets a few drinks in her, most of it spills out her tear ducts. Francesca nearly dislocates her shoulder trying to help with the buttons, but they do finally wrestle her out of the fitted bodice. She is hippier than she should be for this dress. In fact, she feels the first pangs of heat rash coming on under her control-top hose. She slips on her replacement dress, after shaking baby powder down her thighs.

Now Lee is sobbing. Franny instinctively takes her into the linen closet, where many a tear was shed in the summers of pre-adolescence.

Lee is a runny-nosed, mascara-smeared beauty who keeps saying *you grabbed the brass ring, Franny. It's yours, fair and square.* She is clutching the wilting bouquet, taking in deep, hiccuppy whiffs of its dying fragrance. Franny is tipsy, not loaded, but the brass ring analogy strikes her all the same as off-kilter. Her wedding ring is gold, not brass. Alongside the diamond baguettes, it literally weighs down her left hand. But isn't there a line from a nursery song about "if that ring should turn to brass?"

Lee grabs Francesca by the chin, bringing her tear-streaked face nose to nose with Francesca's. She stares cross-eyed at her friend and whispers barely audibly.

"I don't know if you love him."

"What? Me?" Francesca stutters back.

"Well do you?" They both recoil, as if the question is too hot to the touch.

"Yes. Lee. I do."

"You do what? Say it."

"I love Alec." It sounds so strange coming out of her mouth like that. *I love you* is far easier, she now knows. And she *does* love Alec. Sometimes she wonders if he actually loves *her*. Because she is not sure what love looks like; everlasting, lifelong love, beyond hot lingering kisses and solemn proposals and marriage vows.

"Well good." They hug messily.

Francesca is crying because she has had one too many glasses of champagne but possibly also because she is not sure if she knows how to be a banker's wife in Manhattan's Upper East Side. Up until now, since right out of college, she has been a party-hopping magazine journalist in the lower East Twenties, who spends her entire salary every month on fun and frolic. Or maybe she's crying for the little girl whose skin condition "ruined her beautiful face" but, once she learned how to apply make-up, met and married Prince Charming. What happens when she takes off the make-up?

No one at that lavish reception would ever suspect that Francesca Wilson, the newly minted Mrs. Alec Carlton, a fun-loving young socialite with the flashing green eyes and the alabaster neck and the rough and ready complexion would to this day think of herself as a Gila monster with one scaly claw still in the swamp. But Lee Poehailos knows. Gila monsters need love, too.

If that ring should turn to brass…there is something about that weepy interlude in the closet near the close of a magical day that smacks of a fairy's curse. Alec Carlton is an up-and-coming young banker with excellent prospects, good breeding and long eyelashes. And now he is Franny's husband. She shudders—for a moment she thinks she might wet her cerise silk going-away outfit there on that soft pile of clean towels in the ladies' locker room closet—she shudders at the thought of all she has won in marrying Alec Carlton and all she now stands to lose. Her mother comes looking for her minutes later, the spell is broken (but not the curse) and she staggers out of the closet and into the bathroom, where Muth instructs her to stick her finger down her throat.

"You need a fresh start, Pumpkin. It's been a long day." They festoon her in clean towels and then as effortlessly as blowing her nose, she regurgitates half a bottle of metallic-tasting cake batter. It works. She actually stays alert for the afterglow in the cramped little honeymoon suite upstairs.

❖ ❖ ❖

She wakes up to the sound of Elizabeth screaming at Daniel not to touch the remote. Katharine is pounding on the crib slats with her Cow Jumped Over the Moon lullaby gizmo. Alec snores on. She storms off to silence the big kids and haul Katharine out of her cage. Katharine runs to the TV before Francesca can change her diaper so she traps the toddler on the couch and performs the stinky operation there.

"Gross, Mom!" She ignores her nine-year-old daughter, who finds anything to do with bathroom ritual abhorrent. Daniel, age five, ignores all of them.

"Goss!" chirps Katharine.

Francesca stumbles back to bed, issuing orders the whole length of the hall.

"Get some cereal but eat at the counter! And put your bowls in the sink when you're done. If I hear any fighting over channels, the TV goes OFF!"

She should snap off the TV now, and get out a board game since this is the one day in the week when they don't have to rush around in a panic, but she needs time with her husband, doesn't she? Don't the experts concur that the primary relationship in a home should be that of the parents for this is the relationship that gives children even more security than knowing their parents love them unconditionally? Not that she loves anyone unconditionally. As long as her family doesn't give her too much trouble, she's all theirs. On the weekends, anyway. After she snuggles with Alec a little longer. After her run. And her shower. It's not that she resents her kids, you could hardly call it their fault, but each of them arrived at the most inconvenient time! The first pregnancy announced itself just as they were planning to go trekking in Nepal, but her morning sickness was too intense for even a pleasant stroll through the park so there went Nepal. The next baby came when they were moving to Boston and it complicated everything, having a newborn in tow. Katharine was altogether unplanned. They had intended to stop at two, but they got sloppy.

They spend Saturday in the usual fashion; moving stuff around the apartment until it looks like it all fits. Alec and Daniel take the winter coats down to storage, temporarily reclaiming some fourteen inches of hanging space in the hall closet. Summer is always easier on the closets, but tougher on the floors. Francesca makes a mental note to tell Merly the housekeeper to air the rugs. In the afternoon, they all go to the Natural History museum. The kids first like to stop and say hello to Mr. and Mrs. Earlyman—the hairy little couple who stand behind the glass in a tucked away corner of this subterranean permanent exhibit. The husband has his arm around his diminutive Neanderthal wife. Their footprints disappear off into the ash-covered terrain, to suggest they have come a long way, but that there's still a long way to go.

Then it's off to the new Amazonian frog exhibit, featuring every neon color under the tropical sun. They spend a good two hours choosing favorites, cooing through the glass, searching under fronds for tiny little peepers with markings as elaborate as any leopard. They lose Katharine briefly, and Daniel has a tantrum in the foyer when he is refused a trip to the museum store, but he's tired, and everyone is hungry and as far as Francesca is concerned, Monday morning can't come soon enough. She feels differently after dinner, when the whole litter is snuggled on the couch with Mom and Dad balancing sundry limbs in their laps. This is when all the conditions are right again, and everybody is feeling the love. Tomorrow is church and then the second half of the day will be spent with some combination of kids while the parents divide and conquer. Alec has a business trip and will want to pack. Their Brazilian nanny Margarita, or Ga Ga as they call her, is actually coming tomorrow afternoon because Alec has an early flight on Monday and Francesca has to take Elizabeth to tennis camp on her way to the office. Ga Ga will stay home with the other two, and be paid handsomely for figuring out what to do with them all day. She normally has everyone half days during the school year, except of course Katharine. No use planning for Katharine's day—she wouldn't do what you say anyway. That, in a nutshell, is the aspect to parenting that Francesca has questioned, to put it mildly. From the mighty spike on the volleyball court that signaled a new era of self-determination, to the honeymoon in Quebec she planned from start to finish, and the return trip for their first anniversary,

Francesca maintained a formidable stranglehold on her personal fate. She chose as her consort a man who was quite happy to let her take the wheel, as long as he was given plenty of freedom to scale the ranks of professional success, making his own hours, and leaving his worries at the office when he finally did get home. She took care of all social engagements, family obligations, domestic arrangements, and trips, and he suited up appropriately for any and all appearances. Then the babies started showing up and Francesca's grip on her happily-ever-after unraveled somewhat, to the point where, three babies later, she doesn't dare wish for anything beyond the next nap.

Two weeks from now, they leave for Block Island. She has a slight problem because Ga Ga thinks she's coming with them again this summer, and Alec thinks she isn't. Francesca hasn't quite yet figured out how to tell Ga Ga no, because there is very little hope of her changing Alec's mind. They agreed at the end of the last beach trip with Ga Ga that it would be her last. Ga Ga is a voluptuous, to say the very least, bottle-orange Brazilian narcissist. More than once Francesca has come home to Ga Ga showing off her artwork before the kids show theirs. But hey, at least they're doing artwork. At the beach, Ga Ga wears a thong bikini as dictated by her motherland's cultural mores, along with a low-slung boob hammock to catch what doesn't sit up anymore, and in this get-up is about as aesthetic as a Sunday roast before you cut the strings off. Not that Francesca would have wanted her to look any better in a thong. The kids barely notice, they're so used to her sprawling all over their furniture in strange low-cut, tight tops and hot pants, but Francesca could tell Alec was a little depressed at the sight of Ga Ga's big brown bottom cleaved in two by a polka-dotted strap.

But then Ga Ga took the kids to Coney Island last spring, and they all started making plans for this summer's trip to Block

Island, and next thing you know, she is jotting down the dates in her little black book and Francesca is in deep trouble. They wait all year for those blissful two weeks in the charming, squeaky clapboard cottage they rent with a view of the sound from the screened-in porch. It's crowded, but they are rarely inside; the kids tear around the beach like dogs off-leash, skipping off to the penny candy store or the ice cream shack on a whim, and after a barbecue dinner, they like to build great big castles with moats and shell accents as the sun goes down on another day in paradise. But that's not until the second week in August. For now, it's summer in the city and all that moist heat; no matter how many trips you make for ice cream. And Ga Ga thinks she's going on vacation soon, and she's right about that, but just not where she thought.

People wonder why Francesca works, given the banker husband. Bankers are, by definition, great with money. They know how to make it, and they know how to use it to make more, and they love to spend it. Just as she is not a typical Upper East Side wife (she works full time, for starters), Alec is not a typical investment banker. He lives with the constant, gnawing fear that his success will somehow turn on them, and they will lose it all. He will be indicted for something a boss did that he didn't even know about. The markets will fail, the industry will tank, the young MBA's will take over the world and all the nearly-forty-somethings will be out of work. This is just a sampling of the scenarios she has heard over the years, and the main reasons why she keeps working, currently in an academic publishing house supervising production of French textbooks. Oh sure, they could be like everyone else they know and rent a place in the Hamptons for a month, and piece together some other little adventures to keep them out of New York's steam. But that would mean giving up her job. If you can't stand the heat, get a new life. The other reason she works is for the money. Her money. No one else's.

There is an apocryphal story that Muth tells of the first time, as a newlywed, she mentioned wanting to go shoe shopping. Apparently Dad looked up from whatever he was doing and said, "You already have a pair of shoes." Muth decided then and there that she needed to get a job. After she got through birthing and weaning her babies, and sending them off to school, she got first a part-time, then a three-quarter-time, then a full-time job at Yale, where she worked for the next twenty-five years. She had her own salary, her own credit card, and lots of pairs of shoes. Francesca has taken a chapter from Muth's book and she, too, has lots of shoes.

Plus, she likes to work. She loves her kids, but they are extremely juvenile and she has to say, the buzz she gets from being taken seriously by colleagues and clients helps compensate for the tedium of tantrums, endless, inane questions, and surly attitudes that greet her at the end of each working day. Yes, they are adorable and funny, but they can also be loud, cloying and uncooperative. Especially Katharine, who is two and orders everyone around, including her sitters, and nobody ever tells her 'no' because she can be rather dramatic and it is painful to be on the receiving end of her outbursts.

It may cost them the equivalent of her entire salary to employ the necessary help to keep her sane, but that is a small price to pay. Ga Ga from Sao Paolo has lasted longer than most. The former barmaid in the tight fuzzy sweaters that accentuate her voluminous "peellows" runs a fairly tight ship, which is more than Francesca feels she could achieve.

So Alec doesn't spend money needlessly. That said, there is a certain bar under which you simply cannot possibly pass here in Manhattan (read Upper East Side again), and that would include private schooling, classes for the kids, sports, travel, the basics. Of course when Francesca's Midwestern sister hears tell of a no-frills resort, she snorts down the phone—they go camping for their annual vacation—but it's important that Alec is at least perceived as swimming in the same waters as the bigger fish in his tank. Alec has to make small talk with the people who may be promoting him and that means knowing something of the good life. He has to look the part of the well-rounded executive he considers himself to be, and that costs money.

Not that he earned all that much in the early days—New York is outrageously expensive for young professionals who are clawing their way up the corporate ladder. They lived from paycheck to paycheck. They got lucky in the technology sector later on, and for two years running, Alec got huge bonuses. By then, they had two kids with a third on the way, Francesca's job at the publishing house was more demanding than ever and there wasn't all that much time left over for indulgences. But they were comfortable. They *are* comfortable. Distracted, not the best communicators, occasionally overwhelmed by their responsibilities as professionals, parents, and partners, but by no means in any sort of real pain. Comfortable.

Chapter 7

Today Alec has taken the airport limo straight home from one of his day trips to corporate America, skipping a late afternoon stop at the office in favor of actually seeing his children before bedtime. Rarely does a conversation with Alec take place before dinner, and never before the children's dinner, because he doesn't get home until after the kids are in bed most of the time. Alec's surprise appearance and the ensuing conversation, while the kids watch a video and she scrambles around the kitchen, takes an ominous turn.

"Has the sun set over the yardarm?" says Alec in Muth's mid-Atlantic accent, reaching for the liquor cabinet door. It means *is it time for cocktails?* from who-knows-what historical period, but Muth has been saying it since the beginning of time. Francesca knows it's a nautical term, but she has never actually looked up *yardarm*. Alec delights her with stock phrases from her childhood—the best way he knows how to prove he has been listening all along. It would be hard to know, otherwise. He is somewhat inscrutable.

"How was your day?" He asks oh-so nonchalantly.

When Alec asks first about *her*, it means he has something *he* needs to talk about; just as in the conjugal sack, he tends to her needs first, before arranging and rearranging her in a half-dozen unlikely positions with gleeful, manly abandon. She and her friends call it origami sex. She doesn't remember being folded into quite so many interesting shapes earlier on, but then again, origami takes many years of practice, and they have been practicing for over ten years.

"Long," she says, as she pokes at the ravioli in the roiling water. She could go on at great length about the galley proof she just got back from the printers; here textbook—her *baby*—looks like it got switched at the hospital, so many screw-ups and missed instructions did she find, and that was only flipping though it on the way home in the cab. It is going to require a week's worth of careful proofing, time she did not budget for this project. Time they cannot afford to spend. She is going to be up late. But she reveals none of this. Something tells her from her husband's furrowed brow that it would fall on deaf ears.

"What about you?" She knows better than to sound too concerned, or he will back off altogether and it will be days before she finds out what's troubling him. Several days, and probably an unrelated argument that will set him off, at which time today's news will be delivered in a seething *staccato pianissimo.*

"How was *your* day?"

Alec sighs. He hacks off another helping of cheese and pops it into his mouth, giving Francesca time to take down the wine glasses, rinse them, dry them and put them on the eating island before he has swallowed sufficiently to answer. He throws back the last of his sherry. He will be more lucid after a couple of ounces of Amontillado. She should have known something was up when he pulled the dusty bottle down from the shelf. The last time they had sherry, he announced over cheese and crackers that he wasn't willing to have a vasectomy after all, his excuse being that if she got killed, God forbid etc. he might want to start a second family. It took every one of his vertebrae to let her know this, because they had developed quite a consistent pattern by then of Francesca calling the shots and Alec acquiescing. *Alecquiescing* as Mac calls it. He learned from the 'chance' encounter in front of the Pie Hole that Francesca had a fine mind, strategic smarts, and these would serve the family well. With all he had to do at the office to make his mark, he was only too happy to delegate the emotional life of the family. From birthday parties to family planning, Francesca held the reins. And that has worked very well for them both. It is unclear how an abrupt change in the couple's dynamic will affect the very equilibrium of their lives together.

"Remember that biotech company in Austin that does spinal fusion technology, the ones with the kryptonite rod?"

She remembers very well. The CEO, Arnie Something, took them out to *La Bergere* when he was in town last fall and she had the *Moules Bergeres*. Whenever there are mussels on the menu she orders them, out of a transferred patriotic duty. *Moules* are *de rigueur* in Brussels and it is in Dad's honor that she sips the salty wine broth from a half shell woven through the tines of her fork.

"You mean that Arnie guy?" He had the *sole meunière* because he is a bland Texan. He didn't eat his roll or his rice but he ate every olive on the table and he ordered an extra side of creamed spinach. Clearly a man on a crash diet of no carbs and 100 grams of fat a day.

"Right. Arnie Adler. MNS. He called today out of the blue. I haven't spoken to those guys in ages. I mean it's way too soon for a private placement for their scanning package. They're still writing code."

Whatever.

"Is he in town?" She has wanted to try the new Portuguese restaurant on West 85th.

"No...it turns out he called to tell me they're launching a sub-sidiary that makes a new kind of artificial bone, and they're looking for a CFO. He wants to fly me out next week."

"To Texas?" She squeaks as she mentally reaches for the sherry, then remembers the Chardonnay in the fridge.

"That's the engineering plant. Headquarters are in..." As Alec forms the sentence, her adult life flashes before her: here she finds herself a mother of three, still firm in the derriere, if not the thighs; the breasts less so—a robust specimen. She runs a small but highly successful department producing the very latest in French textbooks, complete with CD-ROMs shrink-wrapped to the latest edition, and unlike so many at-home work widows, she lives a life "crowded with incident" as Muth would declare, from sunrise to sunset.

While Alec is away (even if he is a mere twenty blocks away, restructuring deals until two in the morning), she covers the whole spectrum of urban existence: cultivating work, friends and prog-eny, not necessarily in that order, but usually. She runs a mean meeting, she organizes drinks after work a couple of times a week, laughing all the way to the bank for another cash withdrawal to cover one last glass of wine before it's time to hand what's left over to Ga Ga.

She and Mac share a running joke about not remembering the birthdays of their own kids, but knowing every last detail about their competitors. The publishing industry is rife with espionage and underhanded scoops and they are ruthless at keeping informed of the latest industry developments. Lee, childless, manless, but worst of all, guileless, just does her job thoroughly, keeps her head down, shaking it helplessly at the antics of her two scheming friends.

When Francesca returns from the battlefield that is her work-place, bruised, bloodied, but exhilarated, she engages in bedtime rituals with the kids with the grit and determination most people reserve for the gym. They talk to her about their days, albeit in condensed form, and she parses any morality lessons she can invent from the sparse data they offer up. They read a few pages of a book together, and they say prayers. She skimps on none of it. When she considers her life in New York City at age thirty-eight, it is a disciplined life, a good life. And she is fierce about collecting memories, as proof that the life was lived. She fills boxes with the kids' output, though she often neglects to date its contents, and she must work on that. She is merciless about what gets saved. If it is unrecognizable, that is, if it needs any annotation by Ga Ga ("A house on a hill"), it's down the incinerator, heave-ho. You can't be too sentimental; there just isn't the room. She intends to scan the best pieces one day....

She thinks of her children, whom she loves (how could she not?), as beautiful, priceless charms on her favorite bracelet. She wears this charm bracelet with pride, with nothing short of awe, and she tucks it away carefully at night, relieved that another day has gone by without her losing or breaking it. She hires sitters to guard the door to their home and she stands outside of it, listening to them triple-lock up before she takes in a poetry reading, a play or a movie. For this is how she is fed.

With one word, one new job, Alec could take all of it away. Of course, she'd get to keep the charm bracelet.

"...the most visited city in the world, apparently. You'd have thought it was London or New York..."

"Is it? I wouldn't have guessed."

Tokyo? She really must stop thinking so loudly. She misses half of every conversation, especially ones with her otherwise recalcitrant spouse. But Tokyo? How could they possibly?

"...maybe even take up sailing..."

She is flummoxed. Orlando?

"There are something like five yacht clubs in the San Francisco Bay Area alone!"

Got it. Of course. San Francisco. The most visited city in the world except by Francesca. She has never been west of Cincinnati. Alec, with his Chemical Engineering degree from Stanford, sneers not so subtly at her euro-centricity, suggesting that until she has traveled from sea to shining sea, she has no business going abroad on quests for breathtaking beauty. She, in turn, pities this man who has seen most of the wonders of the world from a ten-year-old sofa, though she is equally impressed by how he retains all those sociopolitical, cultural and historical facts gleaned from his one-dimensional travels.

"Since when are you interested in sailing?" The sherry, combined with her glass of wine has rendered her ever so slightly belligerent, but she masks it with an ironic grin and squint—something she learned from her first-ever boss, who squinted and grinned whenever he had anything critical to say about her writing, which was the majority of the time. She learned a lot from the old goat: mostly when to grin and squint when confronting an adversary.

"It's the best way I know to teach kids about physics, and we'd get to be out on the Bay."

Physics? They learn about physics every time they heave a toy at the other's head, or turn a somersault down an incline and bite through their tongues. Physics, gravity, momentum...all of it there for the asking and no sails required. She hates boats. She hates the smell of them, the way they slap along the water making her want to throw up all over the foc'sle or whatever they call the part of the boat where she huddles, on a so-called pleasure cruise with the wind and salt merrily tangling her straight, fine hair. Physics belong in the classroom. Psychology, less so.

And it is psychology she deploys now, as she turns to the task of reversing the possibility of a move from Manhattan. Psychology and her carefully cultivated guile.

"Wow. Leave New York? I thought we left Boston because you didn't feel like you were at the center of the action…"

"The San Francisco Bay Area is the center of the action, for biotechnology."

"I mean, you're the guy who always says if you can't get it in New York, you can't get it."

"Yeah, well, I was probably talking about out-of-print silent movies at two in the morning."

"I just figured it meant promotions, too." Everyone in investment banking knows that the only people who get the really big breaks are the ones sweating it out at head office. In the provinces, you're lucky if your Division Head has ever even heard of you.

"I mean, it seems like we just got Boston out of our system, and now this."

"Boston was different. It was still banking and it was a promotion and besides, you love Cambridge." She went to college there, after all.

"I love New York more." She feels like a bumper sticker that no one bothers to read.

She tries to look extremely involved in the pasta she is boiling; not all that interested in this hypothetical discussion. Yet she can feel the sweat trickling down her back and thighs as she plots her next several moves.

"I'm just going to talk to them. It probably won't come to anything." Like a rat in a maze, Alec senses that the cheese is off in an entirely different direction. He needs to stop and puzzle out this roadblock. She needs some food in her stomach before she starts shaking someone. The day ends in a stalemate.

Chapter 8

*I*n the first days of kindergarten, the curriculum centers on rules, what they are for, why we have them, what would happen if there were no rules. They usually give the example of a road system without any signs or traffic lights. Teachers wring their hands over the chaos that would ensue if there weren't traffic signals to keep the cars running safely! Next, they go over the rules of the classroom, the play yard, the library and the wider school and finally, they settle into a gluing project involving red, yellow and green circles as these pint-sized citizens step onto the surface roads of life.

Another aspect of civic participation, which is less well understood, also has a parallel in traffic symbology. That would be what they call in the tabloids "road rage." It comes on suddenly, powerfully, when you feel an overwhelming sense of injustice on the roads. Someone might cut you off, take the parking space you were about to back into, or make a maneuver without warning you first. Whatever the indiscretion, it sets off in you a kind of ferocity that you didn't even know you could feel, and the next thing you know you're tailing a Toyota into a bad section of town just to make a point. Ever since Francesca's little 'fender bender' with Alec, she is overwhelmed by rage. They had made a deal. Two years in Boston in return for the rest of their lives in New York. While she doesn't have it in writing, she always assumed that was the plan. She cannot shake a new feeling of intense antipathy for this man whom she always considered a life partner. Suddenly, her longed-for marriage feels more like a life sentence.

Their move to Boston was part of Alec's scheme to increase his value in the banking world—you make yourself available to be poached by another financial institution, ideally one with a different set of strengths, to comply with the non-compete clause in your contract, which most people ignore anyway, and you make this move at a substantially higher salary. Then, after everyone has forgotten how hard hit they were when you left, you make overtures about coming back. Alec always had such a squeaky clean reputation that when he announced he was moving to Boston for personal reasons, they actually threw him a big going-away party and gave them season tickets to the Boston Pops. Two years later, he let them know that they were moving back to New York, again for personal reasons, and p.s. he was now much more valuable with all of his high-tech contacts, a booming industry at that time. His former employers lassoed him right back at an appreciable increase over his earlier salary. Francesca stood on the sidelines and watched, rather in awe, as he pulled off this scam. Alec had gone from St. Francis of Assisi to, well, at least to Abe Lincoln, whose "ambition was a little engine inside of him." (See daughter Elizabeth's biography of the 16th president of the United States of America.) This elaborate hoax confirmed something about her seemingly unassuming husband. Alec's self-worth is directly correlated to his net worth. Francesca went on to have another baby, which, after the first twenty-four hours, when you get to be Queen of the Universe (mighty tiny universe: a birthing room with an automatic bed and a privacy curtain), is something of a burden; you are right back at zero again, twenty to thirty pounds overweight, and half-dead from exhaustion for months on end. Looking back on those grueling early years, she would say her self-worth has little or nothing to do with their children, and everything to do with how she has managed to maintain her sanity in spite of them.

During the two years in Cambridge she got to see plenty of her mother, who was retired from Yale by then and would come up from New Haven on the train to help out after Katharine was born. Not that she actually babysat, having gorged herself on the other grandchildren. The initial thrill behind her, Muth was happy to hold the baby while Francesca brought her tuna fish sandwiches and V8 on a T.V. tray, and Elizabeth and Daniel watched cartoons at her feet. It was a relief to get back to New York, where Francesca could pay the hired help and get back to work, where she belongs.

Leave New York? How could she ever survive without Mac and Lee? But Alec is proving to have a once undetectable itch to step out of what he is suddenly describing as a rut.

"What do you mean, a rut? You talk about your work as if you couldn't survive without it."

"Actually, Cess, that's true. We couldn't survive without it." When it comes to dialectic discourse, Alec would have given the ancient Greeks a run for their money.

"You know what I mean."

"Well, what I mean is that yes, I work hard, and I stay focused. But you know what, Cess? I am sick to death of playing fairy Godmother to the REAL players. I guess I'm just getting tired of paving someone else's yellow brick road, you know?"

"What is that supposed to mean?"

"Investment banking—what it boils down to is we're all about helping other people realize their dreams. We help them set goals and then we find the resources to get them there. I am just so sick and tired of standing on the sidelines. I really am."

"Why haven't you said anything before now?" This is not asked in a nurturing fashion.

"Because I guess I wasn't aware of how I felt, until someone asked ME to be a player. It's like I've been wandering around with blinders on."

"Great. Just great. The timing sucks here, Alec."

"When big opportunities present themselves, the timing never feels right. But if the outcome is anything like what Arnie described in our first conversation, this could be very big." She may not have known about his mid-career crisis, but one thing Francesca does know for certain: Alec does not make financial promises casually. *Very big* could mean owning an apartment at last. It would mean walking away from her little fiefdom at Cooley, but there might be some kind of stop-gap position for her in San Francisco...still... leave New York? Leave New York *again*?

There are several less obvious reasons why she doesn't want to leave New York. One, the crowds. She happens to derive great comfort from the fact that there are millions of New Yorkers all around her at all times, bustling from A to B without a single solitary interest in where she is going. It's like a huge dysfunctional family, and no therapy bills.

Also, she loves doormen. She just loves a man in uniform waiting for her no matter what the hour, ready to receive her or her cargo without a hint of resentment about any of it. You don't have to hide bulging shopping bags from your doorman. You can't hide them, truth be told. It's that enforced honesty that makes the relationship so refreshingly open, and so dependable. Oh sure, they go off duty, and new faces appear on the scene, but it's always the same livery and that uncomplaining acceptance that she savors.

And their apartment building: she never feels safer than when she is surrounded on all sides by other people's homes. Forget rolling green yards. They scare her silly, especially after dark.

She even likes pigeons. She admires the way they adapt to urban settings, hustling along with the crowds and using their wings strategically, to make the short trip from French fry to pretzel part. She marvels at the way they pirouette awkwardly in front of their *pigeon du jour.* And she likes the fact that when you come upon them, they scatter in great festive clouds of pigeon wings and then settle nearby, like pets. They rarely get run over, unlike most vermin. She prefers her infestations airborne.

But the main reason why she can't leave New York is she just spent the better part of a year getting her son into Collegiate, a school she would have laughed at back in New Haven, when she was a swaggering seventh grader with ripped jeans that pooled around her ankles and huge, baggy sweatshirts. The boys at Collegiate wear trim little coats and ties and if that isn't enough to set them apart, they are also terribly well mannered. When you have a four-year old boy of your own, suddenly well-mannered little preppies make a lot of sense. However, gaining admission to a private elementary school on the Upper East Side requires more political savvy, social connections, and stamina than running for mayor. The applicant pool is vast, the class sizes minute, and nowhere in the Western world is there a greater concentration of perfectly designed five-year-olds vying for these spots. Note that preschool isn't just for four-year-olds anymore. They're great strapping young men of six before they even darken the doors of kindergarten. All held back for the good of the social order, apparently.

Not Daniel. He is four and three-quarters and proud. She once overheard a mother at his preschool declare *if you don't hold them back, you can kiss the Ivy League goodbye.* That mom had just signed her preschooler up for his second year of fencing and was starting him on French, the language of diplomacy, culture, gastronomy and The Association of Independent Schools.

They had just moved back from Cambridge, where Elizabeth had spent two very happy years at a respectable all-girls K-8 private school. She transferred without any fuss to Nightingale, arguably the best girls' school in Manhattan, where the Head of School at that time had been college roommates with the Cambridge Day principal.

Daniel was three when they moved back to New York. He had been groomed by his older sister to dress Barbie dolls, to play school under her grim tutelage, and to play the part of the silent sidekick in all of her living room theatrics. Francesca had taught him to sing snatches of Italian opera as a cheap party trick, but he was otherwise just a scrappy lisper from leafy Massachusetts without too much to show for his first three years.

That all changed when they got back to New York. She never considered herself a particularly competitive type, but the level of achievement among Daniel's peers was enough to kick her into high gear. It seemed all of his classmates were ahead of the curve—doing 30-piece puzzles, spelling their names, counting by 2's to ten...she began coaching her three-year old after hours so that by his fourth birthday he could recite *James James Morrison Morrison* while doing somersaults down the carpeted hall outside their apartment.

From there, it was a simple matter of touring all the local private schools and playing the mating game with the various admissions officers. She even got the Dean of Alec's business school to write Daniel a letter of recommendation. He wrote primarily about Alec's tireless community involvement and hinted at his limitless earning potential. Daniel, he knows less well. With everyone getting so frantic about the limited supply of local private schools, Francesca found herself getting whipped into a mania she could no longer control. This was not how she had intended to handle the kids' education, as some kind of arms race. She just wanted them to like to learn and to make some nice friends along the way, as she had. But she was swept up in the frenzy. Suddenly she wanted Collegiate more than she had ever wanted any man. She wrote love letters to everyone she met there about how perfectly she felt their school would complement her son's many burgeoning talents and skills.

Back at Eastside Preschool, where Daniel was newer, shorter, and possibly brighter than any of his classmates, she maintained a devil-may-care attitude throughout the application process. She was bobbing and feinting at pick-up, never really letting on where they were hoping to go, for fear of causing a stampede. She would just smile and shrug and say, oh, aren't they all pretty much the same? And all those poker faces would nod at the newcomer that, yes, they were all much of a muchness.

When they finally heard from their second choice, not to name names, she had twenty-four hours to accept. Luckily, it was a Friday afternoon, because no letter from Collegiate came that day. She felt like a heroine in a Kabuki drama. Even as people heard from their first choices, no one was letting on from their expressions what the final results were. You could tell at pick-up time that no one had yet heard from Collegiate. You could hear the collective inability to draw a deep breath.

Francesca didn't sleep the rest of the weekend. She went through the motions with the family, but even Katharine the baby knew that she was delicate. On Sunday afternoon Alec took all three of them to the Bronx Zoo, leaving her to languish on the settee.

Monday finally rolled in and so did the letter from Collegiate. It was fat. That was a good sign, though in her paranoia she actually had herself convinced that the school had mailed their entire application back to them. She stood in the lobby of their building, her hands trembling as she tore open the envelope. Then came the Academy Awards moment of suspended animation as she read the letter, and tears of gladness and relief at last spilled down her front. The doorman on duty brought her a tissue and she threw herself at him, pinning his arms, wetting his lapel. It was the joy of the delivery room that afternoon.

Now Alec is asking her to give Daniel's place to some sniveling little pipsqueak on the waitlist. Someone the academy deems slightly unworthy. Of course, she gets to keep the letter of acceptance. Frame it!

The news travels in yelps along underground cable crisscrossing the Upper East Side of Manhattan.

"California?"

"Have you ever even been there?"

"Francesca, you can't!"

"But how could he?"

"Leave banking? Why?"

She tries whining, she tries sulking, she tries lecturing Alec on the merits of job continuity, especially when raising a young family, but he is determined to "weigh his options," as he so calmly describes this Kamikaze act. She resorts to scheduling three dinner parties over the next two weeks, in the hopes of curing Alec of his lapse in judgment. One at home, one in a restaurant before an Off-Broadway show, and the *pièce de résistance*, a party *chez* Minotte, a fellow Nightingale mom who would gladly throw a dinner party and claim it for her own to trap a spouse in *n'importe quel crime*. Minotte is a very well-off *divorcée*. They have never been all that close, but extreme circumstances demand extreme measures. A mutual friend hooked them up and Francesca knows she is in capable hands. The dinner party at Minotte's is her silver bullet. Great food, great wine and liberal helpings of fascinating people just might woo Alec back into his natural habitat from which he has so thoughtlessly strayed.

"Who's invited?" asks Minotte, taking command of the covert operation with the flip of a pad. They are sitting up against the gilded wall in the vestibule of the Nightingale upper school, waiting for their kids to tumble down the sweeping stair.

"The best and the brightest. Alec has to see and feel for himself what, or whom, we would be giving up by relocating. I'm going to see if Rosemary and Ben are in town. Did you ever meet them? He's the Booker prize finalist." She feels slightly manic.

"We could ask my brother-in-law, if you want a cultural attaché," the socially connected Minotte offers up.

"Oh, yes, please," as though she were choosing from a menu.

Alec is called away from the first party to put out a blazing fire—anxious underwriters want new terms and he has made himself an expert on rewriting terms. He gets home two hours after everyone has left. She is more desperate than ever, for this was an unforgettable evening with six wonderful friends: three couples with whom they are uncommonly cozy. They vacation with Declan and Carrie and their three kids, they travel with Max and Linda, and they swap kids and other essentials with Beth and Marc down the hall. This dinner party was like attending her own wake. She couldn't help picturing them all, backlit by the barge lights on the East River, silhouettes in gales of laughter, a mural of friends with her rubbed out. They ate and drank too much and laughed until they cried as Linda the psychotherapist described a client's anxiety over choosing a new lipstick shade and Declan told them stories about his crazy Irish family back in County Cork. Alec gets back in time to dry the glasses and she can't seem to retell a single funny story, though they had her gasping for breath hours earlier.

The Off-Broadway show is a highly original one-woman show about Edith Sitwell but Francesca's heart sinks as Alec's sings, when they read together in the program notes that the play originated in San Francisco. Strike Two.

Three weeks later, dinner *chez* Minotte features a dazzling array of *tout* New York. Well, maybe not *tout*, but certainly *beaucoup*. Francesca is seated next to the cultural attaché and spends a goodly portion of the meal comparing and contrasting French and American cultures. It is one of those mid-summer night evenings where everyone is half-enchanted and the conversation, like a gushing stream, turns the wheel of social ease. She feels like nobility at Minotte's table, tossing out *bons mots* with a distinguished French diplomat. Then she notices the former Dior runway model opposite her swing her head in a panicky swivel. She has never actually seen someone swoon, but she is certain that is what she is doing and before you can say *Qui mange bien, vit mieux*, (Eat Well, Live Better) the hollow-eyed waif starts vomiting up Minotte's famous, but tainted oyster stew. The chain reaction is positively operatic.

Nothing is working. Alec is going ahead with the multiple interview process, and Francesca has run out of diversions. It is time for some cosmic rearrangement. The next Saturday evening after dinner and a movie, as Alec holds the cab and Francesca goes in to release the sitter, the smelly couple from the 11th floor, Mr. and Mrs. Stinkbomb, as the kids call them, barge past her, wafting into the lobby, back from some late-night outing, reeking of cigarettes and oily hair. Normally, Francesca would dawdle by the mailboxes so as not to have to share an elevator, but tonight, she rushes in to stand close to Mr. Stinkbomb, close enough to count the raked furrows of greased hair, even to count the flakes of dead skin that balance on individual follicles. She breathes through her nose, taking in the heady odor of this rancid twosome.

"Nice night out tonight!" she offers, cheerfully.

"Yeah, some enchanted evenin'. The traffic tonight is a mother. Paid more for the cab than the tickets."

"Yes, it was pretty bad on Madison." She inhales deeply. The perfect propitiation. "What did you see?"

"*Tamin' of the Shrew* in the park. Done modern. Good show."

"Fun!" There. She has spoken to Mr. and Mrs. Stinkbomb. She has inhaled them for good luck. They ride up together in the elevator and she breathes through her nose the whole way. At the 9th floor, she waves them off exultantly, coughing and sputtering for the next two floors.

Chapter 9

Dear kids,

I am sending this email because I want you all to hear it from me in exactly the same way all at once. It will cut down on confusion. I have suspected over the past few months that Dad was getting a little forgetful, and that of course comes with the territory when you get to be our age. In the last couple of weeks, though, I have wondered if his memory problems were not a little more serious than I thought. I took him to see Dr. Baratz, and they ordered all kinds of tests. These we have just gotten back, and it is confirmed. Dad has Alzheimer's. We will start him on medication and discuss possible treatments, but I am afraid it is only about maintaining a certain quality of life because this is not reversible at this point. This will be hard for all of us, but I know you kids will do your best to give Dad the patience and understanding this disease will demand of each of us. For now, Dad is fine. He can still drive, go out alone, and best of all, he can still play table tennis over at the club. Really, nothing has changed, except that not all recent events seem to cling to the old memory bank as they might have once. Franny and Alec are nearby, so that will be helpful, not that we want to be a burden—

She can't read anymore for the tears bobbing in her line of sight. When they start landing on the keyboard, she worries she could short out the wiring so she pushes back her chair and stares, dumbfounded, at the screen with its blurry lines of rebuke. You can't stop things from happening by riding in elevators with smelly neighbors. And you can't stop this. She reaches for the phone.

"Alec? Can you talk?"

"Sure, for a sec. What's up?"

"Dad has Alzheimer's." Silence. "Are you there?"

"I'm here."

"Muth wrote us an email. He has it. It's definite. Why didn't I see this coming?"

"Cess, honey, I'm so sorry. How does she—"

"They did tests on him. We can't leave, Alec. They need us."

"Well now wait a sec. They're going to need us a lot more when his symptoms get worse, sweetie. If he has just been diagnosed now, it could be years—"

"Are you kidding me? Dad has Alzheimer's!"

"I heard you. Listen, we did a financing deal for a Swiss biopharm and I read an eighty-page report on the disease progression. Your dad is going to be living with this for a long time. What did your mom say?"

"I haven't called her yet. I didn't want to have to tell her we're moving to *California* on top of everything else she's going through."

"Now slow down, hon. We're not definitely moving to California. I still have interviews…"

"You know you're going to get it."

"No, I really think you need to slow down here. You're upset, this is terrible news, but why don't we take this one bite at a time, OK?"

"Well, actually, I'm done. I'm full." Silence.

"OK, honey. We can talk more tonight. I'm sorry. I really am. Everything will work out, you know that."

"I'm not going to California."

"We'll talk later."

"Don't you make me do this."

"I never make you do anything you don't want to do."

"That's because you make me want things I don't even want, like Boston."

"You wanted to move to Boston."

"See? That's what I mean. I didn't at first."

"OK, OK. I love you. But I gotta go, OK?"

"Bye."

At home that evening, Alec takes special care to keep the kids out from underfoot. He is always their parent of choice when it comes to roughhousing or make-believe because he is so compliant. He gives turn after turn when twirling, hefting or riding them around the apartment or the park, and as for make-believe, he will be whatever he is instructed to be, no questions asked. A crane? He'll stand with his arms straight out in front of him until they are called to dinner. An old woman? He'll tremble and sway and squeak until the kids have moved on to a new game and forgotten all about the stooped old crone waiting patiently in the TV room for her next line. Francesca doesn't allow 'physical play' inside, and gets overly involved in make-believe scenes, to the point that her kids are taking direction as if they were under contract and underpaid. They prefer Daddy. Francesca takes advantage of the free time to read everything she can find on the World Wide Web about Alzheimer's, none of it bringing her any comfort at all.

In response to Muth's all-points email announcing Dad's diagnosis, her brother Henry sends an open email back, asking specific questions about Dad's condition like, *Does HE know he has it? If so, does he want to talk about it? How are we supposed to handle it when he doesn't remember something?* As if you can be handed a flow chart on your father's gradual mental disintegration and it will guide you through. Muth prints out the email, Dad finds Henry's email in the printer tray and the gist of the ensuing conversation with Muth is that he just doesn't want anyone to worry about him. This offline exchange tells them three things. One, Dad knows he has Alzheimer's, two, he is more concerned about the rest of the family than he is about his own condition, and three, Muth is a convenient go-between for any questions they might have pertaining to the disease because no one, not even Pat, feels comfortable talking about it directly with Dad.

"Hi Muth."

"Hi back."

"Is this an OK time to talk?"

"Oh, sure." So far, no change in Muth's breezy demeanor. But one of them has to speak the truth out loud. It might as well be Francesca.

"I got your email." She hasn't rehearsed what to say next, and Muth isn't helping. There is an expectant silence on the other end.

"That's some practical joke, Muth."

"Ha ha. I wish it were."

"I'm still trying to take it in."

"Me too."

"Poor Dad. Poor you. Poor all of us, but mostly poor you."

"Poor all of us."

"How did you figure it out? Why didn't we notice?"

"Well, it's going to sound really crazy... I did have some suspicions about his memory, but I finally sat up and noticed when he stopped opening the mail. I mean, I think I've suspected for a while, but you don't want to believe your husband's losing his marbles…and I didn't want to worry you kids…"

"Please don't ever spare us. We can take it, OK?"

"Maybe so, but I just wasn't willing to see what was right in front of my nose. And then the mail. He has always taken an interest in the mail. And his business magazines. But suddenly he just wasn't opening the mail. And it occurred to me that he wasn't opening the mail because he couldn't follow it anymore. Or he didn't remember the people writing, or both. Anyway, I knew something was off."

"Wow. That's so…perceptive of you."

"I am pretty canny, aren't I?" She sounds like her old vainglorious self, but it is a hollow sound.

"So you took him to the doctor?"

"Yes. And they asked him all sorts of questions, and took a blood draw, and ordered an MRI, and then I got the call two days later…"

"Oh Mom."

"It's not an easy thing."

"I know there's never a good time for bad news, but this comes at a particularly awkward time, Mom."

"What does that mean?"

"I have some news…"

"You're pregnant." Her mother is heading into a shriek of excitement. This is Muth at her most irritating: when she wants things for her kids that they no longer want.

"I am not, nor will I ever again be pregnant, Mother."

"Then what?"

"Alec is being headhunted for a job in California."

"California!" she can almost hear her mother's pulse racing.

"Near San Francisco. Near Stanford University."

"Where will WE live?" If Muth says things in a disarming way, and she often does, she can always fall back on the fact that she is 'only joking,' if called out. But Francesca knows she isn't half-joking and would never call her out.

"He hasn't got the offer yet. I don't even know where we'll—"

"I'm only joking!"

"What about you guys spend the winters in California?"

"Darling, don't you know Mark Twain's famous quote? 'The coldest winter I ever spent was a summer in San Francisco.'"

"What does that have to do with spending the winters there?"

"Well, just imagine what the winters must be like."

"How true."

"If Alec gets the job, we'll just rent out our place and come live in your attic."

"Oh, I'm sure we can make room for you in the basement; near the dryer so you can stay warm on those freezing cold summer nights."

It's much easier to joke about these life-changing events. What she really wants to do is throw an old-fashioned tantrum. But that is not the way they communicate. Whimpers are for wimps. There is always a bright side if you squeeze your eyes tight enough shut. Instead they talk about the time frame, for how long dad might be able to function well, and the window of opportunity to let Alec chase this dream. Her mother is of the school that brings girls up to make way for their men. There is no mention of Francesca's job in New York, no mention of the kids' adjustment...just plenty of breathing space for the breadwinner. And starry-eyed imaginings of what all of this could bring in the way of material success.

"Daddy wants to say hi." She always says that when she is done talking. Dad never actually asks to speak.

"Who's that?" he always starts that way.

"It's your favorite youngest daughter." She's relying on the old favorites but this time she feels panicky and unsure of how to speak to her newly afflicted father.

"And how is my favorite youngest daughter?"

Relief.

"I'm just fine. How're yeeeeeew?" she drags out the word "you" the way they have all done throughout the whole of their family life together. In an introductory anthropology course she learned this kind of in-speak is known as animal noise. It's an intimacy constructed between tribe members to create solidarity. Their animal noise echoes through generations of the tribe. Can 'closeness' be genetically passed on? It would appear so.

"Surviving. What's all this about California? I overheard your mother." He still seems entirely on the ball.

"Alec might have a new job out there."

"Which bank?"

"Not a bank, actually. A high-tech company. They are coming up with new material for making synthetic bones."

He chuckles indulgently. "It all sounds terribly important."

"Absolutely. I wouldn't marry a man who didn't have something very important to do."

"Well I have something very important to do. I need to get my Rockports re-soled."

"How many miles today?"

"Six this morning, four yesterday. Your mother has walked precisely none."

"That's because I have too many meetings!" Muth has been listening in on the other line. Like a heartsick lover, she doesn't want to miss a word.

"It's because she doesn't like hills."

"He keeps walking in the hills without a cell phone."
"I don't need a cell phone. I need to re-sole my shoes."

"Well, I'll let you two get on with it then." She can imagine them bundling off into their Subaru for an afternoon of errands and Frappucinos. Holding hands in the pedestrian parts. Truly happily married. Now she imagines Dad's tall, lean figure start to break up, starting with the inside of his head, until he has disappeared altogether.

"Dad, do Muth a favor and carry a cell phone, OK?"

"Anything for peace and quiet!" Another stock phrase. You can hide a lot behind stock phrases.

"Call me when you know more," adds Muth. Her three adult children's lives play like a favorite T.V. series. The plot lines, the surprise guests, the comedic turns, all are performed for her entertainment. She passes on the highlights to her many acquaintances, who, no doubt, have more news of her offspring than they do of their own. But as the plot thickens, Francesca is the one looking on in helpless fascination. Muth and Dad close the conversation in their usual fashion, in unison:

"Love you to pieces!" Always the same tune: A A A A F sharp.

"Ditto!" B A flat.

Chapter 10

When Francesca's sister Pat calls, the conversation about Dad is characteristically unsatisfying.

"There's not a lot any of us can do right now. He's purportedly still well enough to drive and so on. So says Muth. I think he should stop, but no one listens to me. So, I hear you guys might be moving to California?" She has heard their news from Muth, who is the clearing house for all the family gossip, even at times when she has been instructed not to say a word, which isn't the case about California, though Francesca now realizes she should have tried to keep this quiet during the torturous waiting period.

Pat is a hardheaded public defender in St. Paul. She was once a thrill-seeking hippie pothead. She wore Indian print everything and never shaved her legs. She had pungent boyfriends and a black light in her bedroom in the turbulent town of New Haven, Connecticut in the 1970's. She swore off pot after leaving a very expensive dulcimer on a Greyhound bus in a stoned haze, a work of art crafted from willow and cherry that she had saved up for two years to buy. Talk about a bad trip. She reasoned that it could have been a child she left on that bus, which Francesca always found a little overblown, but you don't argue with Pat's logic. Like the Woman at the Well, or the Road to Damascus, the Dulcimer on the Bus became a conversion story that led to a rather extreme Christian devotion.

She accepted Christ as her savior at an outdoor concert in the Berkshire Mountains where kids were having hallucinatory breakdowns and Pat was the only sober one there apart from the medical staff. That spiritual awakening led to a life of service, defending the very people with whom she used to cavort as a wayward druggie. The family always knew Pat would be an effective litigator. She is compelling in and out of the courtroom. They hear about her cases over email. They are all on her distribution list, though as their brother Henry the dentist points out, that's because there isn't an option to unsubscribe. He is a hardheaded Republican who makes his living off of other people's decay. Pat's stories fill Francesca with hope for a "kingdom on Earth" where the poor are fed and the outcast are brought home, and justice is served. They make Henry laugh out loud, and shake his clean-shaven, close-cropped head in disgust.

Pat thinks Francesca is spoiled rotten, but she would never presume to let on. To Francesca. Directly. Things Muth has let slip lead one to believe Pat thinks her baby sister is absurdly wealthy and possibly undeserving. But Pat doesn't know absurd wealth. Francesca's kids go to school with the absurdly wealthy. She works very hard to keep their heads screwed on straight when all around them drivers are dropping their classmates off and whisking Mom away for another day of shopping and self-care before the nanny collects them for the remainder of the afternoon and the personal chef prepares them an early supper. Finally somewhere around ten, a kiss is delivered to their sleeping profiles before the cycle repeats itself again the next day. The Carltons are not that. Francesca would love a driver though.

She considers herself a basically giving person, though she could do more volunteer work, but with a full-time job and three kids, it's hard to fit it in. She does help in the Sunday School class-room once a month. Not that those kids are exactly crawling with flies in there, but hey, you do what you can.

Pat is the eldest child, which partly explains her vocation. She went to an all-women's college (she was calling herself a "woman" when she was a senior in high school, just as soon as she turned eighteen and could vote and smoke in front of the parents) and those women's colleges have a knack for minting leaders with con-sciences. Plus, and possibly most importantly, Pat gets to be the one in the courtroom addressing the judge, and she loves that aspect of the work; where she is exalted by association.

Growing up, Pat invariably took the starring role in their living room theatrical productions. She would play the tortured protagonist and Francesca would be the maid, the hairdresser, the neighbor, or her bewildered daughter, while Henry would man the lights. They were Rheostat. Their father installed them him-self when they first came out in the early seventies not because they provided a whole new spectrum of moods to every room, but because he thought, wrongly, that you could save on electricity. Henry would fade up, fade down all afternoon while Pat impro-vised wrenching dramatic scenes that would have given *A Long Day's Journey Into Night* a run for its money. Swathed in the one mint condition cocktail dress Muth had tossed into the dress-up trunk, Pat was a natural as the hectoring diva. Indeed, that is how the life roles were ultimately assigned.

Pat, of course, sides with Alec, because she sees this move to California as some kind of rite of passage designed to teach Francesca about self-sacrifice. Again, she doesn't say so, but you can always tell what Pat's position is, by the way she forms her carefully constructed sentences.

"So I guess you'll be needing our covered wagon!" The family was all a little shocked when she left her law firm in suburban Massachusetts for the city appointment in St. Paul, Minnesota three years ago. Pat encountered no resistance from her husband Ted, though, because he is a tradesman and can live anywhere. He is a carpenter, and that's not the only thing he has in common with Jesus Christ. He is possibly the most self-sacrificing soul she has ever encountered up close. They never had kids—they couldn't, or more precisely he couldn't—though they still talk about adopting boatloads. He would make a wonderful, patient father. Pat would run a tight ship.

"Don't hitch up the team yet!" jokes Francesca. "We don't actually know if this is going to happen."

"Well, I hope for Alec's sake that it does. It sounds like a really exciting opportunity for him." For him. She thinks she is being subtle. Francesca has been her sister too long not to know how incisively Pat harnesses the power of language. She doesn't waste a word.

"Yeah, well, it's not that great a time to be moving..."

"Oh, I don't know. Daniel isn't even in school yet and Elizabeth is so resilient. And of course Katharine—" she is masterful.

"Daniel _is_ in school. The hardest school in Manhattan to get into." Francesca regrets the ferocity in her tone, but can't seem to help it.

"Then he'll get in again, when you move back. I hear it's only a temporary move, until Alec strikes it rich? Or should I say rich*er*? Just like the Gold Rush!" Francesca chooses to ignore the subtle dig. She raises the small matter of her career in publishing.

"Can't you find a job out there?"

"I don't want to find another job. I like the job I have. They're hard to come by, and I have one, and I want to keep it."

"Ah well, marriage is about sacrifice, after all! You'll be so glad you gave Alec this chance to try something new."

Something a little too cheerful in her demeanor makes Francesca wonder if Pat secretly hopes Alec will fail so she can watch her pampered little sis unravel. She is losing ground in this sparring contest, but she can't help going one more round.

"I guess I kinda want to be near Dad, while he's still in good shape."

"You know, I've thought about that. Here we are all the way out in St. Paul, and of course I don't want to miss out…but think about Dad for a sec. He would hate to think we were putting our lives on hold for him. You know he would. He has always wanted his kids to reach beyond their potential, you know? He would love to see you take this risk."

Waving the white flag, Francesca changes the subject. She asks Pat about her job and Ted, and the weather and their travel plans for Thanksgiving and Christmas this year. That's a bit of a stretch, since it's early August.

"Maybe we can come out to California for Thanksgiving!" Pat isn't done with her yet.

"We would love that, Pat."

The call with Henry is even more unsatisfactory.

"I told her to get a second opinion. They are so trigger-happy with diagnoses these days. Especially Alzheimer's. You forget what you were going to say a few times, and you've got Alzheimer's. I'm sure he's fine."

He obviously hasn't heard anything about California yet, either. He may or may not hear about any of it until she's moved in and miserable. And Dad is worse.

Chapter 11

*F*inally, some good news. There are three strong candidates for the position of CFO at MNS. One has more industry knowledge and has actually been a CFO before (Francesca is betting on him), one is an internal candidate, a woman, who has been in the finance department since its inception and is very close to the whole enterprise (they ought to hire her, but won't), and the last is Alec, whose two years in Boston gave him direct experience with high-tech financing. He comes from the other side of the financial equation—the credit side, and therefore has contacts in the financial community that the other candidates simply don't have. But his wife secretly hopes that by leaving banking, he would burn many of his bridges, and therefore would not be as valuable to his would-be employers as they think. She has actually considered sending them an anonymous letter to this effect. That is how desperate she is to stay home. To keep her job. To be near Dad.

More news: it turns out Alec knows someone at MNS in the research and development department. He knew him vaguely at Stanford where they were both chemical engineers. The guy, Troy Howard, has good inside information and reassures Alec that this company is going places. What else is he going to say? Nobody likes to think the start-up they have bet their livelihood on is going anywhere but skyward. The more she hears about the job in Santa Clara, California, however, the more she has to accept that it isn't just the job that is luring Alec away from the only life she wants. The job is really just a symbol for change—big, challenging, thrilling change. Ever since he entered into negotiations with these people, he has had a renewed vigor about him; a bounciness in the morning, a chattiness in the evenings, an intensity in the bedroom she hasn't seen since they were dating.

She is quite the opposite. With every hopeful indication, she becomes more sluggish, less able to fake enthusiasm for this outlandish opportunity, because she has come to hate change. There has been so much of it over the past several years. They have made babies, moved to and from Boston, upgraded apartments a couple of times, birthed another baby, traded in one school for another, and another, she has changed departments, jobs, hired and replaced half a dozen nannies, and throughout, she has assumed that Alec's career is the one constant in an otherwise convulsive existence. She has expected him not to budge from his rung on the corporate ladder, unless it is to ascend. Bankers who work past midnight are either passionate about their work, or passionate about someone else. Since Alec and she have enjoyed fairly steady, satisfying sexual relations, she has always been secure in the knowledge that he falls into the former category.

She is more afraid of change than most. If she were to analyze it in-depth, and that is not really her style, she would say the reason she doesn't like change is it takes her back to her college years when she couldn't get even a toehold on the sheer cliffs of social success. She watched as all around her, at various points along the timeline that is marked by semesters and summers, the socially anointed scaled those dizzying heights. She was still on the ground when others had planted their poles. She was still lacing up her boots. As the acne spread, so did her social anxiety.

It even became awkward at home, at the holidays when the five of them would reconvene for short bursts. Her entire family, usually crackling with energy, gunning for a good tease, a harsh reminiscence, or a shared belly laugh at anyone's expense, suddenly became quiet and sincere around her and her bumpy outer layer. For she was handicapped now. Her face had ceased functioning in its prescribed role. It was meant to express openness and friendliness and an eagerness for life, but all it did was pulse with self-loathing.

After all of his success as an investment banker, all the promotions, the bonuses, the elaborate deals he has helped arrange, Alec has grown tired of waving the magic wand at the legions of business professionals whose fortunes ride on his ability to make financing happen. Apparently, it's his turn to have his wishes come true.

And here she thought they were making a life together; forging a future in tandem. Now she sees that no matter how much she has dictated the *style*, or perhaps the *logistics* of their family life, Alec has actually been the one calling the shots, and she has been so skillfully accommodating his every whim that she has failed to even notice. Francesca is confronted once again with the fact that she is not the princess in the fairy tale after all. She's actually the one reading the fairy tale out loud. The one who says, *ooooh, I wonder how this is going to end?*

Later in the week, with the kids tubbed and scrubbed and drug off to bed, she clears the apartment floor and its furnishings of sundry small plastic parts and personages while the bathtub fills. For Alec, the bathtub is simply a place to stand to perform his perfunctory morning ablutions. For Francesca, the bathtub is a means of transport. Armed with her current book, a shameless romance from her summer reading list, her plastic stemware and her Green Tea bath salts, she leaves her earthly concerns on the bath mat once and for all, the uncertainty of the move—the tangles forming in her father's brain—and slips, unnoticed, into an aquatic realm where she is at last weightless, alone, naked. Prenatal. Her feet barely reach the taps, as she fumbles with the extreme temperatures and bobs in the rising waters. She has an unspoken rule that once her feet leave the floor, her hands must remain dry, because a book that has been exposed to the merest droplets of mist is like a snail doused with salt; shriveled and buckled and no longer fit for the natural order. She plucks the paperback from its perch on the clothes hamper, and her journey through time and space is underway. Before too long, she is standing on a windswept hill overlooking a fishing-village in County Kerry. Cowbells tinkle in the foreground and in the distance, a low-riding fishing rig heads toward the harbor. The young captain is racing in a squall at sea. He is blessed with a fine catch and is unaware of the squall awaiting him at home, where a bright-eyed neighbor girl of seventeen has just discovered she's in the family way. The doorbell rings like a fog horn. Startled, Francesca dips the book into the now lukewarm bathwater. Damn it, Alec.

She lets in a swaying, cross-eyed version of her husband. It is so rare to see him in any way impaired, at first she thinks he is suffering a stroke.

"I goddit!" His shining eyes catch the hall light and glow like a cat's.

"What?" she queries, dripping and confused.

"I god the big gest op-portun-ittee uvvour lieevs! I god the job!"

He takes her into his arms by propelling himself at great speed into hers. They tumble backwards and the hall table tips over, spilling a bowl of odds and ends across the floor. They end up in a heap amongst the keys and pens. He is laughing crazily and she is crying just as hard. He is really going to make her go through with this.

Minotte calls. She got the hiccuppy message about the new job.

"How could he?" She is more insulted that her underground operation didn't work, than she is sad to see them go. The immutable fact about Minotte Grosbois is that she will always have a steady supply of adoring friends. She is, after all, *adorable*.

"I will find you friends in *San Francisco*." She says it with her heavy accent. Apparently, the French love Northern California for its fine weather and fine wines. Minotte has a cousin who emigrated to Berkeley in the 80's.

Francesca has actually considered the possibility that there is a hidden camera recording this elaborate prank and any minute they will all have a good laugh and Alec will go back to work downtown. Because how can she be expected to wrench the kids out of the two most prestigious private schools possibly in the *world* and then find them a soft landing place 3,000 miles away in a matter of weeks? It is August, school starts in September, and they are supposed to be leaving for two weeks to Block Island the day after tomorrow. As if in a trance, she cancels the rental and gives up their deposit. Still no hidden camera crew. At least she doesn't have to tell Ga Ga she isn't invited to Block Island this summer. Instead she has to tell her she is out of a job.

That conversation doesn't go well. They are both crying: Ga Ga because she loves the children, and Francesca, because she loves New York. She promises Ga Ga a month's pay and expects they'll only need her for a couple of weeks.

Francesca uses the time she should be buying them their uniforms for the fall, maniacally researching private schools in Northern California. They don't even know what town they will live in, though Alec says Palo Alto is the best choice. Where the hell is Palo Alto? He also says the school district in Palo Alto is outstanding. That's what his new employers at MNS tell him. There's only one problem. Francesca's research has revealed that California ranks in the high 40s out of 50 states in terms of its public schools, so 'outstanding' is a relative term. *Not Palo Alto* insists Alec, who has never got over his four years of undergrad at Stanford. *It is the jewel in the crown.* It is the jewel in a very shabby crown, but when her research turns up precisely no openings for either of the kids in private schools, she realizes she has no other choice but to home school them and that would be a travesty.

Besides, in the critical second year of this exciting new venture that is MNS, their first year in California must be a year of extreme sacrifice. For one thing, there will be no bonus from the bank in January. Considering that sum makes up half of their income, they are in for a shock. Alec will of course draw a six-figure salary at his new job, and that should cover the cost-of-living, but the rest of their reserves must remain in reserve.

"Let me get this straight. I am supposed to give up my wonderful life, my job, which, incidentally, was ABOUT to include a new edition of *Sights and Sounds* and I was going to get to go to Paris to find our recording artists, in case you were wondering how MY career was going, but never mind, I don't want to distract you from YOUR career...all my friends, and the things I like to do, the kids' schools, Block Island, all of it, so I can come to California with you and have no nanny, no cleaning lady, no family vacation, no gym membership...."

"We can still go to Block Island. Next summer."

"Alec!"

They are standing in the master bathroom in their bulky terry robes, each gripping a toothbrush in an impromptu duel. Before the double sinks and the mirror-lined wall, she sees herself at her ugliest, her mouth in a sneer, spittle flying, eyes dark and menacing, hair pulled back in a frayed hair band, revealing every rough facial surface. She looks like a gargoyle.

"Pash."

He plays his trump card.

"Pash...I'm sorry."

Early on in their courtship, Alec arrived at her apartment unannounced and out of breath. He gripped a small paper bag in his fist and demanded she guess its contents. Her only clue was that he thought of her when he saw it. Imagine trying to guess what made a new beau think of you—not one of her guesses was remotely what she hoped for, but she had to show restraint. What was she supposed to say? She guessed a book, a CD, a chocolate chip cookie...Alec's patience thankfully expired and he plucked from the bag what looked like an over-ripe dark purple plum, the skin as crumpled as the bag that held it. Her heart sank like a broken elevator yet Alec's eyes were shining with excitement and lust, and not a hint of her confusion crossed her expression as she smiled mutely back at him.

He rewarded her charade, shouting "You are my passion fruit!" and she felt giddy again, though she would have preferred to be likened to a sparkly gem. They fed each other juicy slices of the sticky fruit, seeds and all, and rolled around noisily on the carpet, her roommate gone for the weekend.

She was his passion fruit and later that shortened to Pash, and she called him Jiggy, which was short for gigolo because Alec is seven months younger than Francesca. Ten years later, Pash and Jiggy are Cess and Alec and the only soft fruit she has hand-fed anyone comes out of a small jar with a picture of a baby on it.

"Jiggy, you are pulling the rug out from under me."

"I know I am but I am going to make you so glad we did this. You're going to have that apartment overlooking the park you've always wanted. I can get that for you. I promise, it will be worth the sacrifice. Besides, they love you at Cooley. You know they'll take you back. And you can have a much deserved break."

"Who said I wanted a break?"

"Well, wouldn't you like to take it easy for a year or two, and enjoy the California sun and fun?"

"No thank you. I like to work in case you hadn't noticed."

"OK, OK, then work! Anyone would be lucky to have you. Please, honey? Will you jump with me?"

"I will make this sacrifice for you because you want me to. But don't go trying to make me want it, too, Alec Carlton."

Alec describes the possible pay-off. Based on his back-of-the-envelope jottings, they stand to net a total of ten million dollars over the next five years. Five million in the first two years. Hard as it might be for someone, from say, Kansas City to believe, to buy a co-op apartment for a family of five in the Upper East Side of Manhattan requires a minimum of five million dollars in liquid assets, which you are required to reveal to the board of governors of the building. This is to match the original five million dollar cash outlay for the place. They insist on cash. This is not an urban legend. There are plenty of people who can abide by these terms though the Carltons are not among them. For the past several years, they have been paying an average of $10,000 per month in rent for the privilege of enjoying use of this precious real estate. However, if Alec's projections are sound, and he is nothing if not conservative when it comes to financial analysis, they'll be tearing down walls and ripping out plumbing with the best of them before she is 43. Just.

Over the next ten days, she keeps saying *but are you <u>sure</u> about this?* And he says *nothing in this business is a sure bet.* She second-guesses him once too often: the last time she begins a sentence with *Are you absolutely sure, because if I make this move*—Alec loses it. He looks at her with what appears to be revulsion, something she has not registered before on his sweet baby face, and mutters,

"You're acting the spoiled child."

It's the way he says it—like a line from an Edwardian drama—*You're acting the spoiled child, Francesca!* Where did that come from? She is speechless. But she quickly recovers.

"The only thing spoiled around here is my life." Sometimes even mommies can sound like 12 year-olds. She stomps out of the room.

With a slam of the door, *the spoiled child* launches a campaign so subtle, so dignified, and yet so passive-aggressive as to disprove her husband's assertion once and for all. This day marks the start of a period of such extreme self-deprivation that she will prove beyond a shadow of a doubt that she is not the least bit spoiled. A martyr, perhaps, but not spoiled. It is a gloriously selfless act, for she has grown rather used to the life of a senior editor married to a New York investment banker. Alec would have made partner in two years, the bonuses would have gone through the roof, and their stock portfolio would have swelled as timber after a mighty flood.

When the kids find out they are moving (it was thought preferable to wait to the very last possible moment to break the news, because until the ink is dry, things can always change), they expect tears and recriminations. These they get in spades, especially over the part about leaving Ga Ga, the only mother figure either of the younger two has ever known. *And that's some figure!* Alec would say. Both parents are a little terrified of how Elizabeth will react. She is their oldest and most sensitive by far. Francesca's strategy is to play the victim right alongside her. After all, this was not her choice. Alec will have to bear the burden of everyone's resentment; it is part of his remuneration package.

When they inform Elizabeth that she will not be returning to Nightingale, her familiar little sheltered world, she doesn't throw a tantrum like the other two. She doesn't slam her bedroom door and refuse to come out for the rest of her life. It is much worse. She looks at Alec with those sleepy brown eyes and says,

"You need to stop changing jobs. It doesn't look good." Then, this family therapist trapped in the body of a nine-year-old turns to her mother and adds,

"If you spent less, he wouldn't need to earn so much." Then she stands up and walks out of the room and hasn't spoken to any of them since. Alec even left a new portable CD player in a slick black leather case on her bed last weekend. They had agreed to wait until she was twelve, but apparently drastic circumstances require drastic measures, though he might have consulted his wife first. Elizabeth simply plugged herself in and tuned them out for good. Daniel thinks he's going to meet real cowboys and pan for gold in California, so he is increasingly reconciled to the move. Katharine will probably have a pierced belly button and a Valley Girl accent by the time they move back to New York. What. Ever.

When Francesca turns her attention to housing, she expects they will find a spacious house with a backyard pool and spare rooms for family visits, working well within the parameters of their rental rates in New York. She can't even find property that comes close to their rent of $12,000 a month. When she starts to focus on a couple of really great houses, with porches and eaves and lots of square footage, and all of them under $8,000 a month, she emails pictures to Alec at work. The phone rings within minutes of her hitting Send.

"Hi," he says warily.

"Did you get my email?" She sounds excited about the move for the first time.

"I did. We have a problem." This is the first time Alec hasn't sounded solicitous and cajoling.

"What?" she demands.

"Hon, our housing budget. We need to stay under $3,500 here."

"What?" she shrieks.

"Our circumstances will have changed considerably, Cess."

"You make that sound like it's MY fault!!" She is a little hot under the collar.

"No, it's just that we haven't had a chance to communicate about this…" Alec assumes the voice of reason, while she continues to plumb the depths of her role of mad housewife.

"Communicate as in what? What are you trying to say?"

"The budget we need to follow for the next 18 months or so takes into account our new salary." She has always appreciated the way Alec refers to his salary as "our salary" and same with their yearly bonus, but right now he sounds so patronizing she could throw the phone.

"There won't be a bonus coming to us at the end of the year like we get at Solomon, and you already know my position on our principal assets…" He trails off because he knows she knows all of this.

"I thought you said TWELVE months of sacrifice. I didn't expect to spend what we do in New York, obviously—and anyway, how do YOU know there won't be any bonus?" She sounds quite immature and out of her depth at this point but she throws caution to the wind.

"Because I'm the CFO." He tries hard not to make this last statement sound arrogant, but he can't help what she hears.

"Well excuse me, Mr. C.F.O. if I had KNOWN we were only going to spend $3,000 a month, I could have saved myself a lot of trouble looking at houses that are clearly way out of our price range."

"Thanks for understanding. I have a meeting. Gotta go. Love you." Notice he didn't correct the $3,000.

The choices on the Internet are all a little too "perfect" for the asking price: Perfect for a growing family! Perfect for downtown living! Perfect for entertaining! In the end, she decides that they had better get to Palo Alto, the town they have chosen as their new home, before they choose a house.

Chapter 12

*T*he Three Graces crowd into a booth at Paradiso, sharing three kinds of salad, which they stab at dolefully.

"We can still have our con calls," offers Mac.

"It won't be the same, I know I shouldn't say that, but it won't." sighs Lee.

"Conference calls, and emails. Whoopee." Francesca is beyond gloomy. Lee tries to repair her earlier damage.

"We're going to do a road trip, right Mac?"

"That's right," Mac rallies. "We'll fly out and then we'll pile the kids into the car and we'll head for the Hollywood Hills."

"Daniel gets carsick." Francesca, remembering a smelly trip to Madison Connecticut, is in no mood to be cheered up.

"We'll bring a bucket!" trills Mac.

"Can someone please explain to me how all this happened exactly? I used to think I had a handle on my life." Francesca slumps in her seat.

"Like a suitcase." adds Lee.

"Exactly. Everything neatly packed and ready for me when I need it."

"Honey, you still got a handle on it. It's just that your suitcase got a little heavy," Mac explains.

"So now you got wheels," adds Lee. "Hey, Franny, about your dad, I hear the drugs these days for Alzheimer's really, really work! I bet he'll be in a steady state all the way till you get back!"

"And Saint Alec will make boatloads of money and give it all to you to spend and then it's time to party!" Mac rises to the occasion. It isn't working. Francesca can't rally. The evening ends in front of her cab pointing to the Upper East Side.

"You sure you don't want us to come to the airport?"

"Positive. I want to remember you like this. With stuff in your teeth." They laugh mirthlessly. Lee sniffles. Mac claps Francesca on the back.

"Be great out there. And if you can't be great, at least be yourself."

"Huh?"

"That didn't come out right. Be yourself out there. No one else is qualified."

"Better qualified…"

"Quit editing my work. Can't you see I'm struggling here?" They hug three ways. They strike the Three Graces pose, which makes them all giggle halfheartedly.

"Save my place?" says Francesca as she climbs in her cab.

"Till the cows come home!" cries Mac.

"Or you do!" adds Lee.

Westward ho. Alec's interpretation of Manifest Destiny has won out. They are pointed toward San Francisco at a cruising altitude of 38,000 feet. Francesca skipped breakfast (and coffee) in all the rush of getting her family on the trail and is consequently lightheaded and cranky. Why not just stuff her life in one of the overhead bins, so much like *his* piece of carry-on luggage does she feel on this, Alec's Great Adventure.

They are at least comfortable. There are so many Magic Miles in Alec's travel wallet that he has upgraded the whole family to Business Class. With the five of them dotted about the screening room/cum seating section, Alec next to Katharine because Francesca is in such a foul mood, and the older two sitting together across the aisle, you would never know they were a family. Elizabeth is a miniature version of a jaded rock star. Dressed all in black, and plugged into her portable CD player, she doesn't appear to notice she is airborne. Daniel chomps on a large wad of gum "for his ears" and is riveted by what looks to be an R-rated movie, R for violence. Katharine snoozes on Alec's arm while he reads business magazines. Francesca cracks open <u>House of Sand and Fog</u> because it is set near San Francisco, but that turns out to be a big mistake because that book ends very badly.

The trip from SFO in a battered airport shuttle van is deadly quiet. They are headed down the San Francisco Peninsula to their new temporary digs at the Mountain View Residence Inn, with its spacious kitchenette and plaid fold-out couch. They arrive so late 'their time' everyone is in an exhausted, grouchy heap when they finally finish dragging in their oversized, overweight luggage. Francesca and Alec get the kids ready for bed as if under water. Katharine wails piteously while Alec scrubs her teeth and Daniel tinkles on the bathroom floor in a passive aggressive act of rebellion when forced to pee "one last time." Alec sits on the toilet seat after the family is finished in there, punching away at his cell phone for a late-night call to the other side of the world. He barely looks up when Francesca turns out all the lights except his. Elizabeth wears her portable CD player to bed so she doesn't have to listen to her family making annoying little noises all night.

Alec abandons them the next day for meetings in Santa Clara, so she takes the three kids on a hunt for a home in their realtor's silver Lexus. The perky little brunette is Cookie; an energetic woman of somewhere around sixty with a page-boy haircut and upside-down tinted glasses sliding down her altered nose. She shows up at their motel room this morning faster than a pizza delivery. The only snag is she misunderstood the message Francesca left on her general office voicemail and thinks they are looking to buy. This is revealed only after the kids are strapped in to the backseat, Elizabeth plugged back into her portable CD player and Daniel sucking on his fingers, which he hasn't done in public for two years.

"All the way from New York City!" Cookie crows as she starts the car. "You're going to love it here, is it Francesca?"

She nods, not in the least bit able to match Cookie's gushing enthusiasm for any of this. Though it is a beautiful day. Not a cloud in sight.

"I know just where to take you first, hon." She pats Francesca's arm. "There is a peach of a Spanish Mission that just came on the market yesterday, no one has even been through it yet, but my colleague got the listing so I have an in."

"How much?" Francesca is not even sure what Cookie means by Spanish Mission, but she is won over by her conspiratorial air.

"They're asking two point three but I think we can get it for under two. It needs landscaping, and some roof work." Cookie is patting the wrong arm here.

"Um, did you get that we're renting? We're only here temporarily..." Cookie is less adept at hiding her shock.

"You're renting?"

"Wuz matter, Mama?" Katharine pipes up from the backseat.

"Yes, we're only here for a short time, a couple of years —"

"'Till I'm ten!" calls out Daniel.

"Hush, guys," she hisses, feeling her blood pressure start to rise. Cookie may be annoyed, but Francesca is frantic. They are running out of time here.

"Well, with housing prices going up the way they are, you really ought to re-think your strategy." Cookie has a new sharpness to her voice that makes Francesca inadvertently check the exits.

"I'm really sorry for the confusion, Cookie. I thought I made it very clear in my voicemail that we're looking for a rental..." Cookie is executing a dangerous U-turn half a mile from the Residence Inn. She doesn't seem to be listening at this point.

"I know little to nothing about the rental market. We're not the best outfit for that. Why don't you pick up a copy of the Daily News and see what you find in there? It's free," she adds.

Francesca calls Alec's cell phone from the motel room and leaves an urgent message.

"We need a rental car here." They have two days before school starts back up. For some reason the Palo Alto public schools begin before Labor Day weekend, so they have already missed the first couple of days. Now they have the holiday weekend, to get their bearings.

She circles options in the Palo Alto Weekly and after fourteen hours of wrong turns and self-guided tours of inadequate living space, by Labor Day, they have found a suitable dwelling. Suitable for a family of opossums, anyway. It is what they call in the industry a mock Eichler. Apparently, a post-war developer called Mr. Eichler designed and built hundreds of flat-topped houses with balsa wood walls and heated concrete floors for the expanding middle classes, and these have since become modernist collector's items for people who, rather than choose to tear them down and start over, consider them to be ultra-chic. Francesca is a little surprised that some other, long-ago developer saw fit to copy Mr. Eichler's Kleenex box-design. She doesn't know about California chic but she worries about all of her heat buried under the floors while the wind whistles through the joins in the walls. But for now, it is brutally hot in Palo Alto, and all those floor-to-ceiling windows scorch the living-room/dining area. They have a DECK (apparently a special feature since it was spelled out in capital letters in the ad), with an up-close-and-personal view of a sagging, rotted fence surrounding a dappled strip of dirt. Daniel can play trucks out back, but who is going to wash those windows? The kitchen is no bigger than the one she had in Manhattan, but the appliances have some catching up to do. All in all, this place is a dump. But it's within budget. Francesca the Martyr is more than satisfied with her compromised circumstances. Saint Alec is relieved that his wife seems to have resigned herself to a more modest lifestyle.

"I'll take you to Bermuda when we're back in New York, just the two of us. Remember how much you liked the Queen Victoria Inn? I haven't forgotten!" But Francesca has forgotten. Like a monastic, she has eschewed all of her worldly pleasures and treasures for a life of total self-denial.

"I'll need to make floor-length curtains for the living room."

"My little homemaker." He kisses her on the nose and wraps himself around her on their blow-up mattress. The movers will be here in two days.

With the kids caught up on their inoculations and registered in the Palo Alto Unified School District, her biggest unresolved problem now is finding somewhere to put Katharine all day. She would have been starting at Eastside Preschool had they stayed in New York, but here in Palo Alto, there doesn't seem to be a single opening anywhere. Francesca has called dozens of nursery schools, and with each new lead, she is exposed to increasingly esoteric child development theory and practice. When she finds herself touring the nut-free, gluten-free, all organic Peas in a Pod experimental Nursery, where children make their own lunches using only what is grown in the school's plot at the municipal gardens, she realizes she has lost her focus. What she really wants is to pay someone as little as possible to keep Katharine busy in the mornings so she can at least take some kind of part-time editing job up in San Francisco. She adds her name all the same to the Peas in a Pod waitlist and takes Katharine for a hamburger and shake at the Peninsula Creamery downtown.

Finding a church is a snap: the one that serves their neighborhood is less than a mile away. Muth always says, "You shouldn't choose a church by its preacher," but at St. Matthew's, the preacher does happen to be the main selling point. He looks like Russell Crowe and sings the service like Bono. When father Mark shakes hands on their way out of church, she has the urge to ask him to autograph her belly. He is very magnetic, but not in a sleep-with-the-parishioners way. Not at all. He has a godliness about him that is definitely not put on. You see it especially when he is ad-libbing his prayers of thanks out loud. He is abundantly grateful. And so articulate! She marvels at the way he weaves together a poetic paragraph about the poor, the disenfranchised, and the war-torn, with all these convoluted clauses and lashings of adjectives. He is Heaven's mouthpiece, this guy. And he is very easy on the eye. Apparently his teenage son fronts the band at the groovy five o'clock service and it is just a matter of time before someone signs the kid to a record label, he is that good. She learns all of this from the chatty pre-K Sunday School teacher who keeps her after class to run through the curriculum and sign her up for classroom volunteer time.

How coincidental that it is at church, a week into their stay, where Francesca experiences what amounts to a miracle. Pat would add, *there are no coincidences!* which may be overstating things some-what. At the coffee hour, Katharine is snaking around Francesca's ankles, smearing the inside of a jelly donut on her linen trouser leg while Daniel eats crackers at the food table and Elizabeth reads in the car with the door swung open. Alec is at home enjoying the peace and quiet of an empty house. He doesn't do church, not unless there's a bride coming down the aisle. An apple-cheeked grandma bustles over, and leans down to address Katharine.

"Now I don't know if I have met you before. My name is Faye." She holds out her hand and for some reason, Katharine holds out hers and they shake. This is newsworthy, because Katharine has never shaken hands with anyone; they have been working on hand-shakes at home since she was two but the only ones that she will attempt in public are the 'secret handshakes' Daniel has developed, which include spins and drops, strange throat calls and stamping feet. Usually, when an adult addresses Katharine, she shuns them completely. She really throws herself into the exercise; diving into whatever fabric her mother may be wearing around her lower half. Skirts are ideal, but she will seek refuge between bare thighs in a ladies' changing room if the need arises.

Still holding hands, Faye and Katharine start singing the hokey pokey. Francesca has never seen anything like it. Katharine is the last person she would have imagined "shaking it all about" with a total stranger, but this brazen old lady has some kind of a magic touch. Faye is giggling helplessly to the extent that she may topple over, but she suddenly straightens up and says to Francesca,

"You're new here?" Francesca explains they have just come from New York and Faye asks her which preschool Katharine attends and she explains that they are on two-dozen waitlists and Faye says,

"You come see us tomorrow and we'll find Katharine a cubby." It turns out Katharine just shook her booty with the founder, executive director and head teacher of the Cartwheels Co-op, a preschool that somehow didn't pop up on any of her Internet searches back in New York. Judging by Faye's seemingly magical properties, Francesca wouldn't be surprised if this twinkly crone had conjured up the school with a wave of a wand.

"What do you mean by co-op?" Francesca asks, bracing herself for more organic vegetable soup at lunchtime and gluten-free soy cakes on birthdays.

"The parents own the school. You get a key to the campus, you spend time in the classroom with the children, we have wonderful parties—our fall carnival is famous in this town." She stoops down to Katharine's level again.

"If you come nice and early tomorrow morning, I'll take you to the chicken coop and we'll see if we can find an egg for you to take home." Katharine looks up at her mother as if to say *can I go home with her now?* And Francesca thinks *only if I can come too.*

Monday morning at nine o'clock Katharine is pinned with her very own laminated nametag in the shape of a hen. A freshly laid egg is safely nesting in a monogrammed paper cup in the refrigerator of the full-service kitchen. Outside, Francesca nearly steps on a free-range chicken pecking in the weeds by the door. She tries to be more careful with the free-range children populating the expansive, shady play yard.

Katharine's nametag gives her a new boldness and she heads for the sandbox, eyeing a little girl who is making sand cakes in battered pie tins, which another little girl carries off into a bright yellow playhouse. Like an overworked waitress, the one laden with finished pies asks Katharine to help her bring in more dishes and Katharine takes the bait. Francesca leans against the swing set pole and surveys the scene, relieved to be dropping off her last child at last. *A place for everything*, as her mother used to say, *and everyone in their place,* thinks Francesca triumphantly. Presently, a big-limbed woman in overalls sidles up to the swing set. She wears an ethnic cloth fashioned into a sling with a big bump at the bottom that rests on her pelvis.

"You guys visiting?" she asks, gesturing at Katharine.

"Actually, we started today. I'm Francesca Carlton." She sticks out her hand, which is ignored.

"Welcome to Cartwheels!" Blares the large woman, throwing her arm around Francesca's shoulder.

"We're so happy to have you! I'm Spring. My little guy's Jonathon. He's three and a quarter. There he goes!" She points at a little boy in overalls matching hers, careening by on a tricycle. A little girl steps into his path holding a crude stop sign. Jonathon screeches to a halt inches from her bony legs.

"Whoa," Francesca can't help saying. Spring doesn't seem to notice.

"What's your little lady's name?" The sling emits a fussing sound. Spring unbuckles her front and pulls a plump breast from under her t-shirt. She waves it at Francesca while digging around for the source of the noise.

"Katharine." Francesca looks around to make sure no men can see Spring's massive breast. Because the campus is so large she forgets that she is on private property, not in a city park. There are no men anywhere. But there are a surprising number of women.

"What's your workday?" Spring wants to know.

"I beg your pardon?"

"Which day are you working? Or don't you know yet?"

It turns out that every parent at Cartwheels is assigned to a "teaching team" and she is expected this very Thursday to work from nine until noon alongside six other mothers. They have a "night meeting" tomorrow night for two and a half hours; in fact they have night meetings three out of every four weeks. Francesca learns that she, not Katharine, is in fact the student at Cartwheels Co-op. The school is funded by the city's Adult Education department, and the parents are the students. The classroom is simply a lab for their ongoing study of parenting and child development. The kids are the course materials. What is faintly absurd about it is she is on her third child. What she hasn't learned yet, well, isn't it a little late?

A slightly tanned, carefully dressed mother strolls by in darling pink flats, crisp cotton piped beige slacks and a fitted blouse in diagonal brown and pink stripes with three-quarter length notched sleeves. Francesca can't help complimenting her on her shoes and she, in turn, admires Francesca's hair, a highlight job she had done by her beloved Oscar on 88th and Madison. It's the only thing left on her person that reminds her of better days. This sleek, understated ambassador offers to show Francesca the bike shed and they leave Spring tending to her grunting nurser in the gunny sack. Francesca has that slightly elevated pulse that accompanies a first date or a job interview, but can also flare up when you think you might have found a like-minded friend in a strange land.

"Whenever I have Outside Bikes," confides Mimi Stark, "I give myself permission to dress like a normal human being. Believe me, it's a different story at the art table, or if you get Sandbox and Hose after snack..." It is all too much to take in at once. Francesca concentrates instead on Mimi's eyebrows, which are artfully plucked and appear to be colored. They discuss shopping opportunities in the surrounding area; there's a Bloomingdales, Neiman Marcus and a Tiffany's nearby, and for ten blissful minutes Francesca forgets completely that she has no shopping budget. They are interrupted by Teacher Jody who reminds Mimi to get out more bikes and adds,

"Let's not get Francesca off to a chatty start, now!"

She is shown the sign-up sheet on the wall in the hall where she is expected to choose a booth to run at the famous Carnival in October, to sign up to bake dozens of cookies to sell, to put her name down for two three-hour workshops to make things that will be sold in the Carnival Store (make things?), and there's a six-hour "Maintenance Day" she might as well get out of the way because they are required to do one every quarter that the school is in session. This is what Faye meant by a co-op. She feels bamboozled, but there's the small matter of the laminated nametag, which Katharine wants to wear home at noon. Yessiree, they all 'own' Cartwheels Co-op, whether she likes it or not. They've got the key to the play yard now.

That night, Katharine pins her nametag to her pajama top and later, Alec informs Francesca that he can't possibly get back in time for her Night Meeting tomorrow. He has to fly to Austin in the morning for a management meeting. When she corners Faye the next morning to let her know about the conflict, expecting her to wave that magic wand of hers and excuse her from the whole ordeal, Faye counters with the good news that she can bring her children to these meetings.

"Lots of parents do," says the bright-eyed pixie in the paint-spattered smock. "They can amuse themselves in the music room while we talk about parenting issues in the big classroom."

What she wants to tell the old dame is she doesn't have any parenting issues, except, of course, the issue of having to parent when she would rather be reading a magazine. Now there is the issue of being a co-owner of Cartwheels Co-op where it seems the parents do all the custodial work, including yes, porcelain scrubbing. She can just picture all those little preschool boys spraying the bathroom stall as they perfect their aim over the course of the year. And she gets to mop up behind them.

Each night meeting has a theme, and tonight it's negotiating. They are approximately thirty parents, all seated in tiny kid chairs, facing Teacher Jody, who has the same command over the grown-ups as she did over their squirming spawn at yesterday's story time. She covers the topic of negotiation like a college lecturer, citing current sources, representing all sides of the issues, punctuating her talk with interesting personal anecdotes (it turns out all three teachers and their aides attended the co-op themselves at some time). Francesca's three children are a caterwaul away in the music room, tumbling on mats someone laid out. Elizabeth has her portable CD player and homework, but when Francesca checks on them as the class reconfigures itself into 'break-out groups', she finds her surly 4th grader helping six little kids through an obstacle course of low balance beams, mats and a ladder stretched across two sawhorses.

Mimi Stark has thoughtfully joined Francesca's break-out group, to sit next to the 'new girl.' Francesca admires her Kate Spade saddle bag nestled at her feet. Mimi sees her studying it and gives her a wink. At one point in the discussion, Mimi allows that at their house, they use TV as a carrot, or stick, depending on the situation. A dad, who looks like Gilligan in a business suit loudly interjects,

"You let them watch TV?" Not to be intimidated, Mimi shoots back:

"Not if there's something on I want to watch!" and lets out a gale of giggles.

Francesca laughs along with her and thinks to herself, *I have got to remember to call the cable company tomorrow.* She realizes they are the only ones who are enjoying the joke. A plump, frizzy-haired woman in her 50's says,

"I used to let Audrey watch PBS but now even they have commercials, so it's pretty much nature videos at our house these days." That seems to soothe Gilligan and they move on to the next pre-printed question on the slip of paper Teacher Jody has passed out.

"Why do children tantrum?" reads Gilligan, the self-appointed moderator.

"Why do any of us?" pipes up Mimi. "Because they aren't getting their way."

Story of my life, thinks Francesca. *Alec <u>always</u> gets <u>his</u> way.* They discuss ways to handle tantrums and other forms of civil disobedience. They talk about setting expectations. She could have used this particular seminar about two months ago. At least she picks up a good pointer for those times when Katharine is screaming bloody murder in a department store and threatening to bang her head on the marble floor. Let her.

When they are called back into the plenary at the end of class, she imagines the clean-up facing her in the Music Room. Some nights she still feels like she's on New York time two weeks into their stay. When she finally retrieves the kids at 9:10, she finds them dragging the last mat into a neat pile under the supervision of a truffle-colored Indian woman.

"Your children are very well behaved," she murmurs, and before Francesca can say something clever about how she must be talking about someone else's kids, she finds herself saying,

"Thanks."

Mitra has huge, solemn black eyes, magenta lips and shiny, supple skin. Her tiny little daughter sports exuberant, loopy curls in all directions and a lilac Tom and Jerry nightgown over bright green sweat pants that end in red Elmo slippers. The sleepy sprite takes her mother's hand and they float out of the room in companionable silence.

Chapter 13

*S*o much for the editing job in San Francisco. She has combed
the industry rags and no one is looking for a very part-time
telecommuter. Francesca has resigned herself to one year at least
of "working out of the home" as the "stay-at-home mothers" at
Cartwheels call it. She has taken up her toilet brush and wields it
like an enchanted sword, determined that each swish of the bowl
will bring her one swish closer to her very own bite of the Big
Apple. The fabled five million dollar tree house overlooking the
Museum of Natural History will naturally come with a hard-working porcelain scrubber of its own, with family to feed, near and far.
And she will feed them.

Over the years, she has employed dozens of child minders and
housecleaners, each and every one 'sent' to her as if in answer to
prayer. She considers the partnership — and it must be a partnership between employer and employee if it's going to work — the
perfect symbiosis. In New York, she needed the cleaners to dust
and clean and they needed her to keep paying them to do so. She
needed the sitters to stimulate as well as safeguard her kids, and
they needed her cash and references. It is not easy to explain what
would appear to most people as her over-reliance on others to do

the work she had signed up for as wife and mother. But she had a good excuse: she worked. On the Upper East Side, her situation was as common as cabs on a wet day. The rest of the mommies in her neighborhood did not work, yet they still stole her sitters. They complained about how they had to manage three kids, two schools, and a total of ten activities a week, all in different directions, and all at the same time. Well she had to feed and clothe five people (Alec has no dress sense whatsoever) and entrust them to other people's care. Then, she went to work and managed several editors and authors and marketing staff and printers and retailers and her boss, and her boss' boss, all before heading home to pick up where she left off that morning. Once a week, she went out with Mac and Lee. They took in a movie, a play, a poetry reading, whatever struck them. Just the girls. They liked to take their souls out for an airing. She can hear the bush woman in remotest Africa sur-rounded by her seven children under the age of eight asking where she can get some of that soul food and what she has to say to that is, *you know you couldn't survive any better in Emerald City than I could in the bush*. Francesca's survival took a different set of tools, and that's all there is to it.

She knows her dizzying place in the food chain, but she does have a streak of humility informed by a long-ago crudely con-ceived morality. The Wilsons were always a church-going family, and years of Sunday School and Confirmation Class taught her all there is to know about the three-in-one: Father, Son and Holy Ghost, or Holy Spirit as she is known in the Wilson household (though she's more of a family pet whom Muth takes care of). When Francesca was little, it was "Jesus loves me this I know" and the underlying sense of security this sweet, tuneful message brings. As an adult, her focus shifted to God the Father, the one who art in Heaven. She regards him as the Almighty, and like a

God-fearing character in the Old Testament, she does her best to keep Him happy. She tries very hard not to take any of her good fortune for granted, because she knows that God is listening in. She views Him much the same way she did in her primary school years: as a slimmed-down Santa Claus in loin cloths who knows when she has been bad or good.

When she says "bad or good," she is not talking about murder or sainthood here. Back in the day, "bad" in her household encompassed the basics: lying, cheating and stealing, but what really got her mother riled, and remained for Francesca the final frontier, given her proven ability to avoid most forms of lying, cheating and stealing, was showing off.

Their mother the amateur actress couldn't resist a good speaking part, but she couldn't stand a show-off in her home. Like the Eskimo nation with their dozens of words for snow, she had a million words to express the incorrigible: braggadocio, pomposity, verbosity, gloating, and vaingloriousness— these were the four letter words in their house growing up. As the youngest, Francesca was a novice, and guilty more often as an accessory, but Pat and Henry were worse. Ellen Wilson wanted talented, nimble, and gracious children, but she wanted them with a matte finish: no outshining their creator. That's creator with a small "c." Muth's ego needed plenty of elbow room.

If one of them got going for too long with a story or gag, Muth would twirl her right wrist and ask them to "wind things up." They had five more minutes, as if Muth were the floor director and they were the talent.

"Don't write my scripts!" Pat used to protest. Henry was docile and acquiescent, but he wasn't actually listening. He did exactly as he pleased, nodding agreeably.

Muth regarded Francesca, her youngest, as the perfect under-study. While Muth played the starring role, she groomed Francesca for the unlikely occasion that she might one day take over the part.

"We're cut from the same cloth, you and I. The very finest linen."

They were all raised to believe in their vast potential, with clear expectations about how to employ their God-given talents. If you are brilliant enough, you will attract quality, and this you will add to an immaculate gene pool and the real alchemy will take place in the form of the NEXT GENERATION. Muth often reminded them that her two great-uncles married two Collins sisters—of Collins and Jamieson, Haberdashers. Their respective fortunes helped fund various 19th century siblings' endeavors, from found-ing a mission in Nicaragua to hiring a taxicab to drive from Chicago to Bloomington on a drinking binge. The point is, those brothers had been brought up right, to have wed the Collins sisters. When she was covered in festering pustules, Francesca knew the family secretly worried that hers might be the last stop on the Wilson line. But then the weather cleared, and the sun came out, the band struck up and she was back out on the dance floor of life. If she had been a son, this would have been an even greater cause for cel-ebration, for Henry hadn't settled down yet and Pat was off at law school. Of course it took Francesca several more years to find her 'Collins,' and by then Pat had settled down with Ted, though no children were forthcoming, and Henry had knocked up Margaret and they had Mindy and Tom. Alec came along just in the nick of time. He was a fine specimen and would go places and their prog-eny would rule the world. For now, their progeny are reveling in free-dress days everyday at school, bare feet on the sidewalk, fairy houses and mud pies, hide-and-go-seek, hopscotch and daydream-ing in the grassy front lawn. It's a big, beautiful adjustment to life in California for the Carlton three. The toughest adjustment of all is Francesca's. She has landed squarely on the hearth, with a clear view of a sagging, rotting fence.

Their parents' only friend in California, Troy Randolph, is coming for dinner. In fact, he is Alec's only friend. Francesca has twenty-nine new friends—the mommies at Cartwheels, though perhaps they are better described as comrades in arms. Arms filled with snack trays, paint brushes and easel paper, science projects, vacuum cleaners, paper towels...and weepy preschoolers.

Troy is the guy from MNS whom Alec knew at Stanford. They both majored in Chemical Engineering, but Troy went on to get his PhD in molecular biology and has been at MNS since its inception doing hard-core R&D. He was supposed to bring his girlfriend tonight, but he called yesterday to say he would be coming alone after all. It has been months since Francesca has entertained, so she has gone all out. She unpacked all of their candle paraphernalia (she has Guatemalan votive holders in the shape of exotic flowering vines that take up a great deal of the surface area of the table), and their good china. The older kids polished the silver, and Katharine and she washed the windows. Rather, she washed them, and Katharine smeared the lower two feet with water and graham cracker goo. Now they are only going to be three at the table (the kids are eating pizza in their room with a video). Oh well, more *osso bucco* for everyone.

Troy is twenty minutes late, which renders her warm hors d'oeuvres (gruyere and *parma* on pita chips with capers) chilled and wrinkled. He is wearing a t-shirt that says "Don't Tell Me The Score..." tucked into jeans that hold up a fifteen-pound slab of stomach overhang. Later, when she returns from checking the *osso bucco*, she reads the message on the back of his shirt: "...I'm TiVo-ing." Her guess is, there is no girlfriend. He probably thought he'd keep the option open, in case he found one before today, but given the shape the guy is in, his social grace quotient, which is currently in the negative numbers, and his beard, which grows more consistently on his neck than on his face, he has probably been single for quite some time.

It turns out her presence is totally unnecessary at this little party because so far, the men have touched on three topics: football (Alec gets all of his information from the sports pages because they don't have the luxury of turning on the TV on weekend days), chemical engineering at Stanford, and work. She has not opened her mouth once, except to offer Troy another beer and to see how the kids are doing in the back. She checks the *osso bucco* again. It is ready to slip off the bone on to the floor so she calls the men to the table. She dishes up the homemade pasta, and lays the meat and sauce in their pasta nests before bringing them out with a flourish. The men are talking about a coach who got carded for rushing a referee and don't even notice her steaming dishes, one in each hand, her flushed face. She looks like the cover of a Tyrolean travel brochure. She realizes now she could have tossed Troy a piece of the kids' pizza and she would probably have had a bigger reaction. They eat the *osso bucco* with a Medoc, while Troy has another beer. When she passes around the basket of toast points for the bone marrow, she feels vaguely ridiculous. Troy has no idea what to do with his toast points. She makes a show of digging into her marrow and spreading it lovingly on the toast. Troy reaches for the butter and leaves his bone marrow for the scrap heap.

Dessert is raspberries and cream, which look completely out of place being shoveled past Troy's beard. At one point Alec looks over at his wife with his half-closed eyes, which is meant to read *great job, Hon*, but she will not be mollified, the damage is done. Archly, she suggests that Alec make the coffee, while she gets the kids ready for bed. This is the last they will see of the chef tonight. She climbs into bed with Katharine and stews in her own bone marrow until she falls asleep to the sound of very boring conversation at low volume in the other room.

She struggles out of a deep sleep after midnight and returns to the matrimonial bed where Alec is emitting Medoc fumes mingled with meat drippings. They sleep the rest of the night on opposite sides of the bed.

They say that the biggest problems in a marriage stem from a lack of communication. Francesca maintains the opposite is true. She and Alec communicate far too much. Every little gesture, every pause, the slightest variation in tone, all of these blazing arrows whiz back and forth between them. Alec can tell by the way she answers "good morning" that she is pissed. She can tell he can tell by the way he pauses before asking her whether he should make pancakes for the family. She knows he is trying to build a bridge out of pancake batter but she is unmoved. She tells him he can make whatever he likes, and now he knows she is furious. At least now he can ask her what's wrong, knowing she cannot possibly say *nothing*. She knows this, too. But she can say *you know perfectly well* which is equally powerful.

"You didn't like Troy."

"Why do you oversimplify everything? Is it to make me look shallow?"

"I don't need to make you look shallow." Ah, the famous Carlton *Double Entendre*.

"I never said I didn't like Troy."

"You don't, though."

"And I doubt very much you like Troy yourself."

"That's not the point. He was our guest."

"I would have enjoyed serving a homeless guy off the street more than that slob. He didn't even compliment me on my meal! And neither did you, for that matter."

"I thought the sauce was a little salty. I'm KIDDING." She will not be kidded.

"I'm going for a run." She casts around their bedroom looking for her sneakers, while pulling on a jogging bra.

"Pash—."

"Don't you even speak to me, Alec Carlton."

"Of course it was delicious, Pash."

"DON'T."

"Look, we did the right thing having him over. It will make it easier for me to crack the whip on those guys in the lab."

"Bully for you."

"Fine," he mutters.

"I felt so ridiculous! The little woman with her special meal, the good china...all because you can't afford to take the guy out." But perhaps she has gone too far. She forgot to be Buddhist this morning. She cuts her losses and carries her shoes into the hallway, leaving her husband in bed to ponder her lapse in saintly decorum.

She nearly storms past her three little munchkins lined up on the couch staring at the television. Elizabeth has the remote. She hits the mute button.

"Hey!" scream Daniel and Katharine.

"It's a commercial, duh. Mom, what's for breakfast?"

"Duh." Daniel retorts.

"Duh!" echoes Katharine.

She is not mad at these members of the family. She swoops down on all three with her arms outstretched and tries to hug them at once.

"Ow!"

"Ow!"

"Mom!"

Instead, she gathers her hair in a ponytail and heads for the door.

"Dad's making pancakes."

"Yippee!!!"

She grabs her cell phone on the way. It's Saturday and she has a thousand free minutes to use up before Sunday night.

She waits until the cooling off portion of the run before dialing for sympathy. It turns out Mac has more important things to discuss than Francesca's failed dinner party.

"I swear to God, when he kisses me, it's like he's sculpting me. He takes my face in his hands, and just moves them around like a...a blind sculptor!

"How poetic. Only one problem. He's not your husband."

"Oh, come on. It's a sign of closeness."

"It's a little more than a sign, doll."

"Well, you know what I mean. You certainly can't call it sex."

"You can't call holding hands sex, either. Or snuggling in a movie theater. But we're not supposed to do it with people we're not married to, Mac."

"Here we go again."

"C'mon, Mac! I leave you alone for, what, a few lousy weeks?"

"Cut that out. You're not my moral compass, for Chrissakes."

"Well, you better find one soon before you completely lose your bearings."

"Because I kissed Terry?"

"How would you like it if you found out Hugh was kissing one of his colleagues?"

"I wouldn't care."

"Bullshit, Mac."

"It would be like reading about it in a novel. I feel so estranged from him."

"You would hate it."

"Well I don't hate kissing Terry."

"It's a slippery slope."

"Yeah, very slippery."

"Quit doing it, Mac. Terry is a cheat!"

"So am I, apparently."

"Please? Hugh doesn't deserve this."

"Hugh isn't home. Hugh isn't ever home. Plus, his mouth is too small. He's a lousy kisser."

"Why don't you get Terry to give him lessons?"

"Very funny."

"Quit kissing Terry, Mac."

"I told you, he kisses me. I never initiate."

"There's that slippery slope."

"You've gotten so boring, Cess."

"Nope. I've always been boring."Francesca changes the subject but Mac is not over this. When they say goodbye Mac's hearty leave-taking is forced and overly loud. Francesca finds a quiet retaining wall around the corner from her house and calls Lee.

"Tell her to quit it, Lee!"

"She won't listen to me, you know that."

"Hey! What about you steal Terry away? I hear he's a great kisser."

"He's not my type. I don't go for slimy cheaters."

"According to Mac, it's not cheating. It's Terry being *close*."

"I'm actually quite worried about her, Cess. Poor Hugh!"

"What do we do?"

"I have no idea. We're talking about Mac here. We have never been able to reign her in, you know that as well as I do."

"Do I say something to Hugh? Not to rat on her, but you, know, to subtly give him a heads up so he can take the appropriate action."

"Like rip Terry's head off?"

"Or just stay home for a while. Cancel some of his flights or something." "Plus you know he'll tell Mac. He tells her everything."

"This is crazy. I can't get Mac to listen to reason, I can't tell Hugh 'cuz he'll tell Mac I told…"

"I think I know what to do."

"What."

"Nothing. It's really none of our business."

"This would have been our business…before I moved away."

"It's not your fault, Franny. Mac was due for a rebellion. It's been a while." They also hang up on an awkward, unresolved note. Everything is falling apart.

All of this excitement has made Francesca temporarily forget why she is mad at her husband but then she remembers ol' TiVo-t and she starts to heat up during her cool-down.

At St. Matthew's the next morning, the chair of the Outreach Commission describes an orphanage in the Kingdom of Lesotho the parish is sponsoring. Francesca learns that Lesotho is a tiny country right smack in the middle of South Africa, where poverty and AIDS are so rampant, the only growing industry there is orphanages. The Sunday School kids are raising funds to buy a bicycle for the village where this orphanage is located. The bicycle will serve as an emergency vehicle for anyone needing the health clinic ten miles away. It will also carry cargo, pull crops to market and provide mobility for the disabled. All this from one bicycle. The sermon is about going outside of your comfort zone. Alec is home unblocking the sink, which is a good thing because this sermon might make him the teensiest bit smug, given Troy Randolph.

Chapter 14

*T*he kids settle into a routine whether they like it or not, it's the law. Daniel would gladly 'do time' over going to kindergarten, but at least the jail that is his classroom closes at noon and he can be with his toys again until the next day. Elizabeth is surprisingly fine. Each morning, she beetles off to class, her arm linked with her new best friend Natalie, a darling little neighbor from the next block, with red hair the color of a beach sunset. It is a very different mood at Daniel's door. All teary goodbyes must occur several feet from the classroom before they line up to wait for the locked door to swing open, and for the teacher to announce himself like a game show host. Francesca has to change her shirt most mornings, after peeling off her sobbing son. Katharine squeezes her hand until her fingertips tingle, in anticipation of their own imminent separation over at Cartwheels. That is, when it's not a workday for her teaching team.

Francesca checks her watch, and calculates how many minutes before she is kid-free for two and a half blissful hours. She will spend them grocery shopping (she has never had to take them with her and she is not about to start now) and if she plans things well, she'll give herself a pedicure while watching The Price is Right. She has loved Bob Barker since she was a preteen, snuggling in Muth's bed when home from school with strep throat. Like an indulgent uncle, Bob still gets carried away by the excitement of a big win, and so does Muth and so does Francesca. As a young newlywed wins an Amana side by-side, she can just hear her mother saying *They'll have that for years. It'll probably outlast the marriage!* Or when a grandma wins his 'n' hers motorcycles. *She can sell them. Get a nice little car.*

Then it's time to collect two thirds of the brood; the kindergartener first, oddly enough. Daniel gets out fifteen minutes before his baby sister.

If she is scheduled to work in the classroom at the preschool, she is lucky if she sits down once before the morning is through, at which time she sprints to the car, races over to Green Gables, grabs Daniel by the nape of the neck and speeds back to Cartwheels for her clean-up chore.

Her workday happens to fall on the day of the week when Teacher Teresa comes in to teach the kids Spanish, so she is able to listen in on what Katharine is learning and she can resurrect it in their car rides. Teresa has also produced a cassette recording with guitar accompaniment of the different rhymes and songs she covers in the weekly fifteen minutes. Francesca catches herself humming *La araña pequeñita subió subió subió* and anyone who overhears her thinks it's The Itsy Bitsy Spider. She feels ever so slightly smug, knowing a new song in her rusty Spanish. She can only assume Katharine must feel this way, too. Even Daniel hasn't started a second language yet. But he is studying Matisse in Spectra Art, so she can't complain too much. Green Gables has turned out to be a very satisfactory landing place for her older two. Every other week, she volunteers in both classrooms (cutting into her Bob Barker time, but her kids gave her no choice in the matter), helping the kinders with math activities and discussing literature with Elizabeth's classmates. Both age groups are surprisingly focused, cooperative and motivated. Children move silently from one 'station' to the next, sweeping up used papers on the way and depositing them in the designated bins. They put away classroom supplies without being asked. The older kids work diligently in small groups, negotiating differences quietly, yet passionately. Both teachers employ the same highly effective tactic of speaking in hushed tones when addressing the class. You have to be perfectly silent to be able to catch what they're saying. Elizabeth shares a classroom with another Elizabeth, and it means they are forever being handed back the other's corrected quizzes and homework. Before the situation gets any more out of hand, her Elizabeth decides to change her name to Liza. Everyone is mandated to call her Liza, and should not expect a reply should they fail to do so.

Today is the Thursday teaching team's *Under The Sea* theme day at Cartwheels and Francesca is a floater, since some of the moms on her team are in their fifth year at the school and know the ropes well enough by now to take over every aspect of the day, including the read-aloud, and the science project. Francesca is assigned Outside Art as a fallback position, but today, most of the kids eschew the primary colors at the easels for fish masks and fishing with magnets off the wooden boat marooned in the side yard.

The mommy who was supposed to bring in the book for carpet time totally forgot in all the rush of decorating three dozen recycled CDs to look like iridescent mackerel. Francesca is sent to the OCEANS section of the tightly packed, forty-year-old library and chooses Funny Fishlife, a bold picture book of unusual underwater species. At the same time, she finds Red Fish, Blue Fish, and fifteen minutes later, she is surrounded by sweet-smelling little people with trusting eyes and battered knees all leaning on her and each other in a big colorful skirt spread out on the carpet. She feels their total trust lap up against her. Their little weights against her, their trance-like state as she reads in a slow, hypnotic way, sweeping the book around the group to show the illustrations…it creates a soporific mood that only snack time can eclipse.

Chapter 15

" We've got our dates!" cries Muth down the phone. "How does the 14th to the 25th sound to you?" To Francesca, it sounds blissful. She needs to see her dad, and Muth is always a big distraction. Only trouble is, doing the math, her parents' stay will be precisely three and half times too long for Alec, whose number one rule is Houseguests Leave After Three Days Before They Start to Stink. He had that rule before they married. Even she had to abide by that rule. When you move to New York, friends you didn't even know you had look you up.

"Fabulous." There are always ways to get around the rules, such as sending the parents on an overnight road trip to reset the Guest Clock. "How's Dad?"

"Same as ever. Still taking those interminable walks. No change." Muth would say if things were worse. Now that the cat is out of the bag, everyone is involved in its care and feeding. "I want you to use us when we're there. It sounds like Alec is never home these days! You two need a date!"

"Alec who?" They laugh, both forcing it somewhat.

"I mean it, sweetie. I can't bear the thought of you waiting up for your husband until all hours every night of the week."

"Don't you worry, Muth. It's not nearly as bad as that. I don't actually wait up! But you're right, we need some quality time, without the little scallywags."

"And we need some quality time WITH the little scallywags."

"They will be so excited to see Gummy and Bonpapa!"

"I can't wait to see your life. Visit the schools, meet all your new friends—"

"Such as they are."

"What does that mean?"

"Oh, you know, I mean I wouldn't necessarily choose these women as my friends, you know, under other circumstances. They're just people I happen to have ended up cleaning toilets with, you know? It's like getting stuck on one huge elevator with 89 other families. You can't help getting pretty familiar. But I mean, if you could handpick the people you were to get stuck on an elevator with...I guess I'd—"

"I'd rather have an elevator full of strangers. That way you won't be totally disillusioned by your loved ones when you are finally rescued."

"Believe me, I don't need a stuck elevator to be treated to Mac's craziness."

"What's she up to now?"

"Oh, Mac always has something going on. Tell Dad there are some great hikes around here, but you would hate them. Lots of hills."

"You two can go, I'll baby-sit. How's your I.U.D.?"

"My I.U.D.? Hmmmmm, let's see, it's been three years now, and so far, no complications. None since the last time you asked."

"Just be careful. You only have one uterus."

When she played soccer in high school, her mother was convinced her precious baby girl would sustain permanent damage from all the rough contact. *Remember,* she would remind her, *you only have two eyes! You only have two knees! One nose!* And on and on the list would extend until, by senior year, she had done a full catalogue of Francesca's anatomy. In four years, Francesca sustained only one concussion, and two pulled hamstrings, but that was apparently beside the point.

"Since I only have approximately three healthy eggs left, I don't think you need to worry about my uterus. What about you, how's yours?"

"I have no idea. You were the last one in there." Francesca laughs approvingly. Muth takes this as a cue to run the joke into the ground.

"Judging by your bedroom growing up, I expect you left it in quite a state."

"Now what are you two going on about?" Dear Old Dad has picked up the extension.

"We're talking about uteri," says Francesca for comic effect.

"About what?"

"She's being very silly," Muth cuts in. "I was telling her our dates."

"Our dates?"

"For our trip to California to visit Francesca and Alec and the kidlets."

"When's all this taking place?"

"Not soon enough!" chips in Francesca.

And so the conversation goes, with Dad listening in on a fast-paced exchange between two of the five members of the family who mystify him with their wit, frivolity and word play. It is so much easier to play at communicating than to engage in the real thing. Dad seems just the same, but suddenly *the same* seems fairly compromised. It occurs to Francesca that her father has ceased trying to keep up. Muth now performs this function for both of them.

When Alec gets home, she mentions the dates. She expects a *frisson* of disapproval, given his houseguest rule, but none is forthcoming.

"That is terrific, honey. It will be so good to see them."

"It's kind of a long visit," she probes.

"Not a problem. There's plenty to do, plenty to see...and you'll have some company. And some help. I know you have been stretched in a million directions, sweetie."

"Wow. OK. Great. Yeah, I'm excited." It is amazing how one kind exchange can transform a relationship from mediocre, to marvelous. How one minute, you think your husband is an uncaring creep and the next minute he is the prince you dreamed about as a little girl. This must be what they mean by marriage taking a lot work. It's exhausting trying to keep up with all of the new developments.

Chapter 16

*L*ast night, she retrieved a message from Mac that she is coming into San Francisco this morning. Hugh is flying on to Tokyo, and he will collect her on the way back. Francesca wonders if he suspects something, and is hoping Francesca will straighten out his wayward wife, dropping her off for a thorough going-over. Alec kindly offers to take the kids to school so she can leave early to get to W, a chic new hotel Mac has chosen for their mini-Girlsday. She can't reach her to confirm, but Francesca knows Mac well enough to know that she is expected, schedule conflicts notwithstanding. W is near the train station, so she heads up with the commuters and walks the four blocks to the hotel. She arrives at 9:05, an hour early. Through the glass front doors, she spots Mac right away. She can tell it's Mac from any angle. And she is embracing a tall man in a suit. It's a long, lingering embrace. Terry. Francesca ducks around the corner of the building and waits there, panting, until she figures they have uncoupled. As she rounds the corner, the guy in the suit has his back to her, looking for a cab. She wants to push him into the traffic. Instead, she calls out his name and then starts rifling through her purse as he swivels around. She takes a deep breath and enters the spacious lobby where she spies the scarlet woman sitting serenely off to the side at a table for two.

"You're here!"

Mac leaps up and charges. She hugs Francesca like a drunk hugs a lamppost.

"You're up early!" Francesca points outs meaningfully to her amoral friend.

"Oh, you know, three-hour time difference. You're so tan!!"

Mac has ordered two glasses of champagne, coffee and W's famous donut holes with Meyer Lemon Curd.

"I read about these puppies in *Home*." Mac takes an extravagant bite of the goopy confection and launches into a long-winded description of the other people in her row on the flight over. Francesca accepts the fact that she is not going to hear more about the little rendezvous in the lobby. Mac pushes a flute of bubbly across the table. Francesca pushes it back, prudishly.

"No thank you. Too early. So, what's going on with you?" She reaches for the coffee. She will work Terry in slowly.

"I hate Hugh." Mac delivers this fact in a sing-song voice, the way you might say *I'm fine*. It turns out Mac has decided to divorce Hugh. The kids will apparently not notice the difference because he is gone so much as it is. Her marriage is a charade.

"Don't tell me you're running off with Terry." She meant to do that more subtly.

"Oh, him. Naw. That's pretty much over. Besides, he's already married. Mac sneaks a look at her censorious friend, then looks away again, as she often does when she's being economical with the truth.

"No more chaste French-kissing?"

"This isn't about Terry. Terry is just a symptom. I've been thinking about this for a long time." Her jaw is set in plaster. Francesca gives it her best shot.

"Oh, c'mon, Mac, everyone THINKS about it. It's got to rank as a married woman's most popular fantasy! But that doesn't mean we're supposed to DO anything about it!"

"I don't love Hugh. It's over."

"Have you mentioned any of this to Terry?"

"Quit bringing up Terry! Franny, he's nothing! He's just a friend."

"I'm a friend and you don't make out with me."

"God, you're such a prude."

"Hello? Who was the wanton hussy who slept with three men in one weekend?"

"Yeah, well, that was because you hadn't met us yet. You were looking for love in the all the wrong places."

"You're right. And that's what you're doing here."

"I told you, this isn't about stupid Terry."

"See? You think he's stupid."

"Of course he's stupid. Why else would he be kissing a middle-aged woman with sagging breasts?" And she starts to cry. "I just can't keep going on like this, pretending that I care about Hugh when I don't anymore. He irritates me."

"When a tag on my shirt irritates ME, I cut out the tag. I don't throw away the shirt."

"Yeah well, this isn't the tag. It's the whole shirt. It gives me hives, OK?" She sounds and looks like Elizabeth-aka-Liza, when she is in one of her horrid moods. They usually send her to her room and tell her to come out when she's human again, but Francesca doesn't have that luxury with Mac.

"Have you tried switching detergents?" This makes Mac smile. But then down comes her brow again and casts a shadow over half her face.

"It's time to give the shirt to someone less fortunate."

"But Mac, what about the kids?" She hates to bring them up, but they are the elephant in the middle of their bistro table.

"I am thinking about the kids, Fran! They need a loving couple raising them. Not a pissed off old woman and her fly-by-night toy boy." Mac dabs at her eye makeup with a used napkin. "Now you made me cry!"

"Because it's sad. I'm sad. But OK, if you really think this is what is best for you guys, you know I'll support you." She rubs Mac's forearm. "You've always been able to trust your instincts, Mac. I trust yours more than my own for my stuff," she adds, running on a little at the mouth.

Mac continues to chase tears around her face. "I remember how much I depended on him in college—I would study hard during the week so I could spend the weekends with him. I didn't need anything or anybody else in those days."

"And he needed you, and it looked right and it has been right, because you made those great kids. But you will survive this, babe. You're still gorgeous, and capable and funny..."

"...Don't forget old. Do I look like I've been crying?"

"No. Just wear your shades. Everyone in San Francisco wears shades; they think it'll bring the sun out." There is a pause. Francesca tries a safer tack. She asks about people in New York they have in common. She gets caught up on Lee, who is dating a performance artist who is a complete narcissist according to Mac. They talk about the old days. That fills three quarters of an hour with big long breaks for laughing till they're spitting out their coffee. The old days are always the best days. But then Mac turns very serious as she returns to the present.

"How do other people do it? What makes you so damn happy, anyway?"

They fight for the last of the lemon curd with remnants of the last donut holes.

"I can't speak for anyone else, of course, but we just...um, when problems come up, as they invariably do in any relationship, we...uh...gosh, um...the fact is, I have no idea how we do it. Just last night I was expecting a big fuss and I got a loving hug instead. Go figure."

Mac searches her face for signs of doubt, since misery does tend to love company, but Francesca has nothing to hide. OK, so she never, ever sees Alec. Never seeing him in New York was the norm anyway. Never, ever seeing him is possibly a different story... that's exactly what it is: a different story. The kids and she are in one story, and he is in the other. Hers is probably a happier story.

"We inhabit parallel universes for now. It works fine for us. Some people would hate it, but I've got a lot going on these days." Considering how much she complained to Mac, in the run-up to moving, about how little help she would have in California, her visitor doesn't look too convinced. But the fact is, theater, opera, movies, and book club have been supplanted by real-life plots. Now it's all about book projects, math facts and learning to ride a two-wheeler. All the world's a stage, after all. She checks her watch again. Time to head back to Palo Alto for pick-up.

"Walk me to the train?" She slips on her coat as she stands up. "You don't look like you've been—"

"Just don't make me start again." Mac gathers up her overnight bag, her coat, bag.

"Do you want to put your stuff—"

"I'm not staying here. My hotel's nearby. I just wanted the donuts."

They leave together in unresolved silence.

Francesca collects Daniel at school with seconds to spare. They rush to Faye's, where she and Katharine are in the middle of a game of Old Maid. Daniel takes over from Faye, who leads Francesca into the kitchen for some tea and sympathy. Francesca confesses her worries about Mac.

"My guess is," ventures Faye, "your friend Mac is in a transition time and she isn't too sure what to believe about herself. Her youngest is…?"

"He's eleven."

"It would be too simplistic to call it a mid-life crisis, but it sounds like Mac is re-evaluating her life and the traditional measures of success don't apply. The kids are finding their own way, and she needs to find hers."

"That sounds about right. I should encourage her to get to work on her musical."

"Creative outlets are a wonderful way to connect with your inner self."

She is always a little surprised to hear Grandma Faye sound new age-y. It doesn't go with the picture they all have of her as an old-fashioned schoolmarm. Lined up next to Muth, Faye is more stooped, whiter-haired, crinklier. Yet Muth and Faye are about the same age. Maybe it's all the theatre, but Muth just doesn't seem so old. In some ways, she gets wilder as she moves through the decades. There was that dinner party Francesca threw in New York just last year, when Muth suddenly felt the need to quote Philip Larkin: "They fuck you up, your mum and dad. / They may not mean to, but they do." Her friends still talk about it. Yet today, Faye has her own contemporary sound.

Grandma Faye brings Francesca up to date on the Carnival store. Apparently, they are behind schedule completing the princess wands, marionettes, and bejeweled treasure boxes intended for the shelves in the music room. They need more manpower. Make that mommypower. Ninety mommies times three obligatory hours, that's two hundred and seventy hours of cutting, sewing, gluing, stuffing and turning inside out and that still isn't going to be enough? Apparently, Francesca's job as assistant manager of the Carnival store is to squeeze more hours out of the same ninety mommies to get enough inventory together for the big day. Make that the same two-dozen mommies, for the 80/20 law of community involvement is alive and well, even at a co-op preschool. There will always be those who will roll up their sleeves another inch or two for the good of the social order, and those who skulk out the side gate without so much as a backward glance. Maybe at a co-op it is more like 70/30, after all the required hours are accounted for and there is still far too much to do.

A year ago she would have gone out and bought enough loot to fill the shelves of the Carnival store. Nothing special—a bunch of stuffed animals and yo-yo's would have done it. But this year, she'll be lucky if her budget covers the magic show for Katharine and Daniel. That evening, after the kids are down, she sets up a phone tree and starts punching buttons.

Chapter 17

*L*est she be lulled into the false sense that she is actually in charge of this new life of hers, she finds out by chance that this Wednesday is Back-to-School Night, a misnomer for an event that takes place a full month after school starts. Somehow, she has to find a sitter for her three kids, on a school night no less, two days from now. Where is Ga Ga when you need her? Thank God Francesca is shameless enough to call Faye, because she is free, and willing. And free.

Tonight, Room 10 has the feel of Santa's workshop in the off season. Brightly colored product festoons the walls and ceiling. Instead of the factory-floor safety bromides hanging near bathrooms at the back of supermarkets, here the sayings on the walls seem to protect not so much life and limb, as little souls from injury: "You Can Do It!" "Best Guess is Better Than No Guess!" "When I Feel _____I Try to _____." Lists: HARD feelings / NICE feelings, How To Keep it Friendly, What Good Listeners Do.

She can feel her limbs loosening in their sockets as she lowers herself into a chair in front of Daniel's desk. The cheery bromides are taking effect and she slows her breathing. She relaxes into surveying her fellow parents, searching for their children's name places on desks, and she finds yet again a near uniformity in outerwear. The polar fleece gathered in this classroom would be enough to put a whole sheep station out of work. The extraordinary thing is how fleece is paired with multiple-carat diamond studs and Coach shoulder bags.

The one essential ingredient missing from this bizarre fashion parade of outward-bounders, she realizes with astonishment, is makeup. No one is wearing any. Back home, even the men wore makeup and it was so cleverly applied that the only way you could tell they were, was by the way they snuck looks in their PDA screens. Home. New York is a lot of different things to all kinds of people, but she has never thought of it as 'back home' before.

As the room fills up, her attention turns to the children's self-portraits that dangle overhead. With their huge expanses of pink or brown, and the mostly wide-set nut-shaped eyes and generous grins, they look like one large family of simpletons, staring vacantly at so many hikers assembled at base camp. Alec appears in the doorway with the air of a man who has just stepped out of a time machine. When he is in the least bit self-conscious, Alec looks like he smells something bad, the way he wrinkles up his nose and avoids eye contact. He could not look more discomfited if he were standing in the ladies' room. He is supposed to be in Elizabeth's classroom, Room 18, while she covers Daniel's class. Using her fingers, she mimes the number eighteen. He nods, and disappears. She used to pride herself on the nonverbal cues that Alec and she traded back and forth at parties and other public venues; they were so efficient at getting their messages across to each other and it was all so Cold War-ish and titillating. Lately, though, she could do with a little more verbal. A lot more, actually. For some reason she cannot explain or even guess, Alec doesn't feel the need to speak at all anymore.

She follows the other parents' gaze to the blackboard where the agenda for the evening has been written in prim block print. Mr. Harris is standing next to the agenda waiting for everyone to settle down. Francesca takes him in in great gulps. It is rare to have him at such close range. From the slightly tangled shoulder-length chestnut hair (precisely the same shade and cut as Jackson Brown's) to his too tight, definitely too wrinkled polyester blend beige button-down shirt, his beltless Dockers (the other local regimental uniform, this one reserved for male teachers, civil servants and worshiping Christians), he looks like a laundry bag come alive. His shoes are worn, but clearly well cared for; oiled and buffed: they conform loyally to his lumpy toes. The laces are new, as if he picks up a new set at the start of each school year along with a pack of pencils and a protractor. She stares longingly at Mr. Harris's double knots. This is the kind of basic self-care she craves, new laces in her shoes and she doesn't even wear tie-shoes. Ever since their break-neck arrival on the West Coast a month ago, she feels like a leaky boat the skipper forgot to tie up to a mooring. She has the persistent feeling that she is slowly sinking, and only she knows it. No one in this room has any idea how little unpacking she has done (except maybe Alec, but he is never home), how utterly disorganized the household is, and with no relief in sight. Add to that a fourth-grader from out-of-state (who has never even HEARD of the Ohlone Indians, and it seems her classmates have been studying them on and off since first grade), a kindergartner with separation issues, a preschooler still in Pull-Ups no matter what they bribe her with, and an absentee father/husband/critic bringing up the rear, and it's no wonder she yearns for new shoelaces.

Mr. Harris should not wear beige. He looks like a pasty-faced rocker. She mentally removes the shirt and replaces it with a charcoal ribbed pullover. She immediately feels better. He introduces

their Room Parent, Celia Hartwick, who sounds like the principal. *At Green Gables, we this, we that, we ALWAYS, we NEVER*...her
fleece jacket is providing too much warmth in this overcrowded
room and she is panting and glowing all at once. She winds up her
five minutes of fame and hands out the sign-up sheet for volunteer
positions. By the time the clipboard gets to Francesca, she has the
choice of coordinating a Valentine's Party, designing the class website, or volunteering as one of four lice checkers. She chooses the
party, even though she cannot imagine how she will handle twenty
five-year-olds jacked up on pink confections and raring to play
games that she has designed for their amusement. Yet she prefers
this scenario to a head full of lice.

Mr. Harris tackles his agenda, breathlessly fleshing out his
theories on letter formation, number groupings and spelling prin-
ciples. He launches a discourse on pre-reading decoding while she
undresses and re-vamps the assembled crowd. This blonde should
not be wearing orange. No one should wear orange, except circus
clowns and convicts. That young dad needs to get over his baggy
jeans and put on something tailored and pressed. This couple in
their matching Patagonia pullovers look like an out-of-work comedy team. His tummy is straining his XL, and her sleeves come past
the tips of her fingers. She is so thin she still looks cold in the folds
of fleece and they both look miserable.

When the topic turns to socialization, Francesca snaps to
attention like a Marine. While she is confident her son will gradu-
ate from kindergarten with the necessary tools to handle the first
grade curriculum, the same issue has plagued her since early
September, when they arrived a full week after school had started,
when Daniel would only stand at the back of the line outside his
new classroom, refused to let go of his lunch box, and insisted on
wearing his Spiderman ski cap into the building. Ever since that

moment of agonizing clarity—that her son is a dork—she has fret-ted over his basic survival skills. Mr. Harris describes the Grub Club, carefully constructed encounter groups, for lack of a more age-appropriate term, that meet once a week during snack/recess. Closely moderated, the revolving small groups 'process' social issues that have come up that week. For some reason this makes all the parents murmur. They tingle with anticipation at the range of topics that might reveal themselves. Mr. Harris concludes the highlight of his presentation and turns to play-yard safety and the school's policy on competitive blacktop games.

They are instructed to write their children a little note, to let them know they were here, that they support them in their academic endeavors. She can almost feel the emptiness in Daniel's stomach as he faces yet another morning virtually chained to his school desk, longing for his Mighty Monsters and zoo animals, his cape and masks…finding a love note from Mommy, written in rubrics, meant to give him a lift, but only succeeding in widening the rift between morning drop-off and an overdue reunion at noon. Eye Heart U.

Overhead, the pizza-sized self-portraits hang from yarn lengths and spin crazily in the agitated air currents. Francesca scans the line-up and settles her gaze at last on a large blonde circle with surprised eyes and a watermelon grin. The bridge of the dot nose is doused in big black watermelon seeds. DANIEL. Her bonny, bonny boy. She smooths her fly-away hair—thankfully Back to School Night is only once a year, she is exhausted— and heads out to find Alec in Room 18.

He is standing by the door to Room 10, fiddling with his cell phone.

"She isn't in Room 17. I couldn't find her desk, so I asked the—"

"Room 18."

"You said 17."

"I didn't SAY anything. I held up eighteen fingers."

"Well, I only saw seventeen." They sound like mutants having a marital spat. He is just about keeping up with her, as she sprints to Room 18. Out of breath, she is too late. The clipboard by the door has one slot left unfilled. Lice Checker.

She introduces Alec to Mrs. Wendell and he explains the mix-up while the disappointed teacher heads for Elizabeth's desk and the take-home packet. Francesca sulks in the corner, pretending to be interested in the *Guess Who I Am?* posters covering the wall. Students are required to complete sentences for uniformity of theme and you have to guess from the facts supplied who has authored which poster. She is most intrigued by the phrases "My mother usually" and "My father usually." Kids have written things like *my mother usually packs a note in my lunchbox* and *my mother usually bakes my birthday cake from scratch. My father usually walks the dog* or *my father usually checks my math.* Alec finds Elizabeth's poster first. *My favorite color is black. My favorite pastime is teasing my little brother. My favorite sport is riding the subway. My father usually shows up late. My mother usually makes excuses.* You'd make excuses too, if you were married to this guy.

As they drive home in separate cars, she mentally puts together her *Guess Who I am?* poster.

My husband usually shows up late or not at all or both.

Chapter 18

S ome moments after her grandparents touch down at San
Francisco airport on the evening of October 14th, Katharine
wets the carpet in arrivals, having insisted on wearing her "Dig
Dirl Pants" to meet them. Francesca blames herself for not bringing
a Pull-On, and both generations of Carlton women are shamefaced.
Daniel has brought an impossibly small welcome sign he created
alone in his bedroom. It reads Welcm Hom Gumy and Bonpy! in
faint magenta crayon. It hangs neglected at his side as his officious
mother covers the carpet stain with highly unabsorbant paper towels, clutching soaked panties wrapped in more paper towel in one
hand and passing Katharine over to Liza with the other.

"Ew, gross!" moans her nine year-old.

"Urine is aseptic," she snaps as she strides off to the ladies'
room. She manages to refrain from scolding her semi-toilet-trained
daughter but her body language shrieks annoyance as she huffs and
grunts and sighs and stalks back and forth between the ladies' room
and the trash can nearby. Katharine's socks and shoes are damp
with urine, a fact Francesca has chosen to ignore throughout the
entire triage operation.

Her parents are delivered like widgets on a conveyor belt that is moving too fast for their overworked daughter and they spot the endearing family scene from the bottom of the escalator. Gummy waves exuberantly while Bonpapa escorts her off the disappearing stairway. Daniel waves his illegible greeting and runs to Gummy as Katharine bolts from her sister and leaps into her jolly grandfather's arms. She wraps her wet ankles around his charcoal trousers and moistens both rear pockets. Liza stands nearby, waiting for some attention. Francesca ducks into the ladies' room for a quick rinse and a sit, then returns to the now legitimately loving family circle. Her father has discovered that young Katharine isn't wearing any knickers (he insists on calling them thusly after over 40 years in the U.S.), but he has long ago given up trying to understand the baffling mores of the New World. He assumes the bare bottom is just another child-rearing fad and calmly tucks her little skirt between his hand and her bum.

"Danny may you sigh!" Katharine crows. Gummy and Bonpapa chuckle indulgently with not a clue as to what she has said.

"They saw it." Daniel informs his sister. "Didn't you, Gummy?"

Her mother will not be blindsided.

"I saw you looking a whole foot taller than you did in New York and Katharine and Elizabeth are more beautiful than ever!" She hugs Liza (who says "Liza" into her grandmother's lapel) and whispers in her daughter's ear.

"Saw what?"

Francesca reaches for the sign. "I just love the color he chose, don't you?"

"I DO!" Gummy sounds like a demented bride. "It is EXQUISITE! I will keep it forever! Daddy, put this somewhere safe."

Muth kisses Francesca's cheek so loudly ("mmmWAH!") that her eardrum vibrates several thousand cycles in that one second. She hugs her back, mashing her mother's withered breasts against her padded rib cage, inhaling her signature scent. It's amazing they still make Muth's favorite brand. It smells more like Muth than Muth.

"How was the trip?" Francesca takes her mother's heavy carry-on bag from her.

"Uneventful, except for the man across the aisle who typed furiously on his laptop the whole time. I decided he must be some kind of journalist on a deadline, but when I came back from the bathroom, I had to take a tiny peek and it turns out he was playing a silly computer game. Where you madly tap keys to move the shooter and blow things up. I was so disappointed." She really means this. "Oh well, at least he wasn't shooting me!" she adds cheerfully.

Daniel leads the family over to the baggage carousel, not the correct one, but no one seems to notice this fact for at least five minutes, when Bonpapa suddenly walks off purposefully.

"Where are YOU going?" Muth inquires.

"To get the luggage." For indeed the overhead signage, which her father has been checking periodically, has indicated the corresponding carousel for their flight.

"Daniel, you're so strong, go help your grandfather." Gummy knows how to motivate boys, having raised one and married another. "While we girls go freshen up." She turns to Francesca, gesturing at Katharine's bare bottom under her dress.

"Un petit accident?"

"Non..." Francesca has not yet grown used to being on the receiving end of these Francophone asides. After they returned from Brussels and the Wilson children's mastery of French had more or less worn off, French was once again the official language of scheming parents and the running commentary went right over the three little Wilsons' heads. It wouldn't have been the least bit fair, if said parents hadn't urged their offspring to take up and stick with French, affording them the equivalent of full diplomatic immunity for the price of several years' study. Now Francesca has a firm grasp of French and not a single opportunity to use it. Until now.

"…Un grand." Not such a little accident, actually.

"Numero deux?" The direct translation would be "Number two?" but of course this is hardly French. Francesca cracks up, shaking her head helplessly. The four of them retreat to the ladies' room and companionably preen at the line of sinks while Katharine dispenses bite-sized scraps of paper towel.

"Do you have to go pee pee, honey?" Gummy winks exaggeratedly at Liza and Francesca via the mirror, as if to say *Listen carefully! This is how the pros do it!*

"No, Dummy. I des did."

The first three days of the visit don't count, because Alec never actually sees her parents due to his work schedule. With the bi-coastal time difference, it is at least their two in the morning before he even darkens the door. They are philosophical about his absence; never drawing the conclusion that he is actually avoiding them. They know Alec to be a very motivated businessman and a faultless provider. If they can't enjoy his company, they can at least enjoy the wines from his cellar. He, in turn, hides the bottles he won't share, and unlike the host in the parable about the wedding feast, puts out the least remarkable labels for their mealtimes. In fact, he could uncork, nay, unscrew Gallo by the jug and they would be happy. Gummy is no aficionada, but she does know a good buzz when she catches one. Bonpapa tends to sip his wine slowly, and would be just as happy with a glass of "ginger pop" with cheese and crackers. But his wife of forty-five years is a sucker for a celebration and that includes each and every visit to her grown kids. After a glass of wine at five and a couple more with dinner, she is like a kite on a long string savoring the view from the giddy heights of grandparenthood. She luxuriates in all the comforts her children extend in her direction, smug in the knowledge that they will never be able to repay all the years of self-sacrifice that went into raising them.

And her grandchildren positively glow with intelligence and talent. They are more fascinating all the time. With each glass of wine and superior plate of dinner, Gummy relaxes more and more into the role of Queen Mother — another tippler who loved a party — and she laughs, hiccups, and occasionally snorts her drink at her kids' uproarious stories about their own kids, and even the ones from their childhood where she is unrecognizable as the ditzy, neglectful mother. While her siblings and she share an innate ability to render their mother helpless with the giggles, it should be noted that after a few bunches of fermented grapes, Muth is an easy mark. Dad, on the other hand, has become more thoughtful. Where once he might have leapt to Muth's defense, citing examples of her superior ability to organize all of them, without seeming to even try, now he sits back in his chair and stares calmly at the assembled crowd with a dreamy half-smile.

It is not the cozy familial scene it appears. Francesca overlooks the fact that her parents' presence, albeit unseen to her elusive husband, is all the same most palpable to him. Her mother has been unloading the dishwasher incorrectly; Alec's favorite espresso cup (a former sippy cup from a once matching melamine set) has, for all practical purposes, disappeared. Tissue boxes vanish from their strategic locations. The Wall Street Journal, which he misses in the mornings because of his extra-early start, has been unwrapped and violated in his absence. The empty wine bottles in the recycling bin remind him of how much fun everyone is having, while he has been battling it out with a bunch of fiber heads who can't seem to keep their R&D on schedule.

The work situation renders Alec even more helpless than the visit from his in-laws, because losing his temper at work is not an option. And lose it he does, at 11:00 p.m. on Day Three. Someone, and he hopes very much it is not his wife, has been folding his t-shirts incorrectly. Call him obsessive compulsive, but to Alec, it is a purely practical matter. If you fold them at the armpit, where most shirts are folded in the western world, Alec's many t-shirts do not fit in his drawer. He needs four rows to fit his entire collection. Therefore, they must be folded to one-third their size, meaning the vertical fold is some three inches in from the armpits. Get a new dresser, some might say. But this is a handsome walnut dresser that once belonged to his grandfather, a self-made man who parlayed his mother's homemade boiled sweets into a candy factory that employed half the Midwestern town where he was raised. The graciously bowed drawers in this fine antique are wide, but not deep, hence the specialized folding arrangement. It took months of training to break Francesca into the folding regime, and she has passed the knowledge on to her various domestic helpers over the years. But that was all a long time ago, and it is so second nature to her now that it has never occurred to her even to mention it to her mother, who likes to surprise her daughter by completing little chores when no one is looking. Surprise! Alec has to re-fold half a dozen t-shirts at 11:00 at night, after an extremely taxing day at the office. And that is how she finds him when she stumbles in from Daniel's room, having awoken to the sound of a dead bolt sliding into place downstairs.

"Hey."

"Harrumph."

"How was your day?"

"It's not over yet."

She suddenly sees what he is doing, and the awful truth hits her like a bucket of ice water, just like the one they used this evening, to hold the champagne they drank in celebration of Katharine's first dry day in a while.

"Whoops, Mom did the laundry."

"Whoops."

"I'll do that!" She runs to the wide pile of shirts.

"I got it." Alec sounds uncharacteristically murderous. What has happened to her mild-mannered do-gooder of yore?

"She was only trying to be helpful." If you were to draw a diagram of this exchange, it would not be dissimilar to that of an internal combustion engine. The first stroke of the piston brings the gas into the chamber — that would be her attempt to inter- vene – and the second stroke, when she defends her hapless mother, compresses the gas and air mixture, which meets with the spark that ignites the fuel:

"PLEASE TELL HER I DON'T NEED HER HELP." Bang.

She is not prepared for this outburst. She was preparing to brush her teeth, share any cute stories from the day, perhaps some of Dad's jarring memory lapses with the expectation of getting lots of sympathetic attention, then dive directly under the covers for the next phase of her beauty sleep. She is instead experiencing an adrenaline rush that roars out of her chest cavity, screeches down her extremities and slams into the tips of her ears, fingers and toes. She can hear the distant roar of the surf, and the scowling, unrec- ognizable man who stands before her blurs slightly.

She thinks, *yeah, well, maybe I DO need her help. Because I certainly don't get any help from you.* But this is not entirely accurate, because

Alec <u>does</u> help her. His salary pays for everything she needs, everything she spends on the kids, everything she buys for their friends and family. That is how Alec helped her throughout the arduous early years of child-rearing, if from a distance. Before she went back to work full-time. The missing ingredient is the innocent affection that Alec could summon whenever he stepped out of that elevator, no matter what floor he was getting out on, over many years of marriage. This time, in this little piece of paradise whose weather is so uncommonly bright and cheerful, Alec is mired in setbacks, delays and shifting priorities at work. He could not be less cheerful if he tried.

She watches lamely as Alec's last t-shirt slides into place—like a scene from Cinderella, *sans* plump tweeting bluebirds holding each of the corners. Then, her husband, greatly resembling either of the evil stepsisters, flounces off into the bathroom for a late-night shower. As he disappears into the steam, it feels like he is sending the message to his dumbstruck wife that she is dismissed for the remainder of the day. And all because his t-shirts don't fit in his drawer? What has happened to Saint Alec? Where is he hiding? And how many t-shirts does he need? All reasonable questions. But these t-shirts are more than just work-out wear. Alec has several coffee house t-shirts from his college town nestled near a line-judge t-shirt from a celebrity tennis tournament, and the slightly stiffened muscle shirt gifted him from the winner of a wet t-shirt contest he patronized on a long-ago Spring Break. These clever slogans and whimsical graphics slapped on a souvenir and stored in a drawer may be the last shred of evidence of a carefree youth, when family and high-risk enterprise were a faraway dream, not a day-to-day drain on his increasingly fragile psyche.

Chapter 19

*O*n Saturday, the next cul-de-sac over invites all of them to
their block party. They have rented a bouncy house, and
there's live music—three dads from the neighborhood have formed
a band called Narnia, who play whenever anyone will have them.
They play 70's and 80's rock covers. The Carltons and their elderly
houseguests parade around the corner behind Francesca, who
bears vinegar-based potato salad sprinkled with fresh chives from
her window garden. Muth noisily admires her homegrown fresh
herbs, having never used a fresh herb in her life—as a busy working
mother in New Haven, the great culinary innovations were pre-
cut, pre-chopped, pre-cooked and frozen. Her idea of a pièce de
resistance was a steaming dish of formerly frozen green beans, a
can of cream of mushroom soup, plop, stir, heat and at the end,
sprinkle all over with those onion ring things that come in a can.
Francesca has never grown her own before now. Maybe she feels
a little special for all the attention she is getting from her mother.

The bouncy house is a giant jacked-up Hummer that looks like
it is four-wheeling on someone's lawn as the kids inside it bounce
off the mesh walls. Elizabeth helps her little brother and sister take

off their shoes—it is clear she wants to go bounce but isn't yet sure if that would work aesthetically.

The men stand in the center of the blocked-off street like a ring of mighty redwoods. They clutch their beer bottles by the long necks jammed with lime wedges—a touch of greenery. Affable and towering, they are the kings of the forest. On the periphery of this august circle wheel satyrs on skateboards, and nimble wood nymphs dart to and fro. Francesca's people fill their inadequate paper plates with an eclectic combination of meats, pasta and salad, and start the process of meeting and sizing up their neighbors.

It is an exotic mix: the Israeli couple with a three-legged brindle dog and children ranging in age from four to twenty. The wife, Elisheva, has jet black hair in ringlets past her shoulders and a wry smile delivering very halting English.

"My brudder ees from New York. He make music in de orchester. He plays de Jello." Next to her at the guacamole bowl is a slight, wide-mouthed Asian woman whose husband is in Taiwan on business. She talks about her love of the Rodin sculpture garden over at Stanford—how his sculpture defines a western ideal of raw realism and individualistic physicality.

"He makes muscles look so strong. Big. Bigger than life, but real. That's how you like your art here. Big and real."

Francesca meets a radiant young couple, the wife being six and a half months pregnant, her jersey top stretched tight over a ripening middle. When the husband inquires if Francesca has any children, Francesca surveys the crowd and finds Elizabeth sitting alone, sipping a can of A&W, while Katharine and Daniel hop maniacally in the now-crowded bouncy house.

Pointing to her three, "Those are all mine. My goodness, that makes me sound like I'm talking about…I don't know, household pets!" That first glass of wine has gone directly to her head. But there is something to what she says: her kids are more tethered to her than ever before. All three of them, like kittens in a litter, keep her warm in her cardboard-box home. Their dad noses his way into the scrum now and again. She would purr right now if she had the right plumbing.

Later, Muth finds her sitting on the curb listening to the music and watching Katharine, whom all her friends at Cartwheels call Kat, so Francesca does, too, dance to Stevie Wonder's *Isn't She Lovely?* She is feeling relaxed after two glasses of wine and lots of calories. Dad idles nearby, studying his hands. Muth stands over her dreamy daughter, casting a long shadow.

"I have just met the nicest couple," says Muth.

"Oh?"

"He's a professor of history at San Jose State, and she helps him with his research."

"Where do they live?"

"That house, there," indicating another flat-topped wooden house painted naval grey.

"He is going to be on sabbatical next year and you won't believe this, but they'll be in New Haven! He plans to do his research at Yale."

"Neat. You can see them again!"

"I told them we should swap houses!"

"Really?"

"I'm only joking."

"Well, I'd like it."

"You would?"

"Sure!"

"But I thought I was impossible."

"Says who?"

"All of you."

"You're not impossible, Muth. You're improbable."

"Daddy would never do it." She finishes the date bar she has been nibbling on, and turns her paper plate upside-down, scattering crumbs. This she places on the curb and lowers herself onto it. It serves as an inadequate cushion, but it spares the seat of her slacks from the grime. She leans awkwardly against Francesca's shoulder.

"We're close." She sighs. Francesca can smell a sweet petit Muscadet on her breath, overlaid with crackers and cheese.

"Yes, we are." She plants a kiss on her mother's pussy willow cheek. "Even if we are 3,000 miles apart."

They stay in this position, crouched together on the ground, lost in their thoughts, possibly the same thought, of living around the corner from each other in this strange land, breathing life into a now compromised existence. Dad getting sicker, Alec getting more and more distracted by his work, the kids growing up and needing more of everything…until they're suddenly gone.

"I could introduce them to Claire. She did her dissertation on one of the Greek philosophers and spent months at the Bienecke. Do you remember when she and Uncle Bruce moved to New Haven? You were still at Bradley." She sighs again, contentedly. "I wonder if they play bridge."

Gummy and Bonpapa take them out for their last night here. They choose the Fish Ladder because Dad loves fish and the kids' menu includes a scoop of ice cream. There is a wait, but they amuse themselves by viewing the old-fashioned black and white fishing photos of historic catches papering the walls. A man stands on an overturned bucket, and still he is not as tall as his massive upside-down catch. It is not an easy thing to imagine those little cans of tuna fish coming from this blimp with fins that weighs so much more than the guy who caught it. Maybe these were the kind of fish featured in the parable about the loaves and fishes. It would certainly explain how five fish fed a crowd of five thousand.

If it's on the menu, Bonpapa orders the trout. He asks for it as if he has never had it before. But first, he'll want to know about soup. He has done it in this way, in this order, since she was a hatchling.

"What's the *soupe du jour*?"

At one diner in Indiana, the waitress disappeared off to the kitchen and came back announcing, "It's soup of the day!" Another waiter in Rochester offered him Soup du Jour of the Day. He has a million of 'em. He has the clam chowder, of course.

"And I think I'll try the trout."

They order whatever they want. Muth chooses fish 'n' chips because it's all fried and she doesn't care anymore. Yet Francesca couldn't have fit Muth's wedding dress around her thigh, so slim was her mother back in the 1950's. The kids have hot dogs and fries and coleslaw, and they wonder why American youth are so obese. She has halibut. Dad tells them all the long version of his escape from Brussels sixty years ago on May 10th. Liza drills holes in her mother, *he has already told us this*, and Alec joins them at the end of the meal for a glass of wine, which he has to chug because the kids are restless. At least he showed up. Her parents have hardly seen him the whole visit, and they are off in the morning. He says his good-byes in the parking lot and goes back to the office.

"How can you work after a glass of wine? Have you eaten anything? I would fall asleep at my desk!" babbles Gummy.

"They have stuff in the staff fridge. I'll be fine." He slurs his words exaggeratedly and they all laugh. He staggers off to his car and they laugh some more. His place in the family system has been reduced to thirty-second promos of himself. He leaves them begging for more.

That night, as they say goodnight, before Gummy joins a snoring Bonpapa on the fold-out couch in the living room/cum guest suite, Francesca's eyes water just a little bit. She doesn't want them to go. She likes having her parents in the same house; they make her feel so young. Muth doesn't like tears because they remind her of human frailty and Muth isn't accustomed to frailty.

"You aren't getting enough sleep," she murmurs. With Muth, watery eyes mean her daughter is either sleep-deprived or premenstrual. There are no other options. Mother hugs daughter, patting her back. It feels more like she's burping her.

"Are you getting the curse?"

"No, Muth. I'm just going to miss you."

"Oh, you'll be glad to be rid of us. Get your living room back."

"Mm hm."

"Go on, get to bed. We'll just sneak out early when the limo comes, don't get up."

"OK. Have a safe trip."

"You'll be fine."

Of course she wakes up when they do. First, when Dad goes to the bathroom at three, turning the wrong doorknob, the one to Daniel's bedroom, before he rights his course, and then at six fifteen when the kitchen timer goes off and they start moving around the front of the house like a couple of bungling burglars. They never speak above a whisper, except when Muth stops Dad from taking something out of the front door.

"That's not ours!" she hisses.

Francesca stands in the doorway of her tissue box as they climb into the airport shuttle. They insisted on a shuttle because of the inconvenience of an early flight, but she would have been happy to take them. They are so busy fiddling with their seatbelts, they almost miss her, but the driver points her out to them. They look up from their work and catch sight of her as the van pulls away from the curb. They wave excitedly, and Muth keeps waving, blowing kisses, mouthing something she doesn't get, and they are gone.

Pat calls later that week.

"How did it go?"

"Great, great."

"How was Dad?"

"A little distracted I guess. Otherwise, he seemed pretty much the same. We had a couple of long walks, and when I talked about stuff, he asked all the right questions, just the same as ever."

"Did you talk about his illness?" Pat has grabbed the remote control and is madly punching the Francesca button.

"Not so much." Francesca did have one conversation with him on their walk to the top of a hill near Stanford, a paved walk that snakes over hill and dale in a four mile loop, past a gigantic satellite dish, with views of San Francisco on a clear day, looking like Oz from a great distance. As they passed a steady flow of clusters of mostly women in deep conversation, she asked him if he remembered that he had a memory problem. She didn't want to describe it as a disease.

"Oh I suppose, but that comes with old age, I'm afraid," he had answered heartily. No recognition on his part of the seriousness of the diagnosis. No clue that over time, he was going to lose so much more than his memory.

"Because I don't think it's right for us to let Muth sweep this under the rug, the way she does every little inconvenience," hectors Pat.

"It's her deal, Pat."

"It's all of our deal, Fran."

"Yeah, but especially theirs, at least now, while they can still enjoy their lives together—"

"Get your head out of the sand, Francesca, you're as bad as Muth."

"Look, Pat, don't start in on me. I'm just saying he seems really well. I thought you would be glad—"

"I will be glad when this family starts talking about things that matter. I don't care how many miles he walked. I want to know how much longer I've got my father around."

"A lot longer than the way you're portraying things." Now she sounds like Alec.

"Yeah, well, we'll see about that."

"You sound like you want him to hurry up and fall apart."

"Don't be absurd."

"Well, don't be so—"

"Listen, I gotta go. Talk to you some other time."

"Fine."

"Bye now."

"Bye."

Chapter 20

*S*he has been 'making home' in Palo Alto for a few months now
and she still awaits the miracle. She dots the calendar with
play dates for Daniel and Katharine (Palo Alto is a very social place)
and she doesn't have to worry in the least about occupying Liza's
time, who has found her soul mate Natalie, the beautifully mannered neighbor girl who is also in her class at school. They amuse
themselves in between homework and Natalie's many music lessons
with fairy houses, homemade miniatures for Natalie's doll's house,
original songs and dance moves, and lots and lots of secrets. Sign
language, coded alphabets, diaries with tin locks... she can hardly
believe this is the same morose nine-year old she dragged out of
the apartment on to the elevator when they left New York. She is
suddenly so...young.

But she still prays to The Great Ohlone Mother Spirit for a play
date of her own with a new, perfectly-matched best friend. She had
put all of her chips on Mimi Stark but she had a change of heart
when, one afternoon, long after most families had left the co-op for
the day, she overheard two women from the other classroom talking about 'the incident' last year. She was so intrigued she blocked
out all other noise and what she heard shocked her. It seems Mimi

nearly ran over a child backing her Ford Expedition into a compact parking space. She sent flowers, but around the schoolyard, she still maintained that the child was unsupervised at the time. These mommies were concurring that the mother of the near victim was bending over a bike lock at the time, and her daughter was waiting peacefully by her side when Mimi roared up. The mother screamed and that's what averted a terrible accident. Francesca imagines she would never be able to face the community after such a mishap. But here comes Mimi, bopping through the gate just as carefree as a woman who had never nearly run over someone else's kid. Francesca has subtly distanced herself somewhat from Mimi since she heard that story.

And so her quest for a soul mate continues, punctuated by conference calls with Mac and Lee. They all agree she needs a Palo Alto best friend urgently. These are hard enough to come by in a lifetime, but she doesn't have a lifetime.

Aren't spouses soul mates of sorts? Not her current spouse. In the early days of his new job as CFO of an emerging biotechnology company with plans to go public within two years, there is nothing about Alec that even grazes the hem of her soul. In the first place, you would need to actually see a soul mate occasionally and preferably in an upright position. Alec leaves the house at six o'clock every morning in order to beat all the other world-beaters down Highway 101 to his fancy glass office in Silicon Valley. He works long hours at MNS, and at the end of the day, he either 1) works some more, 2) takes bankers, investors, or clients out for dinner and drinks, or 3) goes to the gym to work off all the dinners and drinks. When Alec finally returns from another highly productive day, his bottom line squarely in place, and his lats a smidge stronger if he stopped at the gym, he leaves his shoes on the concrete step and enters his home with a niggling sense of a job yet completed, focusing the last vestiges of managerial drive on the final frontier; his home.

First, Alec checks all the doors to make sure they are all locked, which they usually aren't. Frustrated to the boiling point, having gone over this particular safety measure at least a dozen times, he checks on the children, to make sure they are still there, given the doors. He notes Francesca's geographic location in case of emergency. She is either asleep in the bathtub, her little white toes wrinkled as walnuts. Or, she is lying in bed with a good book pressed to her cheek. He then returns to the living room where he pours himself a generous glass of wine (to regulate the spike in blood pressure), raids his kids' snack packs, and turns on his favorite late-night hosts for an hour of senseless entertainment.

He is riveted by painfully shallow interviews with lesser stars; there must be a supply of strong drinks in the Green Room because once those ladies slink into the guest spot, they are as cheerfully malleable as blow-up dolls. Every few episodes a real star appears, but Alec is drawn to the skimpy outfits and total lack of irony of the second-string. What we learn about Alec from his late-night viewing preferences is that if you scratch the surface of this extremely hard-working, highly accomplished financial executive, you will find a well-concealed libido whose engine seems to perform best on wine and starch.

The ideal woman Alec spent his late twenties and early thirties hunting down, given the myriad attributes he required, not least of which would be a grasp of world affairs, a talent for high-level entertaining and a knowledge of, and strong appreciation for the arts, has been revised to a more succinct ideal: a flat tummy and long, silky, blonde hair.

From his chosen life partner, all Alec really wants at this point is some cooperation. And these days, he doesn't seem to be getting much. His definition of the ideal nuclear family would be one of seamless functioning from morning to nightfall. He imagines a home papered in lists; to-do lists, grocery lists, lists of chores (even for Katharine, age 3), home improvement lists... all meticulously drawn up preferably with a write-on/wipe-off feature for ease of updating. In this regard, Alec's role model might be Mr. George Banks, from Mary Poppins.

Francesca doesn't agree with Alec's logic of lists: just because you're making a list doesn't mean you are any more able to remember the thing you are going to forget, list or no list. You have to THINK of something to get it on a list, is how she sees it. This is not a chicken or egg situation. It is all about one-directional order. That is, you think of the thing, you pack it, buy it, remember it. If you don't think of the thing, no amount of list-making is going to bring it to the fore. But she does have one list for Alec: all the different ways he has been making her feel inadequate since she took on the full-time job of running the home.

She has spent twelve years in the magazine industry, much of that time writing features on how to catch, captivate, understand and keep your man. She never once in all of those years made a list that she checked off completely. Her work environment was thick with post-it notes, to the point where her workstation resembled Big Bird crouching in a cubicle. Yet, she processed thousands of sides of every possible story for the digestion of millions of readers across the nation. She had her own individual style and an organizational system that worked for her and she was very effective.

What she hasn't written herself, she has read in competing journals. When it comes to female readership, admonishment is a lucrative industry. So saturated is she with the topics of the trade that there isn't a day that goes by when she is not replaying a dire warning about some aspect of her being. This very evening, as she deliberately, yet guiltily skips exfoliating, indeed leaves her legs to grow a fourth day of stubble as she staggers from cold tub to warm bed, she is reminded of a piece her colleague in Features wrote about the 'personality of the pajama.' The story features a spread of gorgeous models feigning sleep in a variety of sultry poses, each wearing different sleepwear combinations. From these choices, apparent 'experts' in pajamachology comment on the personality of the sleeper. For example, one somnambulant subject clad in a ribbed tank top and drawstring pants "combines siren-like quali-ties" (her top half) "with parochial chastity" (the drawstring). Since when does a simple cotton string keep a man out of the cookie jar?

She was not a little dismayed to find no mention whatsoever of the flannel granny gown—her attire of choice since the begin-ning of time. But she doesn't need a soft-porn article making wildly unscientific claims to tell her what she already knows about her nighties; they represent everything cozy, warm and comforting about bedtime. Wrapped in yards of flannel, she is swaddled and safe. And so is her mother and her grandmother before her. It's no secret that if Alec wants access to the voluptuous terrain that lurks beneath the sprigs and sprays, he need only grab hold and start hauling, like a fisherman with his nets. There's quite a catch in amongst the folds if he's willing to put in the work. Francesca once authored a piece entitled Seven Ways to Reverse the Romance Free-Fall. One of the seven tips, which she attributed to Mary, a nurse in Topeka, was to invest in new sleepwear.

The fact is little St. Alec is all grown up now. Not that he has given up on good works. *Au contraire.* He manages to keep his hand in several non-profit pursuits, including some kind of mentoring pro-gram through work that pairs minority entrepreneurs with success stories like Alec. Isn't this all a little premature? Because Francesca certainly doesn't feel like a success story. Not to mention the fact that Daniel is having a hard time with the social aspects of kindergarten and could do with a little male mentoring himself. He's not being bullied, exactly, but he isn't getting much play time in elimination wall ball, the only game anyone at Green Gables seems to play at recess. Alec could take him over to the schoolyard for a few rounds, but he is too busy with his up-and-coming minority business magnates to make time for his son. She needs to schedule a moment to tell him so. She should write it down so she doesn't forget.

Francesca has her very first play date today. Not with an actual prospect — this woman wants her for her volunteer hours—but at least she gets to spend a couple of hours at someone else's house. Her hostess, Taylor Hanson, is her "buddy" at Green Gables: a PTA-conceived orientation program for new families, with a special category for 'marginal' families, those who did not start on the first day of school in August. Taylor is one of the school's Big Guns, so active is she in the PTA and in the life of the school. They sit in the ticking cool of her brushed stainless steel kitchen. Francesca is pinned to a leather banquette that runs the entire width of the room. Daniel plays with little Clayton in the family room, while Grandma Faye watches Katharine at her house.

Taylor is dressed in a lima bean green sheath and Prada sandals. Framed by a row of contemporary-styled breakfast windows with etched glass accents, she resembles a blinking lizard in a terrarium, her minimalist tortoise-shell rectangular glasses completing the reptilian look. Taylor shares with the lizard family a certain blankness. Medication? Social posturing? Utter boredom at the cliché that is her post-modernist lifestyle when all she really wants is to be young and barefoot and free? Francesca could be waiting for a train, sitting with this talkative, yet foreign fellow traveler. She is musing about getting a dog. The more she talks about the benefits to the family of having a household pet, the more Francesca realizes that this is exactly what their family needs. Nothing furry, per Alec's allergies, but maybe something very western, like a tarantula or a gecko. They need something that says *You have a permanent address. Get over it and feed me.*

She learns a lot about Taylor in their time together, not from what she says, so much as how she presents the material: Taylor deftly weaves salient facts about herself into the most mundane anecdotes. After a while, Francesca is concealing yawns between clenched teeth.

"I was driving Timmy back from Jenkins when I saw Mr. Harris's aide, what's her name?...crossing right in front of me at a red light."

Jenkins is an elite local private school serving a mere fraction of the families who would kill to get their children in. It is never revealed what was so remarkable about seeing the aide in the first place, but Francesca does learn that little Clayton will join his big brother next year at Jenkins and here is her opportunity to add that her Daniel had to turn down his acceptance to Collegiate what with the move West. But she doesn't particularly care who goes where anymore. She just wants everyone to have a friend. One lousy friend to see them through the tough times. She knows she won't be spending any more time with this designer-labeled iguana, no matter where her kids go to school.

To expedite this agonizing encounter, Francesca stares into her lap during the rare silences. Possums call it playing dead (we call it playing possum) and it seems to work wonders. Taylor audibly sighs and smiles when Francesca suggests she had better get back to Katharine. Daniel is having so much fun ranging around this lovely huge home that they agree she will come by later to collect him.

She doesn't have to go quite yet to get Katharine, who will no doubt be totally engrossed in Grandma Faye's huge collection of wooden animals. Besides, Francesca hasn't had a minute to herself in what feels like a year. Back in New York, with an hour of free time, she could drop six hundred dollars on a couple of new outfits at Agnes Bis. The women there used to say she got the prize for the quickest change artist, and the competition was stiff. Now she fingers the two quarters in her pocket which she found next to Alec's sink, and swiped, for good luck. She wants to buy something, anything, to remind herself of the thrill of spontaneous spending.

She heads downtown and eventually parks in a quiet side street near the shopping district. She has not yet grown used to the phenomenon of free parking. It may be not be plentiful around University Avenue, where spots stay open for under a minute. But just a few short blocks in any direction is fair game for all comers. The more she gets to know her way around, the more she views the happy little town of Palo Alto, with its low-rise skyline and bounteous tree canopy as the only small town in America she could possibly take after the last few exhilarating years in New York. This is definitely the little apple, but the apple is sweet and you only need a little nibble at a time to appreciate the contrast in scale, cleanliness, and civic order. You can walk anywhere in downtown Palo Alto, and that does not mean scuttling along like a demented beetle counting down the blocks you've covered and subtracting them from the total while casting one wild eye around for a cab with its roof lit up. Here, you stroll along with a half-smile, discovering along the way yet another *trompe-l'oeil* mural on a public building painted for your amusement. Restaurants provide lots of outdoor seating in Palo Alto, affording up-close-and-personal encounters with fashion and food choices. There may not be the derring-do in either category that you would find in New York on every corner, but the people are as pleasant as the weather.

She buys a *New York Times* with her quarters and sits on a bench outside a Chicklet's. She is joined presently by three very smelly people who seem surprised to see her there. Come to think of it, passing pedestrians are giving her strange looks as well. She is squatting, apparently, on homeless property. She might actually be sitting on someone's bed.

Her neighbors ignore her as they settle in for the afternoon. They light cigarette butts and pick up a conversation that began elsewhere. Their smoke doesn't mask the heavy scent of every kind of odor, from sharp personal fragrance to alcohol fumes, and an overlay of unwashed garments. It is time to get back. As she folds her paper, one of her neighbors points to her ear.

"You'll live a long time. See her earlobes?" They all turn their attention to Francesca's earlobes, which, uncharacteristically, are not currently camouflaged by some oversized earrings. She reaches for the vast expanse of flesh, but the soothsayer in the shiny raincoat is not done yet. She waves Francesca's hand away.

"You are going to live to be over ninety. You got kids? Of course she do."

"I have three," answers Francesca, obediently. The soothsayer speaks with great authority.

"They will take care of you. But only if you take care of them first!" She delivers this caveat with a crackly hoot. Francesca stands up, not wanting to appear rude.

"Thank you, I will." She wonders who took care of these people when they were still perfect and new.

She gets Daniel first, who is so jacked up from sugary snacks and action hero overload that it is all she can do to get his shoes on him and wrestle him out the door. He spends the entire ride to Grandma Faye's listing all of the superior toys, weapons, and video games Clayton the Little Terrorist stockpiles at his enormous house with the monorail in the backyard and the swimming pool complete with waterfall. She tries to sound totally unimpressed, as a way of counteracting the spell that Clayton's good fortune has cast over her son, but not-so-deep-down, she, too, wants a swimming pool with a waterfall.

Grandma Faye greets them at the door with a spice cake. Daniel helps Katharine put away the wooden animals and they are off to get Liza from French class. The cake fills the van with a cinnamon and ginger elixir. They are steeped once again in the love of a Swedish grandma.

Chapter 21

*A*ll Kat wants for her birthday, not even a party, is a lemur. Her favorite TV show features a talking lemur and she is smitten. So far, the only lemur Francesca has been able to find costs 75 dollars and is stuffed. She is thinking of asking the grandmothers to go in on it together, but she knows she will lose her nerve and just get it herself, the way she does every time she spends more than they have. The brutal fact is, a stuffed animal is not what Kat wants. She wants a talking lemur that bounces through the jungle, or at least through a realistic studio set, like the one she watches on her days off. Francesca so badly wants to get her a lemur. Is that crazy? But she tells her that it is not legal to own one—they are not zoned for lemurs. She tells her there is a "no lemur" clause in their rental agreement. Kat makes her mother show it to her. Luckily, her youngest can't yet read.

On the way home from French class, Francesca surprises Katharine with her early birthday present. While she was out running last weekend, she passed a garage sale where they were selling a very commodious rabbit cage. She got it in her head that this cage would house something they can have as a pet, and she ran home to get her money and was back before the man haggling over a broken ice cream maker had completed the negotiation. She carried it home on her head, and snuck it into the garage without anyone seeing Mrs. Carlton wearing a very modular hat, not at all sure what, or she should say who, would one day call this magnificent cage home. It wasn't until she was surfing the web a few days later that she realized exactly what to get Kat. She had already ruled out a rabbit. Rabbits are neurotic and get a lot of eye infections. Plus, when they die, which they do invariably, the carcass would frankly be too much to handle. Just too…big and dead. But a box turtle! She had a box turtle as a kid. They do tend to wander, but maybe the huge cage with the marvelous view of the grounds will be enough to convince their turtle to stick around for twenty years. That's how long you can keep a box turtle. And no carcass! Just a tidy to-go box for the trash heap. She can already imagine it walking down the aisle one day with a ring strapped to its back. Their faithful family retainer. They can dig a deep hole under the DECK and place the cage facing south. That way, it gets the natural heat from the sun in the fore-ground, and shade in the back of the cage. You can achieve the same thing with costly heating lamps on automatic timers. A box turtle that hibernates six months out of every year would suit Francesca down to the ground. The four of them stop at the animal rescue shelter, where she has been calling for turtle updates. This is their lucky day, and Kat is about to be a mother. She realizes she would have far preferred a baby lemur, but they will cross that bridge, or throw themselves off it, when they get to it.

One problem. To get to the turtles at the back of the yard where the dog runs are, they have to pass every furry creature in God's creation. There are two sleepy rabbits warming each other in their hutch. A sweet, silky looking mutt with an intelligent look and a manic tail tries to catch their attention as she hustles her youngest along. An insistent chow barks at them imploringly. Kat drops to her knees and blows it kisses through the chicken wire.

"Come on, sweetie. No dogs."

"I wanna kitty, Mama. I wanna lemur."

"We can't Kat,'cuz of Daddy." Francesca's reptilian substitution is losing its sheen with every step they take.

Finally, they reach the room with the unwanted afterthoughts: the pets people thought would make a fun distraction, until they saw how much work it was to clean out their cages, or handle the live food. A boa constrictor waits patiently in its glass home. Two white mice next door chase each other through the mountains of shavings heaped on the floor of their cage.

It is as if their turtle were waiting for them. When they approach the glass case with the mesh top, it is stepping over a large stick, which it has to do in stages, like a three-point turn. Each little hexagon on its tough, rounded shell has a pretty yellow splash of color, creating a very festive and intricate quilt-like design. The turtle comes straight over and heaves itself up on its elegant stripy hind legs, sniffing at the glass that separates them. Its underside is the faded yellow, of a well-worn work boot. It is patterned, like a walnut desk accessory. At first Kat is hesitant.

The eldest comes through in a pinch, as she often does.

"It's so cute!! Look at those little handsies and feetsies!"

"Where?" Kat cranes her neck, looking wildly for the cute handsies and feetsies.

The older two start baby-talking and cooing at the turtle and Kat picks up on the vibe.

"Wittle baby turtle!"

"It blinked!!"

"No, it winked! Mom, it's smiling at me!" Daniel, ecstatic.

Soon they are toting their reptile out to the car in her handy cardboard box with the mesh sun roof. Their box turtle is a girl, you can tell by the length of the tail, as it happens. And she's better than a lemur in many ways, when you really line them up together. She moves around, has interesting markings and eats live worms; isn't that exotic enough? Or at least it is for this afternoon. Liza is going to do some not-so-subtle campaigning in the next few days to upset Kat's choice of names, but for now, Fireball Wedding is the newest addition to their little family.

Chapter 22

*T*he Harvest Carnival is one week away and they are still woefully behind. Puppets are half-finished, the latex paint on the decorated cigar boxes has glued them all shut, and they have some fourteen signs to make, touch up or re-do. For the next three nights, they meet over at school after the kids are in bed and husbands are clocked in. The die-hards that show up faithfully every night are in the same league as their counterparts in the music room, which has been designated as an official sweatshop for the month of October. The only sound in there is the overheated strain of motors; it's not a very chatty group. If you own a sewing machine, you are practically guaranteed a spot at Cartwheels.

Next door, in the big classroom, the hand workers chit chat the night away as they assemble their mediocre handicrafts. Peggy, a mother of three who leads family hikes all over the Peninsula in her spare time, offers to work on posters with Francesca. Peggy is also from the East Coast, but she has been out here for fourteen years now and doesn't ever intend to go back.

"You're serious?" Peggy is astounded that Francesca is anticipating one day a return to New York. "Oh well, that's then and this isn't. Make yourself at home for now. You'll change your mind, anyway."

Together they design signage for every product on offer in the Carnival Store. They decorate poster boards with every conceivable bauble; they re-do all the directions signs with their left- and right-pointing arrows and their street locations scrawled on the back. Then they laminate them imperfectly with giant sheets of clear contact paper that pick up lint, hair and dust on their way to the board. Francesca speaks fondly of Boston in the autumn, of New England, but Peggy hastily reminds her of the snow, the filthy melt of spring, the sweaty summers, the bugs…never has talking about the weather held so much significance. When she lines up their Carnival posters in the front hall at the end of the week, she is amazed at all they accomplished with all the chatting that went on, and so little talent between them.

The day of the Carnival is overcast. Before they open the gates to the crowds of current and former Cartwheels families, they have a two-hour Maintenance Day that involves setting up the entire fairgrounds and putting away everything that might otherwise walk. At 11 o'clock sharp, the festivities begin. By one o'clock the carnival is in full tilt and Francesca is astonished at the sheer numbers of people wandering the grounds of what could be a public park. Kids run around loose waving strips of tickets, winning prizes at every stop, and snatching up their pathetic handicrafts at the Carnival Store. Francesca buys the goofy bird puppet she made as one of her assignments. It took too many hours for her to let it go to another home. It may be the most challenging thing she has ever made, apart from the kids. In costume (strongly encouraged; she is a scarecrow with the broom across her shoulders threaded through her short sleeves), on-call, alert to any situations that might arise in all of this overcrowding, she is filled now with pride for their little school. Alec and the olders are engrossed in a craft project involving glue and colored sand; they are definitely relegated to the sidelines of this experience she shares with Kat. After all, the two of them make it happen here at Cartwheels. She wonders briefly where Kat is, knowing it's somewhere safe, and counting on finding her soon, most likely in a headlong hug.

Chapter 23

*O*ne third of the way into the school year, and Francesca blends in so much at Cartwheels Co-op that Kat hardly seems to take notice of her at school. She has sprouted wings there and flies with her own flock. Francesca watches her playing cats and dogs with a little group of make-believers, down on all fours in the music room going through obedience training together, while one rotating 'owner' shouts out commands. Katharine makes a charming pet, but she is an exceptional trainer. She has her little cohorts jumping through hoops. Francesca would never have thought of her, her afterthought, her 'one more for good luck' to be a leader, but at the co-op, where there are really only three rules, she is free to be who she is meant to be.

The three rules are:

1. You can't say you can't play.
2. Keep it friendly.
3. Keep it safe.

They're still working on rule #1. With Liza, that is.

The kids who stay for lunch (approximately forty of them from the two classrooms, plus siblings) are done eating in less than ten minutes, while their mothers stay screwed to their little chairs for as long as their kids' developmental stages will allow. They are unanimously exhausted from their morning exertions, having been co-parenting, there is no better word, over thirty kids—speaking calmly for three hours solid, negotiating endlessly, distracting, engaging, guiding, cajoling, even wiping someone else's soiled little bottom.

Grandma Faye polices the yard, calling out affirmations to the kids in various guises of play. The other teachers have all scrambled off home. They have older kids who still need them, and lives to manage outside of the thirty, plus parents and sibs, whom they educate all morning. Grandma Faye, on the other hand, has nothing else to do after a morning at Cartwheels, except a lunchtime and early afternoon at Cartwheels. She is their full-time Grandma.

"I see Simone cross the monkey bars! One-two-three-four! Patrick and Noah are making beautiful roads with their bulldozers! Here comes Ilia! Watch the sand, there, Sophie! It's making a little too much dust, and dust can sting our eyes!"

She likes to give parents a chance to talk after lunch, undistracted by their kids, to trade experiences, problems, and solutions that will help them be better parents. At one crowded table, the mothers are discussing bikini waxes.

"I have been doing Brazilians at home for at least two years now. You get a pretty smooth finish, and the cost is a fraction of what you'd pay in a salon." The waxing expert is a stern-looking former human resources executive, now raising her two boys on one salary. Judging by her corduroys and turtleneck, she is not the first person you would think of giving herself a Brazilian. The longer one spends in this schoolyard, the more miraculous one finds God's creation.

"Just don't use soft wax!" adds Marie Claire, from France. "The hard wax grabs the hair, but it leaves the skin. No bumps."

"I see Melanie and James sweeping out the yellow house! Who wants to help them?" bellows Faye.

Francesca gets out a pen to jot down the brand of home waxing kit. Summer may be six months off, but she intends to be prepared. She wants to make the most of the California sunshine while they are out here. As she is writing on Katharine's napkin, Faye marches up to their table.

"Does anyone here know Spanish?"

Francesca raises her hand, and starts to get up, assuming Tita, the widow of Tito, a young father whose heart attack last year left his widow to raise three boys on her own in a country where she is hardly even a beginner in the English language, needs a translation. Sometimes Francesca pitches in, though hesitantly; her Spanish is rusty at best, but it's far better than Tita's English. If Teresa the Spanish teacher is around, Francesca stays out of the way. Faye spots her.

"Francesca!! Yes, of course you do! That really is our great good luck! How would you like to teach the children a few Spanish songs and colors and numbers while Teresa takes a little break?"

She protests that her true proficiency is in French, but Faye is already handing her a black folder binding lyrics to several Spanish-language songs.

"Teresa's parents have moved in with her temporarily and she really has a full plate right now. We would love to have you as our interim, and of course it would be so wonderful for the children." What is she supposed to say? *Well too bad for the children, because I don't want to?* She flips open the binder to songs they have played frequently in the car driving children from A to B and back.

L'araña pequeñita subió, subió, subió
Vino la lluvia y se la llevó

Salió el sol...
Y todo la secó
Y l'araña pequeñita subió, subió, subió

Three days later she is sitting in the only grown-up sized chair in the place, looking down at over thirty little expectant faces. She is a teacher, of Spanish no less! She was never one to shrink from a challenge, so bring on the dancing girls. She starts by saying, "Hello, my name is Francesca." *Hola, me llamo Francesca.* That takes around twelve seconds. Then she asks who wants to try to say *hola* and after twelve or so more seconds, she gets no takers. So far, she is bombing. She tries again, but this time, she asks everyone to repeat after her. This produces a far stronger response from the crowd, and she is suddenly awash with a newfound sense of power. Whatever she says, they repeat. Before the end of the session, they have run through a whole gamut of stock phrases, including "*dos burritos con pollo, por favor.*" They are so in synch, they sound like all those little children in their matching quilted jackets in the People's Republic of China. When she ends the session, the parents on duty that day and hanging around the periphery all burst into applause. She stops herself short of taking a bow.

Being a teacher at Cartwheels gives her an elevated status around campus that she finds intoxicating. Just because she is the one in the big chair holding the read-aloud book and telling everyone to wash their hands when they're done, she is suddenly regarded with more respect and awe. And that's just the parents. The kids treat her like some kind of apparition. She loves to bend down low with all those adorable, if clueless little students before class begins and hear what they have to say to their *Maestra Cessy.* They share strange little snippets of their home lives with her, like *my cousin caught on fire!* Or, *we have a tree! My birthday was Friday!*

When there is a birthday, they sing, *Que los Cumplas Feliz! Que Dios te bendiga y que seas feliz* (subjunctive tense). May God bless you and may you be happy. At first she wasn't sure about using the word God in the classroom, and then she remembered *One nation under God* and don't forget what you say when someone sneezes, and she figured what the hell, Church and State will survive a simple birthday ditty. *I'm a teacher!*

Chapter 24

*W*hen they were still childless, she loved coming home to their tiny one-bedroom apartment—it was a palace compared to her share in SoHo. They would make pasta and salad for dinner, then afterwards they would sit on the couch together getting caught up on the work they couldn't complete that day. Back then, she was always one story short and two interviews behind. She worked like crazy for a pittance, and she loved it. She would have paid them for the privilege of showing up to her cluttered little cubicle each day. She would have taken a second job to see her words in print. Alec loved this passion for her work. He would say "I like your job better than mine," and smile authentically as he read her final drafts, pointing out very tentatively, deferentially, a leap of logic, or a bumpy transition. Mostly, he nodded vigorously and assured her over and over that she was brilliant. Over and over because she needed to hear it.

In Palo Alto, she works like crazy for a pittance and all of it centered around the upkeep of her family, until the Spanish teaching came along. Her babies have lengthened into self-conscious little bipeds and her husband has attained a level of professional engagement that has left Francesca firmly in his dust. Because doing laundry, driving carpools and grocery shopping makes up the bulk of her profession, Francesca has felt somewhat underutilized, until the Spanish teaching gig, that is. And the time she spends in her kids' classrooms. Her own children need her far less than some of their classmates, several of whom are woefully behind the curve and show no signs of catching up. Welcome to public school, where every American is entitled to a nametag taped to a desktop. In Daniel's class, she works in the morning of the week when the kids do their 'journals.' The range of experiences and interests is as varied as the ability to record them. One child is still figuring out what a vowel is, while the tall boy in the next chair writes a treatise on nebulae. She encourages the first boy to sound out 'house,' with very little success (haws), and then in the next breath she reminds the young astronomer to illustrate his pages of text. Meanwhile, in Liza's classroom, she is responsible for seven 'advanced' math students—a rainbow coalition of brainiacs who run circles around her with their questions about googolplex and pi. She hangs on for dear life as they make their first foray into pre-algebra. And now she has the Spanish teaching job, and $75 a week of her very own, hard-earned money.

Fortunately, it rains here some of the time in the "winter" months because if there were nothing but blue skies and birdsong, Francesca would be inclined to cancel Christmas until their lives returned to normal. They have had weather in November that would rival the perfect spring day. At least it's freezing in the mornings. This has something to do with living near the ocean, beside a bay, at the foot of a mountain range, and at the base of a water system that sucks their wind clear to Sacramento, the state capital. She doesn't know any more than that. She just knows it's cold and dark in the mornings and she hates getting up here as much as she did in New York, so that's a comfort.

But she has far greater worries in California beyond intemperate weather.

Once Alec took Francesca as his lawfully wedded wife she never gave the cost of dentistry a second thought. They had insurance, they had health spending accounts, they were good for co-payments of five or ten dollars for every visit. Things are a little different at MNS. There is no dental insurance and what they have found on their own covers services provided by approximately three dentists within fifteen miles of Palo Alto, and none of them specializes in kids. The older two have had to adjust to a less family-friendly environment for their teeth cleanings with Dr. Chen, but Katharine is still forming her lifelong relationship with her dentist, and they want her to come back long after they have stopped paying for her to do so.

Enter Doctor Dave, the pediatric dentist of choice for school-aged Palo Altans. At the offices of Doctor Dave and his fun-loving partners, animated feature films play on monitors mounted on the ceiling. Headphones pipe in the soundtrack and mask the unpleasant sound of the dental instruments that "tickle Katharine's teeth" while she lounges in the "banana chair" before she gets to pick a prize from the "winners' basket." All of this for a mere two hundred dollars a visit, none of it covered by PacifiCal.

This is a far cry from Dr. Chen, whom PacifiCal has assigned the Carltons. Just last week they were there for a pre-Christmas cleaning, to use up their free visits before the New Year. The waiting room is the size of a walk-in closet and has three chairs in it. Francesca had to keep Katharine on her lap until they called her in, but at least the kids had seats until she was done. Daniel "read" a car magazine to his little sister while their mother endured the hastiest, most painful teeth-scraping her mouth has ever known. When she got back, Katharine was on Liza's lap and Daniel was standing next to them, while in the other two chairs, four young Mexican-Americans huddled over what appeared to be their dad's head, and were plucking things out of his hair. Lice? Fleas? Scabs? Her older two kids stared intently at the magazine in Liza's lap but Katharine was less discreet. She was staring from under her too-long bangs, and didn't even shift her gaze when her mother walked through. Because Teacher Teresa has been working on the parts of the body in Spanish at Cartwheels, Francesca soon worked out that these jolly children were pulling the grey hairs out of Papa's head. The Spanish for gray is *gris*, which sounds like *grease* so her kids were utterly confused.

Meanwhile, back at Doctor Dave's, she watches Daniel and Liza pass the time in the whiz-bang waiting room, with its shelves crammed with toys and games and books and kids' magazines, none of which makes a blind bit of difference because of the flat screen TV piping in Toy Story, subtitled, no sound. This leaves room for the muted recording of carolers serving up holiday standards. While the sun warms their seats by the window, *Let it Snow* blankets the atmosphere.

Oh the weather outside is frightful, but the fire is so delightful...

"That song lies," grumbles Daniel. She didn't even realize he was listening.

"It's supposed to rain at the end of the week," she offers, encouragingly.

"No, I mean about the fire is so delightful. Some people don't have a delightful fire or any fire, Mommy. Some people are homeless."

"Unhoused," corrects Liza, not even looking away from the screen.

"What's the diff?" she asks.

"Duh, Mom."

"What?" She is a lifelong learner.

"Homeless means you don't have a home. Everyone has a home. It's just some people don't have housing." She can feel a teaching moment coming on, though these days, she is not the one doing the teaching. Liza continues.

"Home isn't just shelter. It's the people who love you, traditions, that stuff. Housing is where you go to get out of the bad weather."

"Unhoused people don't have fireplaces." Daniel concludes.

Katharine skips into the room with a big smile and a fistful of prizes and freebies.

"I got a cavity!" she announces with a flourish.

Francesca pays the bill and chooses a date for her filling. Have another hundred dollars.

Behind her, her three children examine Katharine's loot. For once, no one is grabbing, whining, snatching back, poking, pinching, wailing, tattling. As one, they herd toward the door.

"Let's go home, guys."

They are no longer expected to call Elizabeth Liza. She wants to try another name and has decided on Libby. Francesca admires her shoot-from-the-hip artistic freedom, but she hopes this is the last time or else she'll be known as the-girl-in-grade-school-who-had-four-names.

In part in reaction to the deafening silence in their tiny home when she calls for "Liza" or God forbid, "Elizabeth," to set the table or to feed the turtle or to give her a hand with the laundry, she adjusts at last, and she actually prefers the way Libby rolls off the tongue.

They have picked Libby up at a birthday party in Sunnyvale. Katharine is passed out in her car seat. Her tiny torso is literally sideways as drool pools on the carpet beneath her.

"Could someone tip Kat up?" Libby makes a huge grunting show of rearranging her little sister, who immediately flops over again when they turn a corner.

"Never mind. She'll be fine." Libby rolls her eyes. It is practically audible.

"When I grow up," begins Daniel, "I am going to live in a trailer. Because it would be big enough for furniture, but it would be a small house so you wouldn't pay so many taxes, right Mom?" Daniel has overheard Alec talk about property taxes in this state post Proposition 13 once too often.

"My trailer will be big enough to have a little kitchen in it so I can cook."

"What will you cook?" It is so soothing, listening to her kids daydream aloud.

"Hmmmm," he ponders this for such a long time that she forgets what they were talking about.

"I think I'll...get a cookbook. That way I can cook things. Yep. It will be a good life to live."

While her son's musings lull her into a pleasant stupefaction, they set off in her world-weary ten-year-old a quasi-allergic reaction.

"It'll stink of popcorn."

A few blocks later. Daniel is still working out his housing plans.

"I'm going to have more money then, more than $135 which is what I have now, and I am going to take it all out of the bank and put it in a wallet and then go buy my house and other stuff, too. But I will definitely get change. Change is good to have. Because then you can buy more and more things."

Daniel's confidence in his future is touching. She wishes she felt that way about her future.

At dinner that night (table for four, Alec is out of state):

"Mom, Katharine is doing that thing with her tongue." Where human foibles and quirks spill into obsessive-compulsive behaviors, Libby is their border patrol. They are all a little grossed out by the way Katharine swallows, shoving the food down her throat with the back of her thrusting tongue, but she can't really help it. It comes from too much thumb-sucking.

"Katharine, tongue up!" she scolds, mildly.

Her expensive new dentist, Dr. Dave, has described the long-term effects of this tendency. By college, she will be so buck-toothed, she will be opening beer bottles with her two front teeth. Consequently, Katharine has to kick two habits: sucking and thrusting. One would be hard enough. With two, she is defeated before she even begins. They gave her the fall to adjust to the new school routine, but now that Christmas is around the corner, they can bring Santa in on the program. He knows when you are sucking, and that has been a big incentive for Katharine to cut back. Still, Francesca finds her sneaking her thumb in sunny corners of the house, mostly behind the couch. Calling her from the galley kitchen, you can hear the familiar pop of the thumb as she prepares to answer.

"I loathe it when she does that."

"That's enough. Show's over." She gets all brisk when one child attacks another.

"Well, dinner is over for me. I have completely lost my appetite." When she gets brisk, Libby usually gets brisker.

"You will eat your dinner now."

"Are you hypnotizing her?" Daniel is serious.

"Why?" asks his little sister, wide-eyed.

"No, my darlings, I am not hypnotizing Liz—Libby. I am reminding her what the rules of decorum are at our dinner table." At times like this, with Alec on the road, she feels like that woman with the two kids on the train to New Haven way back when she was single and free. She had a look in her eyes that was as old as the Sphinx. In fact, she had more in common with the Sphinx than she realized. She knew the answer to the riddle of the ages: *What starts out on her back and ends up with her arms full and her head spinning?*

Daniel deftly changes the subject.

"The good thing about living in a trailer is if you want to go somewhere really fast, you don't have to pack any luggage. You just drive off."

"It sounds like you're getting an RV, then." She has become expert at making her kids think they are being taken seriously, when she is either 1) only half-listening but knows viscerally when to exclaim or 2) is inwardly rolling on her back, laughing like a hyena.

"What's an RV?" queries Daniel.

"Recreational vehicle," says her eldest unhelpfully and she knows it.

"It's a trailer that you can drive, instead of having to pull it with your car," she adds, glaring at Libby, as if to say *this is how you should have answered that question.*

"Yeah, I'm getting an RV," Daniel announces.

"I wanna Arfie." Maybe if she promises to get Katharine one too, she'll quit her thumb.

That night, before prayers, after his book, when they are lying side by side in his single bed, staring into the dark, Daniel murmurs,

"Mom, you know what I don't want for my birthday when I'm in college? I don't want a car from you and Dad. I am going to wait and get my RV with a little kitchen."

"I hope I can come visit you there."

"Oh, sure, Mom. I'll cook for you and Daddy." There is a long, companionable silence.

"I gotta learn some recipes, Mom."

Then he turns over on his side, and like an organ grinder, she starts up the prayers. Anthropologists would have a field day with their standard-issue God blesses. They cover a good deal of the mortal coil, from several generations of dead fish, to people they might have just encountered that day for the first time. They end on "...and for all those people who need our prayers the most." That way, they don't miss anyone. They both nod off. She startles herself awake twenty minutes later and stumbles into the girls' room. Katharine is passed out cold and Libby is reading in her top bunk. She drapes her hand over the side and Francesca kisses it like it's the Pope's ring.

"Five more minutes, hon."

"Mm hm."

And she'll be back in fifteen, and Libby will still be reading and that time Francesca will say prayers and if the Holy Spirit is hovering anywhere in the vicinity, Libby will mumble them along with her.

With Christmas nearly upon them, she is losing faith in her ability to stick to the budget Alec and she devised together in the early weeks of the Year of Austerity. She has already announced to extended family members that this year they will be making donations to non-profits in everybody's honor. That buys her more latitude to satisfy her children's urgent desire for everything they have ever seen advertised. She even mutes the commercials at their house, an idea she got at a night meeting at Cartwheels, but it hasn't made a bit of difference.

"Mama? Know what I want?"

"What, Kat?"

"It's big like this and they can slide and you can put water in the pool and it swings and it comes with a doll and she waves—" with which Katharine sits ramrod straight on the couch and stiffly waves at the squirrels on their deck.

"...because she is a princess I think."

"Well, put it on your list."

There was the time they were at the grocery store and Francesca needed some toilet paper, and Libby called out down the aisle:

"Do you want Charming?" That's how she knows they are muting.

Her parents have already come through town, and Alec's are visiting in the spring, when his father has a board meeting in San Francisco. No one likes to travel at this time of year anyway, so it will only be the five of them. They have their Compucam that allows them to project grainy likenesses of themselves holding up their presents and waving like the princess doll in the swimming pool. They must juice up the video battery because starting this Sunday, all three kids will report for rehearsals in the St. Mathew's Christmas pageant. Because Libby is in the 5th grade, the last year you can participate as a performer in the pageant, she has the pick of parts. Their once urbane, moody goth girl chooses Mary meek and mild. Francesca would have put her money on the Angel Gabriel, with the flashy set of wings. But their barely budding ten-year-old makes a very virginal Mary and that is type-casting at its finest. Daniel is a shepherd and Kat is a lamb. Francesca gets to drop them off at rehearsals. A woman she knows from the Sunday school drop-off asks her to join her across the street for coffee during the hour their kids will be tied up.

Judy Anderson is a fundraiser for third-world economic relief and is passionate about micro business loans. She is currently fundraising for a new kind of credit/debit card that would do away with expensive wire transfers from, for example, the U.S. across the border to Mexico. Through Judy's organization, electronic cash cards can draw on money made available over here, with little banking interference. Francesca is humbled to hear Judy enthusing about this new scheme, the way old friends of hers in New York might talk about a new resort in South Carolina, or a new napkin ring design from Tiffany. When you think of all those "undocumented workers" (Judy says they shouldn't call them illegals; it robs them of their dignity) sending their meager paychecks home to big families, and to think up until now, both ends have had to pay a premium on this hard-earned cash transfer, it's enough to make you want to go home and sell your ridiculous napkin rings and send the proceeds down South. They have two more coffee outings before the Pageant, on Christmas Eve. She feels like an excited little girl about so much: Christmas, a pageant, and a new friend!! One she sees regularly because of church and their kids.

Not that you could ever describe these blue skies and gentle breezes as Christmastime. With a forty- foot palm tree two doors down, she finds it very difficult to imagine Santa Claus and his reindeer skidding across their shake roof on his overloaded sleigh. He had better wax the runners.

One December morning at ten, when the kids are all still in school, she makes a clean sweep of Mitchell's, where everything is deeply discounted. She gets a couple of puzzles for Kat, a clip-on tie for Daniel, books for all the kids, and a really nice sweater for Libby that was originally $105.00, marked down to $29.99.

Later, on the pretense of making room for the imminent arrival of Christmas presents, she loads up the van with everything outgrown and underused and heads for Goodwill. Another tip overheard at Cartwheels: the Goodwill in Palo Alto is not your typical thrift store. You will find barely worn name brands every fourth hanger. They may not be this year's fashions, but they aren't far off. Today the clothes with the green tags are forty percent off.

Even though she is ducking through the front door primarily for the kids, she can't help but notice a royal blue blouse from Ann Taylor Loft for three bucks, and a London Fog in her size for $7.99. She finds Alec a Polo windbreaker and a rugby shirt that are too fine to pass up. She should do all her shopping for the younger two here. She can get good quality, in good repair, and lots of it for the price of one pair of jeans for Libby. On her way back from the toy section, she finds a fancy little black jacket with fake fur trim and Japanese characters on the label, which even her fashion-obsessed fifth-grader will love. But the biggest catch of the day is a tin with a hinged lid filled with over one hundred Pokemon cards. She has just made Daniel's Christmas, for $4.99. One man's former obsession is another man's treasure. At the local Target, she finds fun rubber boots for all three kids and umbrellas she thinks they will enjoy: a frog one for Kat, a camouflage one for Daniel and leopard print for Libby. She gets a black one for Alec and a mauve one for herself and she is truly filled with the Christmas spirit.

The pageant is a twinkly display of everything sweet and good about children at Christmas. The costumes have been handmade by wonderful seamstresses from the altar guild. The Magi's crowns are each more whimsical than the last—satin trimmings, little jingly bells, fake fur trim—and the angels! There are hoards of them in little white gowns and tinsel haloes, waving to parents, tripping on hems, holding hands with their angel buddies. Gabriel is a very tall striking-looking African American with a beautiful tenor voice that he employs to belt out his lines, *Fear not! For unto you is born this day in the City of David a savior!* Her fifth-grader looks beatific in her flowing sky-blue robe, kneeling serenely next to Joseph, cradling a bundle of rags and staring lovingly into the crook of her arm. Kat is swaddled in synthetic lambswool and is instructed to sit next to the manger with the spotted cow and the tired donkey. But when the shepherds show up with their sheep, she gets confused and walks over to them. Mary meek and mild calls *Kat!* in a hoarse whisper, which Daniel hears, and helpfully nudges his little sister. The only problem is, he uses his foot, and suddenly Kat cries out loud enough to be heard in the choir balcony:

"Daniel kicked me!"

The congregation snickers as Mary beckons to the lost, injured lamb. Kat scuttles across the transept on all fours and curls up next to her big sister as the Magi process down the aisle with their gifts for the Christ child.

It's an odd Christmas, to be sure. It seems to go on forever. After stockings at 7:00 am, and presents at 10:00, and ham, green beans and roast potatoes at 12:30, they take a bike ride through Professorville, the part of Palo Alto that was built up in the late 1800's when Stanford University was aggressively recruiting academics from the East Coast, mostly from Cornell, and the new faculty were putting up shingled family homes with deep porches and wavy glass window panes just like back home. The family of four spins lazily through the quiet, broad streets, everyone lost in their own thoughts, Kat pedaling madly on the one-wheeler that is attached to Alec's bike, which makes no difference to their velocity but makes their three-year-old feel useful. They see a car every fifteen minutes or so, when Alec cries out:

"Car on!" and they all tense up and wait for the noisy vehicle to pass and they are once again lulled back into a sun-drenched stupefaction. The only breeze comes from their bicycling, the air is fresh, and no one is complaining about anything. Merry Christmas.

Chapter 25

Room 10 News

School Schedule Reminder
January 19 —No School, Semester Break

Looking Ahead
I am looking forward to getting back into a school routine as the next few weeks approach. It is the most exciting time of the year! I see huge jumps in academic growth during this time and it always takes me by surprise. I appreciate the long weeks and getting back into solid routines. I think it shows in the quality of work the students do, as well as the effort they put into the work.

After the first two weeks of pure blind terror, and a day of transition after two weeks' off for winter break, Daniel seems to feel nothing but brimming self-confidence and an unquenchable thirst for learning. Mr. Harris gets all the credit. He has limitless approaches to the curriculum, and all of it great fun.

Joan Bigwood

Around the World

We will be in Italy next week! If anybody has pictures, artifacts, experiences, etc. and wants to share sometime during the week, let me know and we can figure out a time.

Let's see, does she bring in the St. Christopher's medal she was proffered by the short, muscular student who slow danced with her several nights in a row at the resort discotheque in Alti Pini? They had a lovely four-day affair before he headed back down the mountain to Verona, to University, and to his own kind. She wonders what his name was. Or where the charm is.

Math

This week we have been working on "Crayon Puzzles." They are word problems with varying degrees of difficulty so that everybody is getting a challenge at his/her level. Some of the problems have one answer, some have multiple answers. Part of the challenge is not only to solve the problem, but to be able to determine which problems have one solution and which have more than one! These puzzles are also a great way to review and practice solving story problems. Here are a few sample problems:

> *I have 6 crayons. Some are blue and some are red. I have the same number of each color. How many could I have? I have 8 crayons. Some are blue and some are red. I have more blue than red crayons. How many of each could she have?*

I have three children, and only one of them has done her thank-you notes from Christmas. How did we get so far behind?

Some items in the Friday Folder:
  "Letters to Dr. King"
  We have read and discussed a few books about Martin Luther King Jr. as well as listened to a brief part of his "I Have a Dream" speech. The students wrote letters to Dr. King.

> Dear Mr. Dr. King,
> Thank you for turning our world upside down.
> DANIEL

One rainy Friday in February, they are all sealed in the car, Kat is repeatedly counting to twenty very slowly, painfully slowly, when Daniel announces that he wants to join Little League.

Francesca is so not in the mood to fill out any more paperwork.

"But you're only six, Daniel! Besides, you don't have a baseball mitt." She is shameless when she is not feeling cooperative. Sometimes, though, she has no good reason for resisting the tenth new idea of the week, and this is one of those times. Besides, since when has not having equipment stopped the Carltons from doing anything? When Elizabeth was seven, and they were back in New York, she took riding lessons in Westchester County on Saturdays because they missed Boston's greenbelt so much. She wasn't much of a rider, but she showed up to her first lesson looking like Princess Anne. Francesca went a little crazy because of Alec's bonus. Same thing last year when Daniel tried Karate. He lasted three weeks, but the little white suit fetched top dollar at the school rummage sale that spring. Now it's baseball. She has not put baseball in her budget and she was about to spring for whole-head blonde highlights with some of her leftover grocery money.

"I don't need a mitt. It's t-ball."

"You don't need a mitt in t-ball?"

"I don't think so. You can ask when we go to sign me up. I have the paper for you to sign."

The Little League headquarters is located at the Little League baseball diamond, with its night lighting and real fan stands. She stands in one of the lines formed in front of several computer terminals and their operators. Two middle-aged men, one in front of her, and one behind, both much taller, carry on a conversation overhead, not so *sotto voce*.

"Trevor did CYSA this year?"

"Yeah."

"A lot more travel, huh."

"Big time."

While Daniel counts carpet squares, and Libby reads her preteen paperback with her forehead practically touching the page, while Katharine hops back and forth, arms akimbo, lost to all of it, while Alec nibbles on snacks and sips a cocktail on his way to Denver, Francesca shifts her weight again and waits for the next opportunity to sit. Unless it's in front of a driving wheel, or in front of thirty children on a carpet, she never just sits down anymore. She used to sit all the time in New York. She could leave paper clips and rubber bands out on her desk, even on the floor if one ended up there, with absolutely no risk of choking anyone. She took phone calls, she made plenty, she went out to lunch. The more she thinks about it, the more she misses sitting right now. These men, talking now about technology, might as well be speaking a foreign language. She has no one to overhear. She decides to use the time to fantasize, but she can't think of anything to fantasize about, except her apartment overlooking the park, and that feels like someone else's dream.

Chapter 26

*H*aving found, intrigued, tantalized and married Alec, she hasn't felt the slightest tug of interest in another man. She is sincere about this. To Francesca, marriage is the equivalent of buying your first brand new car— driving off the lot, there is none other on the road that is quite so utterly perfect. Most you don't even notice; some, like Porsches or Jaguars you only dream about anyway; there are the carbon copies, but they don't shine and sparkle as your spanking new model does. That is how she has always felt about her late model husband. He is the perfect size, style, and smell. So, in the fast lane of life, she keeps her eyes on the road.

Nor does she worry about her husband's fidelity. She has never been the suspicious type, unlike a lot of women, who, as part of a weekly routine of home maintenance, systematically check their husbands' pockets and wallets for clues: receipts from strip bars, drinks tabs, expense reports detailing excessive behavior. Be careful what you look for because you might just find it. Some women don't even need to rifle through their husbands' personal effects. They have a sixth sense about them. Take Minotte for instance. She knew her husband was having an affair by the way he chewed his food. When she opened the credit card bill with charges from a fancy resort on the weekend he was supposedly in a different town competing in a triathlon, she rubbed cayenne pepper in his teeny European briefs and served him papers. He had so much more to lose than she did, and unlike the French wives of lore, she expected more from her marriage. Like mutual trust.

Francesca is not vigilant about this stuff. She cares much more about *how* her husband is doing, than *what* he is doing. When he recounts stories from work, she always insists on verbatim retellings. She wants to be sure he is coming off well, because a good reputation is like tenure in the business world. On the home front, she is the Senior Vice President of human relations. She has credentials. Her career in the magazine business has earned her a Ph.D. in People.

It turns out Alec might embrace quite a different marriage-as-car-ownership model. Cars get old. Newer models come along. It is a gradual, almost stealthy assault on the senses, for next thing he knows, he has a visceral urge to trade in. He wants something sleeker, a smoother ride, faster, more fun. The interior must be soft and accommodating, yet durable. His new model must be easy to maintain, or at least have a good warranty. He even wants a new smell. His old model doesn't have the firmness, the springy quality it once did, and it is starting to ping. He wants something quieter.

One sunny Saturday in April, eight months into the Year of Austerity, Francesca enters Alec's Hyundai to look for a Coldplay CD and instead, she finds a long blonde hair embedded in the fibers of the passenger seat's headrest. She spots it instantly. It is so remarkably different from any hair in their family, any hair she has ever encountered in the laundry, the shower, or the corners of the bathroom. She is actually trembling as she pries the hair from the headrest. She looks to make sure Alec isn't rounding the corner on his afternoon run. Dashing in to the house with the hair between her pincers, she finds a sandwich bag in the kitchen and she seals the evidence away, then takes it to the bookshelf and tucks it safely behind a book: Helen Gurley Brown's <u>Having it All</u>. She finds a clearing on the couch and sits. She doesn't know what to think first. Does she get a detective? She knows she is supposed to feel murderous. But she doesn't feel rage. She feels sick. She feels tired. Ugly. Fat. Uninteresting. Unsexy. Old. But mostly, tired. She claws the chenille throw off the back of the couch and gathers it around her bulk. She shoves a puzzle onto the floor and rests her head against the leather arm of this once opulent sectional sofa, now rife with felt marker tracings and sippy cup dribblings. She can hear Katharine talking to her Barbies in her bedroom. Daniel is building a catapult out of cardboard in his. Libby is over at Natalie's.

When she wakes up forty minutes later, Alec is walking through the front door and heading straight for the shower without so much as a *hello*. Is that sweat from a long run, or from a nooner with the blonde?

The phone rings. It's Libby.

"Mom, can I have dinner and spend the night at Natalie's? Her mom said it was O.K." *They never come to this house anymore.*

"Um...do you have any homework?"

"Duh, it's Saturday, Mom."

"Right. No, of course you don't. What about p.j.'s?."

"I'll come and get some. So, O.K. Mom? Yes?"

She feels defeated. Libby wants a simple sleepover, yet it feels more like she and Natalie have found an apartment.

"Sure, go ahead but we're leaving for church at 9:40."

"Do I have to?"

"Yes."

For the next two weeks, she simply goes through the motions of her life. She tells no one of her discovery. This must be what denial feels like, because by not talking about her husband's unfaithfulness, she doesn't have to accept it, yet. But at the same time, it's all she thinks about. She wonders if he is going to tell her, and how. Will he wait until after school gets out for the summer, or will he just keep going with this charade indefinitely? Does she actually have to catch him out?

Meanwhile, they are heading into May and his parents' big visit from Philadelphia. They are very nice people, but unfortunately, Marianne worships her son. It used to be something she and her mother-in-law had in common. They would coo over the cute things he said as a boy (he is an only child), and pore over the photo albums, lovingly studying the young face for signs of the man she tumbled for. Time and distance have mellowed them, but the long strand of blonde hair has driven an invisible wedge between them for good.

She gets through the first part of May putting in her hours at the preschool with thirty distracting three-year olds who help keep her mind off her misery. She comes away from her workdays completely spent, yet at the same time, renewed. How can you be depleted and replenished all at the same time? It must be like running a marathon; you push yourself until you are literally about to collapse, and when you reach the finish line, you have just enough energy to carry yourself to the snack tables where you dose up on potassium and glucose and all the electrolytes you lost in the race, and you are left with an overwhelming sense of accomplishment.

At Cartwheels, little people come to her from across the play yard to show her buried treasure they have found in the sandbox; often nothing more than one battered sequin. That's all. One teeny tiny piece of hexagonal shiny plastic clutched in a grimy fist and revealed with great ceremony. They wonder together how it got there in the first place—was it pirates, fairies, or ancient civilizations who buried it beneath the stretch of sand? The children beg for the hose to be turned on (there is a special key for the hose pipe only the grown ups can wear around their necks). When the water flows, they carve out Amazonian jungles, dinosaur habitats, shipping lanes, or construction sites, until they are soaked from head to toe and are crumb-coated in coarse sand, like walking chicken strips. The keeper of the key hoses them off and they stand patiently as sundry mommies peel the children's clothes off and dress them in spares from their labeled shoeboxes. Kids walk around in pants two inches too short left over from the fall. One tough little bulldog of a blonde boy named Carter, whose shoebox contained only a pair of green socks due no doubt to successive wet playtimes, had to wear Disney princess panties from the *Spares* box because after a particularly wet, warm day, all the other dry pairs were taken.

Spanish class is a highlight of the week, now that the kids actually know a few words. It is especially gratifying to Francesca when a visitor looks in on them, and her kids sing the rainbow song, jumping up when they get to the color of their shirt. She introduces puppets into the curriculum, going on the assumption that they will provide entertainment and a chance to hear the language spoken, incorporating the words they have learned together. She brings in a dog puppet named Mario and a girl puppet named Maria, introducing the concept of simple everyday conversation. Mario *el perro* is yapping on about the weather when suddenly one of the kids near the back lets out one of those armor-piercing wails that come twenty seconds after they have actually started crying; the kind of wail that is really more about finally catching a breath than yowling in pain. A little dark-haired girl in a pair of pink corduroys and a maroon sweatshirt is cowering in her mother's lap (thank God it is her mother's workday), sobbing inconsolably, while Francesca carries on with her little dialogue about the sun shining in the blue sky. It turns out the wailing girl, Chloe, is afraid of Mario the dog. They have a quiet tête-à-tête during snack, where the bashful little girl gets to hold him, stroke him, put him on, and make him say *hola*. She doesn't actually say *hola*, but Mario moves his jaw slightly, and her tentative mother makes a stab at *hola*. When Chloe is satisfied that this dog is not real, nor is the girl puppet, and that no one is in any danger, they part ways, both sides with relief. Francesca has learned something very important about her young students today. Some of them are total sissies.

She is also learning about what educators call differentiation, which is a fancy way of saying the elevator doesn't always go to the top floor. One day, she was teaching the kids how to conjugate a verb, first in English and then in Spanish. They ran through it a few times, always as one voice, and then at the end of the fifteen-minute class, she wanted to recap the pronouns; I, you, he, just those, no conjugation this time. So very slowly, in a sing-song, she began:

"Yo... tu...—" and before she could get to *el* and *ella*, a little boy in the front yelled out:

"Three!"

We each progress at our own pace.

Grandma Faye takes her aside at lunchtime, when the kids are running off the steam the teaching team wrongly assumes they had completely used up in the morning, and gives her arm an urgent squeeze.

"Your gift with children," she says, as if she already knows about this gift, "it is something that cannot be learned." Francesca's first thought is, *then why do we have to go to all these night meetings?* and her next thought is, *I have a gift!* She doesn't know what exactly she is supposed to say next: *That's nice of you to say?* Faye doesn't say things to be nice, only grips her arm tighter.

"I hope you can keep working with children because our children need you, Francesca."

"I will," she says, and that seems to satisfy this bright-eyed old dear who hobbles off to find her next target. Francesca feels as though she has just earned her wings as she flutters around the play yard interfering with make-believe play and shouting out instructions to children on the play structure. She has a gift! Then she remembers the blonde hair. She also has a rival.

Back in the wood-paneled tissue box, this foreign strand of hair has put a damper on marital relations. Now when Alec crawls into bed after midnight, Francesca just keeps breathing evenly. He doesn't have to choose between the two women in his life because one of them is unavailable. It suits both of them, she guesses.

Chapter 27

O ne of the mommies at school has posted a sign-up for an MNO in San Francisco. That's Mommies Night Out. Or Girlsday, in the vernacular. Francesca is tempted to go, because by now, nearing the end of the school year, she feels quite chummy with several mommies. They are overall a decent bunch. Possibly a little further down the loopy spectrum than she was used to in New York, but what matters is whether their kids and yours can tolerate each other during the narcissistic preschool years. When you scrub toilets alongside the same five or six people all year, in her case, the Thursday teaching team, you develop a kinship that goes deeper than anything you can accomplish at drop-off or pick-up in grade school. It is a kind of sisterhood at this point. They know each other's children about as well as you could know what was once a stranger in the fall. They celebrate their kids' wonderful qualities (they all have a couple of those) and they help them with their "work-on-its."

She signs up for the MNO mostly because she needs to get away from her self-induced loneliness. She so wants to tell someone about Alec, but when she plays that out, she's got two friends in New York insisting he isn't good enough for her and demanding that she walk. She cannot walk, and it's not just because of the money. Not entirely. Up until now, she has only had to inform Alec what is on the calendar for his kids. What camps they are attending, what friends they are having over, and when. If they split up, she will have to do all of that stuff in advance, in writing, through a lawyer practically. That is about the only thing that she can think of, that would be worse than being married to a cheater and trying to make it work. Being divorced from the guy and having to make that work. The MNO is on a Saturday night. She arranges for Alec to be home from his few Saturday hours in the 'office' and signs her sorry ass up for a trip to the City. He is last seen playing Chutes and Ladders on the floor of the crowded living room with all three kids. They are stretched out on their stomachs, radiating from the board like a sunburst. Why is it that when Daddy is around, the atmosphere becomes charged like a professional sporting event?

Dinner is at a divine Italian restaurant in North Beach, where all the divine Italian restaurants are. They have fresh herb-speckled pasta, curly salad with pancetta, tiramisu and *vino rosso*. It is enough to make her forget all her troubles, and God, do they laugh. They laugh about their kids, they laugh about their husbands, they even laugh about their waiter. They can't exactly stop laughing. Patty Russo tells the story of being home one morning with the baby, who was asleep, so she began to weed out her drawers to make more room. She came across a frilly Victorian corset-like teddy she had gotten at her bachelorette party and decided to try it on, to see how it would fit after two babies. It looked pretty good! She was crossing the living room to the kitchen to put the water on for a cup of tea when the doorbell rang. She saw through the peephole that it was Grandma Faye, and dove under the piano near the back of the room, in case Faye peeked in the front windows. Because her car was in the driveway, and the stroller was on the front porch, she would appear very much at home, so she decided to just wait things out. Imagine both of their surprise when Faye came around the back to see if Patty and the baby were outside, and instead spotted Patty crouched under the piano in her satin get-up. Faye just waved cheerily and left a bag of lemons on the back porch. By the end of this story, the shared mirth has accelerated to group hysteria. Francesca's abs haven't smarted this much since her gym membership back in New York. One of the mommies taps her wine glass and announces a new game.

"Let's go around the table and share something no one knows about us!"

They start at the other end, and women start spilling their guts about high school boyfriends, trips they have taken to the antipodes, an archeology dig in Cairo...and when they get to Mimi Stark, they are unprepared for her share.

"I nearly killed a child! She was OK, but I have such nightmares, to this day—" The table goes very quiet, and her two neighbors begin vigorously rubbing Mimi's back and arms, as if to erase this moment. As if to erase Mimi.

Sally, a beatific madonna-like mother who has taught her four-year old boy to knit, says quietly, but loud enough for the whole, stunned table to hear,

"You're forgiven, Mimi."

"Yes, you are." Someone else adds.

"Forgive yourself," says Laure, from France. "Because we have all forgiven you." But she says it in French, which Francesca understands from hearing her parents argue in French, and then make up. How heartfelt it sounds in a mother tongue. That sincerity is authentic. Laure has a remarkable, yet indescribable earthiness about her, coming from a part of France deep in a valley, surrounded by magnificent mountains, where generations of families have farmed and multiplied and survived together. Her wisdom is harvested from the loamy French soil. She does not let down the group, breaking into English. "My grandmother lived by a man whose sick donkey turned the cart that broke away and killed a neighbor's child. My grandmother would tell this story to remind us to forgive in others what we find inexcusable in ourselves." Laure looks expectantly at Franny, who is seated around the table corner from Mimi, for it is her turn to share. With a flushed face, Franny cries out,

"My husband is having an affair with a perfumed blonde." This makes the 'other woman' sound like a scented blow-up doll. And that is exactly how Francesca regards Alec's recent acquisition: as a toy for a spoiled brat. But since when was Saint Alec a spoiled brat? Since he parachuted his entire family into the dot com boom?

If it were even possible, the table goes more quiet still. The whole restaurant seems to pause. Franny looks down this long line of once complete strangers and sees instead a gallery of kind faces, faces that speak of overcoming hardship, of insecurities buried deep beneath a determination to be the best mothers they can be, faces that care about what happens in their communities and are willing to work to make things better. Faces that love their children so much they are luminescent. These are her people now. What binds them together more than anything else is love. She has had too much wine.

"What a loser!" The first volley sends them into a frenzy, as the mood boils up like vinegar added to baking soda. Women are shouting and clattering and half-standing in outrage. Francesca is agog. If there were pitchforks within reach, there might be a lynching, but suddenly one, and then a handful of the women are screaming Karaoke! and soon all of them are standing up and getting their coats and carrying Francesca off in a wave of grim retribution.

They leave the restaurant *en masse* and parade down the sidewalk. They pass a scrubby urban park dominated by a Catholic church whose gothic spires belong in Lyon. This pokey patch of public dirt and grass, with its tattered, its poor, its snoring drunks, this cement-striped oasis fenced on all sides against a noisy, stinking thoroughfare, feels more like home than anything so far. Someone uses her cell phone to call information and after a long chat, they decide that the best Karaoke bar is at the Hotel Nippon. She gulps the stiff breeze and follows her sisterhood to the parking garage, and from there, to Japantown where apparently they will exorcize the demon of infidelity once and for all. Francesca feels like a Mayan virgin being prepared for sacrifice at the altar of Donna Summer.

Candy Whang, a redhead from Houston who married John, a Chinese American computer programmer she met at work, has her arm clamped across Francesca's shoulders and is describing an affair she had when she was engaged to John.

"I had the hots for the guy, what can I say? I can't resist muscular arms, you know? Really bulging biceps in t-shirts? I just think that is so sexy. But what I am trying to tell you is, I didn't actually LIKE the guy. Not at all. It was weird that I would want to sleep with him, and that I actually did it three times, engaged to John and everything, but I was using him, Francesca, that's what I want to tell you. And I bet your husband is using that girl and she is the one who is going to get dumped, you know what I mean? Not you."

In a bizarre sort of way, this story comforts Francesca. It doesn't sit too well with her that Alec "has the hots" for another woman, but as long as that is the extent of his interest...no, this isn't working. She doesn't care if he only wants the blonde for her body...what about HER body? The body that carried three kids until the skin stretched beyond the stretching point? It's not fair.

It's not fair that her boobs don't point upward anymore and the blonde's probably do. Or that the blonde has perfect porcelain skin. Maybe the comfort lies in knowing that upstanding citizens like Candy are lying, cheating low-life, too. In the end, no one's perfect? Not tonight. Tonight she will hate Alec with an immense fury and indignation.

The minivans convoy with the wind at their backs. Just having a plan, however simple, makes Francesca feel in charge for the first time in many weeks.

The Karaoke bar is situated at the far end of a long, deserted breezeway nowhere near the Nippon's lacquered hotel lobby, with its glass-encased bonsai garden and subtle recessed lighting. When the gaggle of oddly dressed mothers enters the bar, Francesca notices a tiny, perfectly proportioned Asian lady in a skin-tight mini dress and matching red stacked heels sitting on her barstool like a permanent display. This rowdy group of dowdy middle-aged mothers lumbers by like a herd of prey passing by an exotic migrant bird. The perfect little Asian makes Francesca feel less ready to sing. Then a tin-eared man in a short suit steps up to sing *Ooh, I Get By With a Little Help From My Friends* so poorly that she is ready after all. At least she can do better than the Beatle-wannabe, no matter what the state of her marriage.

The herd of mommies, fourteen in all, takes up residence. They order drinks, which are placed on tables no bigger than butter plates. She spies the DJ in the corner of the room, and near him a neat stack of papers and a can of pencils next to the pile. Someone hands her a binder full of songs and she obediently flips through the pages, landing in the I's. The last time she belted out *I Will Survive* her boyfriend in college had dumped her for his roommate. He spun tunes for the campus radio and had tight little curls through which she constantly raked her needy hands. When he told her he couldn't keep up the charade anymore, that he was gay, she pretended she had always suspected he was, and this thrilled him. He hugged her like a best girlfriend and gave her one final squeeze before twirling off into the sunset with his emaciated artist friend. They were able to laugh about it at the tenth reunion. He is a campy costume designer for international opera companies now.

Suddenly, a laconic waitress with a tuxedo top, kicky skirt and shiny thigh-high boots appears at her side with a glass of champagne.

"Dat gentehman over deh would like you to haf dis champagne." She lowers her eyes in the direction of a dark corner, and Francesca glances over to see a lone bulk in a booth, but she looks away before she appears to be making eye contact. The rest of her party has got wind of the exchange as if by instinct and women all around her begin hooting and whistling. In the old days, she would have blown a guy like that a kiss, and gone back to whooping it up with her girlfriends.

"Please tell the gentleman thank you." She tips the bored waitress showily, as if to say *dutch treat* to the gentleman with the expense account. Except that the tip is only a dollar bill. She raises her glass to the shadow in the booth and takes a sip. More whooping from her entourage. She wonders if she should sing after all. She feels unsteady and swept up in a mass hysteria. She is fairly sure someone set him up for this. Just then, the DJ motions to Francesca that she is up to bat.

When the electronic orchestration begins to swell, she looks out over the audience and counts four single men dotted around the room, plus the mannequin at the bar and the bartender who is aggressively pouring her drinks. Yet at her feet, in the soft edge of the runner lights rimming the stage, is a great wall of friends, waving and cheering and egging her on. She is no longer alone in her secret torment. She is upheld by her friends' fierce good wishes, and that, for tonight, is enough. She belts out Gloria Gaynor as she makes small adjustments to her delivery, her subtle dance moves, and the speed with which she chases the words up the teleprompter. As she fades out and takes her bows, she realizes the dream man she conjured up as she sang of hot love bears a striking resemblance to her husband. She is pretty sure she doesn't want any other man. She realizes she wants hers back.

Back in Palo Alto, that hand gripping the mop is not a steady hand, not since she forswore her own husband. But all around the school, like little leprechauns, her sisters are keeping a close eye on her. Kat is juggling a deluge of after-school invitations and when Francesca turns to a school chore, such as tidying the carpet for story time, she catches sight of another member of her teaching team sliding the last wooden block into place.

Francesca wishes Alec well because she needs him in good health if they are ever going to make their financial goals. He is the lynchpin, as best as she can tell, for the financial fortunes of everyone at MNS. Obviously the product has to be right, but you can't get the product right if you don't have the funding. And this is a particularly important product: fake bone that will keep people intact, not to mention in good shape far into old age. No osteoporosis in those bones! No fluctuations in density, none whatsoever. Eventually, this revolutionary new material could be used in plastic surgery to correct aberrations of all kinds. It would make a great cheekbone enhancer. Supple yet firm, it is easily contoured in the laboratory. She must stay the course for the sake of her children.

Alec and Randy, the CEO, are in the third world finding someone who can produce these bones, or at least the standard-sized ones, for the cheapest possible price. She is left behind in the first world confronted, once again, with single motherhood. She could sell t-shirts:

> *If I had wanted single motherhood,*
> *I would have opened an account*
> *at the local sperm bank.*

This is actually a very common occurrence out here on the Left Coast. Since moving to California less than a year ago, she has met four children with anonymous fathers. It's the latest craze. She has also met a man at a party who makes a steady living donating his sperm to the cryobank near Stanford hospital. He actually told her this himself. It was all she could do to keep from looking down at his income producer. When she tells Muth about the serial sperm donor and his partner—yes, that's right, this man is gay—she might have given a little too much information because Muth scrambles up onto her high horse again.

"What happens when all of these babies start dating each other in high school?"

"Well, according to you, they will all be gay anyway and therefore not procreating." She loves to bait Muth. It's a slightly more humane form of catch and release.

"And when one of the little lesbians decides to have a child, and she unwittingly chooses her father's frozen spermatazoa?" Muth demands. Francesca has never heard anyone else call it by its proper name, but it comes with the territory, if Muth is up on her high horse. This phone conversation proceeds along the course of a Celtic knot. Daughters and fathers are procreating and all she wanted was to tell her mother about an interesting person she met at a party.

Chapter 28

*T*o her credit, Lee didn't mean to kill her cousin. Mac calls it scum-slaughter. He was lunging for her, so at least he was doing something that he loved at the time of the murder. Lee knows the part she played and so does Devinn, but she'll never see Devinn again. Lee had been running late to work and was trying to hail a cab on a rainy morning. She had way too long a jog, not to mention the puddles, to make an important meeting with a group of fellow editors. She finally saw a cab appear, but with no light on, so still no luck. She stepped back into a puddle as the cab suddenly pulled up in front of her. The door opened and out stepped Buzz. Bald cousin Buzz with the intermittent teeth and that mischievous sparkle in otherwise dying eyes. Buzz of the sudden moves because she got to be so quick, dodging him. It was at the age of thirteen that Lee found her love of running, then of riding…anything fast that got her out of the house and far away. Buzz had hip dysplasia and didn't like to walk much. Certainly couldn't ride a horse. But at home, he made up for miles in speed and could give her a run for her money in the laundry room. He threatened terrible violence upon her family—he owned guns, or so he claimed and what did Lee know about anything this sick, slick nineteen-year old boy might do? Back then he had his teeth and could charm all the grown-ups with a simpleton's guile. This morning, twenty years later, he shoved her in the cab in a swift move and piled in after her, slamming the door.

"Where do you work?" He leaned forward to give the address to the driver but she butted in:

"Just to Metro Center!" She sounded an overly cheerful note. Buzz turned to her quick as ever and leaned in too close.

"I got your address off of Mom's Christmas card list," he leered. "I was in New York City for once in my life and I wanted to find you just to come...say hi." Then he cocked his head and his eye fixed on hers while his head slid back and forth and he said in that stare *just to remind you, I can still kill any or all of you.* It was time to get out then and he pulled a crumpled five-dollar bill out of his pocket. She handed more over to make the tip and they got out, Lee hustling ahead of him with a purpose, Buzz scuttling after her. He had a day pass and knew how to use it in the stile. They cleared them and he kept up. She was striding now and he still kept up. At the portal to her track, the crowd converged and surged as the beginnings of a train rumbled along the track. She rushed along with everyone to the edge of the platform in the hopes of losing Buzz in the swells but instead he moved faster and bolder with hands reaching for her ass and when he lunged, her muscle memory threw her to one side, a maneuver that could occasionally keep her out of harm's way. So she dodged, to save herself from toppling over, so formidable was his momentum, and he positively flew into the oncoming train. As he soared, she saw the pupils and whites of two eyes, fixed on her like they were speaking, and they stayed that way long enough for her to read on the chest below, Devinn, which was the last thing she saw as the train absorbed the impact of Buzz. Devinn's eyes swiveled with the same kind of lightning speed around what felt like a crowded room, back on Lee, and then one eye winked. With a surprisingly low voice, under a pencil-thin, feathery moustache, young, resourceful Devinn bellowed, "He just ran at it! He just ran at it!" and the crowd surged then parted then swayed as Lee was carried away.

All of this Franny hears right before Daniel's teacher conference and is consequently fifteen minutes late and shook up. She had made the appointment for 4:00, the last one available, so Alec had a fighting chance of making this one. He missed the November conference, but she was able to fill him in on Daniel's tremendous progress in cutting and pasting, patterning, and lower-case letter formation. The spring meeting, by definition, promises to hold much more progress in store.

Seventeen minutes past the hour. She has given up scanning the street beyond the chain link fence for The Lovemobile. She imagines Alec hastily tucking in his shirt and smoothing his hair, having spent a long lunch hour at *her* place before the appointment. She imagines Buzz in pieces all over the walls of Metro North. At twenty past four, she and Mr. Harris dive into the charts and stats that he must prepare for twenty kids at the pleasure of the school district. She can barely follow all the sub-categories of performance that he describes; she just looks for the placement of the check marks and sees that Daniel is "meeting the expected standard" time and time again. Mr. Harris reminds her that "meeting the expected standard" applies to the end of the year, which is still two months off. He is extremely pleased with Daniel's performance, especially given the circumstances. She reddens, thinking for a split-second that Mr. Harris knows.

"What with a sudden move from everything familiar, a new town to get to know, friends to make…" So he doesn't suspect her husband is having an affair, but he seems to know how lonely she is. Her eyes water involuntarily and she looks up, as if to ruminate on these challenging circumstances, but actually in a vain effort to tip her tears back into their ducts.

"He is a wonderful boy. Very mature, cooperative; you are obviously doing a very good—is everything OK?" The tears she was trying to recapture roll down each cheek. Mr. Harris puts his hand on hers. She is so surprised that she nearly yanks hers away, but she checks the impulse. An unmarried man has his hand on her.

"We're under a great deal of stress at the moment." She tries to pretend her face isn't wet, that she is a mature woman facing a small rough patch. He has brought his other hand to make a threesome. She finds herself thinking *we could meet after school. Take walks with the kids and hold hands while they run ahead. He would love Daniel for who he is, Katharine is still young...Libby would get over it.* She looks him squarely in the face and says,

"My husband's never home."

Does she mean *so you can come over and we can make love while the little ones watch cartoons and Libby does her homework?* What Mr. Harris hears is *Daniel is missing his father* and he says,

"That takes a toll on a child. Is there any way you can reserve some family time each week, even just an hour or two, to give him a sense of continuity? I worry that Daniel doesn't allow himself to feel disappointment..." Mr. Harris is tucked back onto his side of the conference table, making all kinds of sense. She liked it better when they were feeling sorry for her.

"We're talking about getting away for a few days," she lies. "Maybe Disneyland." This is exactly what she needs right now. Scary rides that end well. Alec can stay home and work, hopefully miss them, and ultimately realize what he has given up for a morally bankrupt blonde. Mr. Harris pats her arm. It is the pat of a man who teaches her son and nineteen others how to read and write and sort counting beads.

"I think that's a wonderful idea. If you need to use a weekday or two, Daniel can afford to skip. Just don't tell Mrs. Heilman," he adds in a mock whisper. The principal. "It'll be our secret. Daniel's going to be fine. You too." She smiles bravely and realizes they'll need to take Alec with them because she can't possibly leave him here to his own devices. She finds her cell phone under the car seat on her way out of the car and into the house. It has two messages from Alec afraid he won't get out of his meeting in time.

Mac calls. BIG NEWS.

"I think I might have found a composer, but this one is a real one, Cess."

"Tell."

"You know how my mother sings in that little choir that goes around to deathbeds?

"Oh yeah, didn't she write a song or something?"

"That's right. She got her song on their latest CD. Well, anyway, she has been singing to this old guy who is dying, he really loves their singing and he is still able to sing along a little bit..."

"Aw..."

"I know. I mean do you get how good that makes my mom feel? She says she is totally comfortable with death now that she has been doing this work for a couple of years. At least one of us is. I cannot imagine what it will be like to have to bury my own mother..."

Conversations with Mac are so complexly rendered that they need a machete to get back to the original point.

"So, a composer?"

"Yeah, the old man's son was visiting from the city, and when they were done singing Mom and this son got talking and it turns out he's an opera composer!"

"Is it an opera now?"

"No, no, no. That's the amazing thing! She says, you don't know anyone who writes for musical comedy do you?" And it turns out he has written four musicals for a summer stock camp, and here's the killer, she says, do you write pastiche?"

"Remind me what pastiche is again?"

"Different styles of music. You know, like Mr. Boddington sings in a classical style, while Marguerite is Victorian Music Hall. Fedora sings the blues..."

"Got it."

"And he says, oh sure, I do pastiche."

"Wow, Mac, that's awesome." Silence.

"You didn't just say awesome, did you, Cess?"

"I think I did. Sorry."

"You're worrying me, Miss California."

"Mrs. to you."

"At least you didn't say *totally awesome*."

"Oh, totally."

"Now you've gone too far."

"I'm so happy for you, Mac. Keep fighting the good fight! I better get going. I have three kids to feed and no food."

"Cereal night!"

"That was Friday."

"Eggs."

Good idea. Omelettes-to-order.

"Sooo...how's everything going, at home?" Francesca wants to know that someone else is in a marital tailspin.

"Oh, great. Hugh is being a doll. He wants to take me to an island and leave the kids with his parents."

"That's progress!" She is only half-pleased for Mac.

"Yeah, well, I figure, if you can do it, I can do it. It's only thirty or so more years, right?"

"Easy peasy." Francesca is discomfited by the new-found ease with which she'll discuss the blonde with her gang at school. Yet Mac would take the debate to new levels, and she isn't up for it.

They sign off for another week or more.

The next teacher conference Alec actually makes, on time! Libby's teacher, the impossibly strict Mrs. Kosminsky, is no-nonsense, no fun. They sit up straight and listen, mostly. Apparently, Libby is ahead in everything except social decorum. She spends too much time with Natalie. Francesca figures hey, it could be worse. She could be spending too much time with Amanda, the overdeveloped harlot in the leopard prints and sassy t-shirts that say My Brother Did It in camo iron-on lettering. But she promises Mrs. K. they will talk to Libby about branching out and they thank her for her time. Jamming her hand into her jeans pocket, she gives Mrs. K. the finger on the way out. The way he lopes alongside her to the car like a high school basketball player, she can tell Alec is still riding the wave of Libby's academic success, and probably didn't even register the psychosocial stuff. Apart from hating him for cheating on her and thinking she doesn't know, she has always appreciated the way he leaves the emotional life of the family to her, just as she leaves their basic survival to him. It has been a very convenient arrangement up until now. But the lines of psychological wellness and basic survival have blurred in recent weeks and now she doesn't feel like either of them is qualified to be in charge anymore.

Since *The Hair in the Passenger Seat*, she has developed new rituals. For instance, in the early morning, when Alec is in the shower and she is supposed to be making the kids' lunches, she grab his keys and runs out to his car with her portable teensy-weensy book light. Kneeling in the passenger seat foot well, in the cold, fog-shrouded pre-dawn, she painstakingly sweeps the light across the length and breadth of the seats, searching for microscopic clues: hair, fibers from a fluffy sweater, a clump of dirt formed from a high-heeled shoe, stains…one morning she is rewarded with a whiff of a foreign perfume; not the rich scent of her vanilla base; more flowery, like jasmine, or lily of the valley. From then on, she takes to snatching Alec's shirts from the clothes hamper and sniffing them furtively. Katharine finds her one morning with her face buried in one of his shirts.

"Whachoo doin' Mama?"

"I'm seeing if this shirt is dirty," she says, as if finding it in the hamper weren't enough.

"Dat's disdustin'."

It is disdustin'. Just look at the levels to which she has sunk, and to what end? How long, exactly, is she going to go on accumulating evidence? Until after the initial public offering? The fact is, she can't leave Alec now, on the brink of all that enormous wealth. If she leaves now, she walks away with enough money to cover groceries at her parents' house while the kids go to the deplorable local public schools in New Haven and she gets back on her feet in the magazine business, which pays lousy.

She is staying for the money. Money is the language that Alec speaks best and she is staying long enough to take half of it away from him. Then she will set up home somewhere a little less desirable than Central Park West, maybe she'll get a loft in SoHo and the kids can take art classes from real artists, and they'll fill their home with music and laughter and they'll make new friends that Alec will never even meet, who will admire her for the way she is raising the kids without their father to help her show them right from wrong.

But the more she fantasizes about a better life five years from now, without this snake in the grass for a spouse, the more she knows deep down that she cannot let this thing go on any longer, however many million dollars are at stake. What if he loves the blonde? Then what? Then she will have to find someone else to love her and she doesn't see how she can do that when the only time she is around men is at Maintenance Days at Cartwheels, and drop-off at Green Gables at eight in the morning and in all cases, these men are taken. She has no intention of breaking up any more families. Maybe the blonde cheated on someone, and she can have <u>him</u>. They already have something in common! She stows these thoughts away until she is feeling stronger. She doesn't know how she got herself into this mess but she is having trouble figuring out a solution that doesn't result in total financial collapse.

One Friday night, when Alec is in India big-game hunting for software engineers, she is feeling at particularly loose ends about her life as an unhappily married single mother of three. As the sun sets over the yardarm, she opens the high-end vodka Alec got from his Finnish client when he was still working at the bank. She decides to mix herself a drink before dinner. She has yet to decide what dinner should be.

She mixes a fairly strong vodka and diet 7-Up, because she doesn't have any orange juice. Halfway through it, she decides they haven't had pizza in a while and why not? She has no one here to help with the kids, the dishes, no one who cares what she cooks, no one to help with bath time…she deserves pizza. She is delighted to find her coupon for two for the price of one at a place that delivers, and phones in her order. With no food prep to worry about (she rips open a bag of carrots for the side dish), she refreshes her drink and drains the soda. She can hear fights breaking out all over the house—little border skirmishes, nothing serious, and she ignores the sound of warfare as the pizza people slide their pizzas into boxes and load them into their delivery van. She is sitting at the breakfast bar staring at the hood over the stove when the doorbell rings. So lost in thought is she, she can't imagine who is at the door. The kids know, though. They charge like the Queen's Corgis. She comes to her senses and brings the man a twenty in exchange for two heavenly-scented cardboard boxes. She hunts for a bottle of red wine, since they got one pizza with pepperoni, a red meat.

They eat the pizza in front of the television, something they are unequivocally not allowed to do. She remembers the rule as Libby knocks over her stemware and red wine splashes all over Katharine's white princess gown, which belongs to the preschool. She yanks it off her and pours salt on it from a large canister. It lies in state on the kitchen floor, looking for all the world like the remains of a princess doused in evil fairy dust. She switches to a tumbler and pours herself a replacement glass.

The movie they have borrowed from the library is a favorite from her childhood, about a man who turns into a fish and saves the country from a missile attack. She hadn't remembered how funny it was. It's an absolute hoot! The kind of humor that adults appreciate more than kids, or at least that seems to be the case because she is rolling around the couch laughing 'til she's crying, while the kids sit stoically staring at the screen. She is mildly surprised to see that the bottle of wine she opened for dinner is empty. Then she remembers the spill, which helps explain why it's all gone. She is further shocked to note that the film is over and she doesn't remember how it ended! In fact, everything seems to be happening faster than she can orchestrate it. She tells everyone to brush their teeth, just as they are leaning over their sink spitting out tooth-paste. She helps Katharine to the toilet, and nearly drops her in. That sets off another bout of helpless laughter, and strange, search-ing looks from her preschooler. She tries to stifle her silliness by looking sour-faced and serious, but this only sets her off again. She sprays Katharine with spittle as she doubles over laughing again.

Katharine calmly wipes herself off on a bath towel and walks out of the bathroom without so much as a backward glance.

Francesca suddenly feels enormously tired, and decides a quick lie-down on the bath mat will help her shake off the sleepiness. She awakens four hours later with a tongue so dry she taps it with her finger to make sure it's hers. She has two headaches. One in the frontal lobe, and another wrapped around the hypothalamus, deep at her brain's core. As she drinks thirstily from the faucet, she tries to piece things together from the previous evening. What did they eat? Did she cook? Did she leave anything on the stove? How much did she have to drink? She throws up the water just as fast as she swallowed it, right into the open toilet, thanks to Daniel. She checks the kids. They are all in the correct beds.

As she heads into the living room, she suddenly remembers the phone ringing at one point last evening, but she can't for the life of her recall who was at the other end. She doesn't even know if she answered. She racks her dehydrated brain for a short while, pacing around the messy room (she knows what they had for dinner now from the crusts that are paired with paper plates and strewn about the floor). She can't bear the sight of any of this any longer, and after another attempt at keeping down some water and a couple of Ibuprofen, she heads to bed, where she lies, rigid with anxiety, wakeful, boring holes into the darkness as she tries to puzzle out last night's events. It is all a sweat-inducing, heart-racing blur. Her body is buzzing with nervous energy, and yet she is mentally exhausted. It takes her two hours of talking to herself soothingly to fall asleep at last. When she wakes up, Katharine is poking her arm and saying what sounds like *see her, see her.*

"Who?"

"What?"

"See who?"

"Who?"

"What do you want, Kat?" she says this through gritted teeth and eyes squeezed shut.

"Cer-real."

"Tell Libby to help you."

"I want you to."

"I can't."

"Why not?"

"Libby needs to. It's an experiment." She is about halfway to halfway asleep. Her thoughts are firing from all directions and her mouth seems to be moving on its own accord. She is whispering, because her throat is so dry. She sounds like she is letting Katharine in on a secret. She realizes that she might still be drunk.

"What's a expeppermint?"

A long pause as she dozes, then startles awake when Katharine says very loudly,

"WHAT'S A EXPEPPERMINT?"

"For allowance."

The magic word. Katharine has been asking for allowance for weeks now. She knows big kids get it, even Daniel gets fifty cents a week, and since she is wearing big girl pants full time now, she considers herself a big kid, too. When Francesca invokes Libby's fabled allowance, Katharine is stunned into contemplative silence. With three-year olds, you can practically see the gears in their heads turning like flywheels, small and fast; most of the time they spin out of control. On this occasion, even in her addled state, Francesca can tell she is calling up her little daughter's animal urge for allowance, and her primitive mind is searching for the words about that. The names of coins, the candy she will buy, how many more years before she gets her very own allowance, all of this clicks by.

"OK Mommy. I know about that." She shushes off in her feet pajamas, thrilled to share a secret.

Francesca does not even pause to consider her immediate circumstances, before passing out for another hour and a half. When she finally appears in the kitchen, she steps on the supine princess gown with the pink salt covering the bodice, and three bowls of murky cereal milk greet her on the draining board. The water she has just sucked from the bathroom faucet rises involuntarily and she has just enough time to lean her head over the garbage disposal and aim straight down. The milk smell from the bowls combines with the sight of bright yellow bile as the sound of squeaky-voiced cartoon characters screaming at each other drown out her retching.

No one comments on her behavior of the previous evening, yet she can feel Libby's confusion. She doesn't know what to do about that, except that she would rather her ten-year-old be confused and slightly out of sorts, than think her mother has a drinking problem. Besides, she doesn't have a drinking problem. She has a husband problem. When she gets the little kids alone later that morning (Libby has disappeared off to Natalie's house), she suggests they play a game.

"OK."

"It's called recollection."

"How do you play?"

"I ask you a question about something that has already happened, and you tell me what you remember about it. Who remembers Block Island?"

"I do!" trills Daniel.

"I do!" echoes his sister, but she can't possibly.

"OK, Daniel you take this one. Kat, you take the next one."

"Everything I remember about Block Island?"

"Yup. Whatever comes to mind."

"I remember that seagull that took Kat's hot dog off the picnic table, and I remember the jawbreakers and gummy worms, and that hammock where you and Daddy nap when we lie down on the porch..." and that brings up for Francesca all kinds of wonderful memories of them watching the kids playing on the beach, Alec rubbing lotion on her back and turning it into a backrub and then that morphing into an invitation to join him back at the rental while the kids stayed with Ga Ga. They were so in love!! Daniel finally runs out of memories.

"My turn!" screams Katharine.

"OK, let's see. Last night. The phone rang. Who called?"

"That's easy!" yells Daniel.

"It's my turn!" insists his whiney little sister. "Daddy!"

"And...who talked to him?"

"We did!" the two cry out together.

"Daaaaniellllllll!" Kat is about to cry.

"Come on, Dan Man, it's Katharine's turn. "OK, love, for the bonus point, did anyone else talk to Daddy?"

"No."

"And why not?"

"Because Libby was busy and you were in the bathroom for a looooong time."

"She was pooping."

"Quiddit!!"

"Daniel, this one's for Kat."

"Well you were. That's what you kept saying, anyway."

"I know, but come on."

"Did I win?" asks Katharine impatiently.

"You tied for first place with Daniel." She gets out blue construction paper and scissors for them to use to make blue ribbons to wear as prizes. She lies down on the couch and sips a warm coke while they work on them. At least her husband will never have to know about her memorable little party of one.

Chapter 29

The in-laws are arriving on Saturday. Francesca asks Alec to come home at a decent hour on Friday so they can vacuum under the furniture in the living-room. His mom is sensitive to dust. Francesca has always made sure to have her place thoroughly wiped down for their visits. And once she gets the place ship shape, she gets to spend a whole week preparing meals while pretending to be happily married.

It's seven o'clock on Friday night. The kids are watching a Disney movie in their bed, having had soup and bread and carrots. Whole-grain bread. As Teacher Anna explains it, if you were a fireplace, refined flour, or basically all white starch except maybe bananas, would burn in your firebox like newspaper does. Whole grains are more like the logs. They burn slowly and steadily and give your body the fuel it needs until the next thing, which should be a small snack in between bigger meals and should include a little protein. So they only eat whole grain these days. Even the pasta. No potatoes at all, no popcorn, no white rice. She finds she can go for longer stretches without wanting chocolate. Alec storms into the house. With him wafts a faint scent of lilies of the valley. Like one of Pavlov's dogs, Francesca finds herself unable to resist the bait and positively bellows.

"What is that smell?"

Alec stops dead in his tracks, and looks over both shoulders as he closes the door behind him, as if to block the smell from coming in the house.

"What smell?"

"You reek of lilies of the valley, Alec. Is it a new cologne?" She closes in on him in two brisk strides. Her eyes are stinging with indignation and she is furious, positively furious, that he has forced her into confronting him; she wanted to wait until she was ready, not that she would have ever been ready for this, and apparently neither is he because his eyes widen with a kind of shock of recognition.

"Does it smell like a mix of vanilla and roses?"

She says "yes" the way a witness might say it when positively identifying a murder suspect in the courtroom.

"Damn it, I swear, that is the last time I drive that bitch home. Sorry about my language but I swear to God…"

"What bitch?" she asks. This exchange she had not rehearsed.

"Gillian Castle? The one I told you about who applied for the CFO job? She thinks of herself as this totally committed environmentalist, so she takes the train to work, walks the mile or so from the station, then she works past the commuter hours and asks ME to drive her home since it's 'right on the way.' I want to say to her *for Chrissakes, get a hybrid and quit bugging me!* When I leave that Hell hole at night, I don't want that psychic vampire badgering me with questions about our financial forecasts the whole way home. It's bad enough having Randy breathing down my neck all day…" Randy is the CEO. Three years younger than Alec and an overachiever's overachiever.

He lifts the coffee table at one end while she scrambles to keep up her end.

"She asks me my opinion on all these funding scenarios and then the next day, I overhear her quoting me verbatim to Randy, like she thought it all up on her own. She is pure evil." They slam down the table in a corner.

"Is she blonde?" She is feeling reckless, on the verge of...what is the opposite of an emotional collapse? She disappears around the corner with the floor lamp.

"Yeah, the fake blonde with the fake boobs. I feel like saying to her you know, Gillian, I doubt those boobs of yours are bio-degradable." As he works himself into more of a lather, she feels herself unfurl. Her shoulders lose their hunch, her toes relax, her jaw unclenches, for what feels like the first time in two months.

"Wait," he cries, "you didn't think I had been unfaithful did you? Because of the perfume? Cuz that is totally preposterous."

"Oh, Jiggy!" she coos, rushing back into view. "Of course not! I was just wondering what kind of aftershave you were wearing. Forget about that ol' psychic vampire and come here. I haven't given you a back rub in a looooooong time."

Later that night, when Alec is passed out cold after a particularly vigorous session between the sheets, she steals down the hall to the living room to the computer desk. She opens her email, and searches on MNO, Mommies' Night Out. Once she locates the email Marsha Mendenhall sent about the pair of glasses she found on the floor of the karaoke bar, she hits "reply all" and changes the subject line to FALSE ALARM.

To my sisters in Motherhood:

I am guilty of drawing conclusions from insufficient evidence. Spread the word. I don't deserve it, but please forgive me.

Fran

She shuts down the computer and heads to the bookshelf. She finds Helen Gurley Brown and pulls it down. Behind the book crouches the baggie, which she unzips and carefully retrieves the blonde hair. In the light of the torchière she can see the half inch of dark root. Normally, she would rinse and recycle a perfectly good baggie for someone's lunch, but tonight she tosses the whole contaminated package into the wastebasket and goes back to bed. She sleeps like petrified wood.

The visit from the in-laws is a typical brainwashing session, only this time around, she is especially vulnerable. As an only child Alec is incalculably precious, according to the first woman to lay claim to this treasure they must now divvy up fairly. Francesca has the hang of that—they're not together all that often, because Alec's father sits on numerous boards around the country and his wife travels with him.

While Alec's mother is in town, Francesca sees her husband as if through a lens that has been adjusted to a new prescription. Alec never gave his parents a day of trouble, apart from the time he tried to scrub guano off his father's Triumph when he was a young boy, and scratched the paintwork. After a stellar scholastic career, he attended Stanford, much to his mother's horror. He did a year in Americorps, in Appalachia (more badly needed separation from Mater), which opened his eyes to the grinding pace of governmental bureaucracy, and he decided what he needed was to go to business school before he could make any radical change. But business school opened his eyes to the thrill of finance, and that led directly to banking, where he leveraged his fine mind and knack for numbers. When Francesca sees Alec through his mother's eyes, she sees a hardworking family man who is above all good. He doesn't cheat on his taxes, not a teeny tiny bit; he doesn't lie, even if your jeans DO make your butt look big; he doesn't even read other people's postcards. He is ethical to the last letter of the law. How could she have suspected him of infidelity? One night, halfway through his parents' stay, she asks him playfully if he has ever considered cheating on her.

"I am far too tired to have an affair," he sighs, punching his pillow into submission.

They have only one disagreement in front of his parents. On their visit to Alcatraz, Mr. C. is having a little trouble on the inclines, given the excess weight a man of his stature must carry. Mama C. is pushing him along by firmly pressing on his lower back, and just then, a seagull drops on Libby's favorite Roxy sweatshirt a huge deposit of white poop. She screams as if it were alive. She can't see how to take off her sweatshirt without the poop getting on her, so she starts to cry along with the screaming. By now, Mr. C. has lost his balance and he has sat very firmly on his bottom right there on the path. Mom C. is bending over him cooing. Alec is running around in circles with his hands in the air like a man in a cartoon and Francesca is helping get the sweatshirt off without it touching Libby's skin.

"Cut it off!! Cut it off!" Libby screams.

Once it's off, Francesca folds it poop-side-in and starts to scrounge in her purse for a plastic bag. Libby is still crying audibly and Daniel has started to wander off, and now Kat is following him.

"Alec, get those two."

"Which two?" She misinterprets this question, assuming he is doing his absent-minded chief financial officer impersonation, when he restates the obvious in question form after whatever she says.

"The two children I birthed and raised with very little assistance from you—those ones over there," and she regrets it instantly because 1) how's it going to help? And 2) she realizes her mother-in-law has resurrected her portly father-in-law and they are struggling back up the gravel path to the prison on the cliff. Within hissing distance. She can't take it back.

Alec storms off to round up the youngers. Libby is busy rolling up the sleeves of her mother's fleece jacket and sniffling and shivering in the whipping wind. Francesca is guilty, contrite, and resentful all at once. But at least she isn't sharing her husband with a bottle-blonde.

Welcome to Alcatraz. It is one of the more unusual sites in modern America, for after a self-guided audio tour of this bleak, desolate, now shuttered federal prison that housed Al Capone and Machine Gun Kelly among many other "bad mans" as Kat calls them, visitors are funneled through a vestibule near the gift shop where a former inmate signs a memoir of his stay in the slammer. Did he ever dream, back in the late thirties, as he peered out of the barred windows in the dining hall, listening to the sounds of merriment in San Francisco carried over the water to his island cell, that sixty years later, he would be signing books at a folding table outside the gift shop?

By the end of the week, she has grown extremely fatigued of being charming to Alec's parents and she is ready to go back to taking her husband for granted.

Chapter 30

*I*t is as if the light bulb for Palo Alto, California were replaced with one fifty watts stronger. Spring is here, the birds sing about it all day, and the Carltons are going away for the weekend, not to Disneyland, but to stay at a decommissioned army base hostel across the Golden Gate Bridge, at the Marin headlands. Francesca is looking forward to time away with the family, but first…

Today is Little League Opening Day. Back in February, when she was signing Daniel up for the season, she heard about a used equipment table at Opening Day, where you could pick up all the baseball gear your kid will need for next to nothing. If you had anything to trade, all the better. She has nothing to trade, but here she is, an hour before the parade even begins, her bike chained to the fence, her family still in pajamas back in the tissue box, and she is waiting to pounce on the first little glove and size 13 cleats that come along.

At 8:47 she has procured cleats and a mitt for under ten bucks. She feels so lucky she wants to use the change to buy a lottery ticket. She meets her family at their parking space to stow her haul and help with all the moods and personalities that tumble out of the sliding doors. Daniel naturally wants to wear his "new" cleats and since the parade is mostly over grass, starting in a park adjacent to the baseball diamond, she acquiesces. She doesn't allow him to put them on until they get to the park where the ground is soft, but that is not what he had in mind. She doesn't back down, and he transforms before their very eyes into a small, pink Incredible Hulk. His face reddens exactly like a thermometer, from the chin to his forehead. She stands her ground. He starts to pound his temples with his fists. She grabs his wrists. Alec comes around the driver's side of the van and sees his wife manhandling his son, and because he has just spent the past three quarters of an hour attempting to herd three children from breakfast table to Opening Day, with Daniel dressed in his uniform and the other two in appropriate outfits with socks and shoes that match, teeth and hair brushed, and all of this single-handedly with little to no job experience, he is not at his best when he comes upon this scene of wanton child abuse.

"Francesca!" he roars.

Daniel and she both freeze. Her son is smart enough to know that things are not what they appear and that he currently has the advantage. He also still really wants to wear his cleats. Very quietly, but loudly enough for his Daddy to hear, Daniel says,

"Mommy, that hurts."

And here is why she loves her surly eldest daughter, who pokes her head out of the van where she has been lolling while they gather themselves together. Before her father can call Child Protective Services, she yells,

"Daniel, you little brat. I'm sure it hurt a lot more when you were beating your head with your fists. It hurt Mom so much just watching you that she made you stop, didn't she?" She turns to Alec. "Daniel wants to wear his cleats on the sidewalk and Mom said no."

"No cleats on the sidewalk," intones her husband, who has concluded that he can continue to leave Francesca alone with his progeny for unsupervised stretches.

The parading goes on for the better part of an hour, and because Daniel is on the youngest team, they go first and snake across the outfields, over to third base, where they stand, rarely on both feet at the same time, waiting, waiting, waiting for something to happen. It does. A former minor league ball player comes out to the pitcher's mound and with his back to the stands, he tells the boys, who range from pipsqueaks to needing a shave, that being big in Little League is playing your best and having fun. That's how to be big. He says it's a whole lot more fun than being little in the Big Leagues.

Francesca gets teary-eyed again. She is aware as if for the first time what it's like for her kids to have a hometown that's just their size.

Mac calls at nine at night, midnight in New York. She wants to get a divorce again. She always wants her divorces when Hugh is on the road. But she sounds serious this time. Very clearheaded, rational. Yet, next week he'll be back and they'll have the best sex they've had in months and Francesca will hear about the cute thing he said, the note he left, the gift he brought her. But for now, Mac wants her to go along with this charade. The kids are all in bed, Alec is somewhere else, she forgets where, but she knows it's not with a blonde, he is *too tired to have an affair*, and she has nothing better to do than to talk her friend out of getting a divorce.

"Mac, think about this. Is that really what you want? You've got four kids, who love their daddy—"

"When they actually lay eyes on the guy. He's never home."

"Well, divorcing him won't fix that."

"No, but at least I can move on."

"What, you're going to start dating?"

"Sure. You don't think I'd be able to attract anyone?"

"Of course you could, it's just that you've got all those kids, and let's face it, we're not in our twenties anymore."

"Neither are the men."

"The men don't need to be. I guess I'm just thinking about all the complications, maybe those are kind of hard to see when you're so sure——"

"Who says I need a man, anyway?"

"They're pretty handy when you want to go out to eat, or to a dinner party, or when your car is making a weird noise…"

"I'll get a mechanic."

"If you find one you can trust. But O.K., let's just say you and Hugh both go out and find yourselves new partners. Let's think about that for a sec. He remarries. Suddenly his new wife is parenting YOUR kids part of the time. And let's say she's divorced with a couple of kids—who knows what THOSE kids are going to be teaching your kids when they're at Hugh's house."

Mac is silent for once.

"And you marry a divorcé, because let's face it, you don't want to marry some bachelor in his forties, at least I wouldn't. And now you're dealing with your new husband's ex, and maybe his ex remarries, so now that brings in some other unknown, and maybe your new husband has some kids of his own, and remember what happened to Lee when they let some weird cousin live with them…"

"Yeah, well he's dead now."

"I'm just saying."

"OK. you've made your point. I am doomed to a life of misery and regret."

"Pretty much."

"Great."

"Mac, you can make this better. You and Hugh are friends. Start with that."

"I hate him."

"Today you do. You've hated him before, but you'll love him again, I promise."

"How can you make that promise?"

"Because, Rose McEntee, you are so full of love."

"I thought you were going to say something else."

"That, too."

"OK." Mac is done. "OK. But things are going to be different around here."

"Thatta girl."

"It's time to stand up and be counted."

Mac actually sounds a little drunk. But Francesca doesn't want to spoil the mood by pressing the point, so she doesn't say anything. That's something else she has noticed about Mac. When Hugh is away, she tends to go for that extra glass of wine at dinner, mostly because he isn't there to put the cork back in the bottle. She's not too great at self-regulating. But who is?

Francesca has her own husband issues. Alec spent all of Saturday helping build affordable housing on a newly developed mound of dirt in East San Jose. He got home after dark, sweaty, dirty, achy and beaming with accomplishment. She ladled up a can of soup for him and toasted bread from the freezer before going back to her movie. It had been a long day for her, too, only she was not exactly beaming with accomplishment. Today, Sunday, he accompanies them to church as a special treat, then skips out before the final hymn to join an all-day symposium for low-income entrepreneurs in Santa Clara County. A community bank in San Jose that does micro-loans to minority business owners found out about Alec and asked him to join their board of advisors. Apparently he has a lot to offer in the way of advice and counsel to ladies who want to start nail salons and men who run deliveries with broken-down vehicles.

Alec is very in demand. She doesn't think he realizes just how in demand he is.

The kids and she are planning a trip to the coast to see the elephant seals engage in mating rituals—Francesca has been assured that it is G-rated; they bellow a lot and flap their flippers and kind of roll around, but there is little to no copulation. Anyway, Libby wants to bring a friend, but Francesca was hoping this was something they could do as a family.

"I think it would be fun for it to be just us and Daddy." To which Kat replies,

"Daddy who?" It turns out she thought Francesca meant the friend's father, but still. Daddy who, indeed.

She wants to say to Alec *stop building houses for the homeless and spend some time in your own home, for crying out loud. You want to make a micro-loan? I'll take a micro-loan!* She hasn't bought a stitch of new clothing in almost a year and she is starting to look a little frayed around the edges. But what should you expect from the wife of an ascetic? No, St. Alec has lost his luster somewhat. And no, she is not having the curse.

But she doesn't say a thing. She suffers in a reverse form of martyred silence, since he is the one saving the world one housing project one micro-loan, one mentoring relationship at a time. She calls Muth, who has her own cross to bear. Dad answers.

"And how's my favorite youngest daughter?" How could he be losing his marbles, when he sounds so with it? He is still her daddy.

"Just fine, Dad. How are you?"

"Surviving. Your mother is making us some lunch. Did you want to speak to her?"

"If she's got a free hand, sure." He cups his hand over the phone and announces in muffled tones,

"It's Pat on the phone."

Chapter 31

They have booked a family room at the Fort Baker youth hostel, which occupies a couple of officer's quarters on the periphery of the parade grounds overlooking the Pacific. They bring their own groceries and use the communal kitchen alongside the several hearty guests who have been coming from as far away as Boston every year for the pleasure of self-catering and light house-keeping chores on the edge of this great nation. They will visit the famous Point Bonita Lighthouse, with its 150 year-old multifaceted lens. They will drink in the unspoiled beauty of the rugged coast and write postcards. They will drag one moody child after another down muddy trails, pointing out beautiful vistas and unpleasant character traits. They will change their sheets and sweep under the beds and leave at least one belonging behind, never to be seen again. Life will resume but two nights at Fort Baker will become a tiny new part of their family DNA.

Lee calls at 7:15 on a Wednesday morning when Francesca is assembling cheese and jelly sandwiches and the kids are dawdling in their rooms before breakfast and they have to be on the road in precisely thirty minutes to make the 7:55 bell.

"Am I calling too early?"

"Yes." Lee recently had a business trip to Rome and had a massage in a ritzy hotel where she fell instantly, deeply, in love with her masseur. They have exchanged a couple of emails since. Francesca is the poorly qualified translation service.

"It'll only take a sec, though."

"I only have a sec, Lee, can't it wait?"

"What does a-b-b-r-a-c-c-i-o mean?"

"Hug."

She doesn't even know how she knows this. When you have spent a year working as a chamber maid in mountain resorts around Europe, buying fruit, taking buses, ordering cokes, disco dancing with the locals, you tend to pick up the vernacular. Plus, all these romance languages are basically interchangeable. But she all the same reaches for the Italian/English dictionary that is on the travel shelf an arm's length from the kitchen doorway. She flips to the Italian side as Lee completely mangles a sentence about *la mano non puo comprendersi, sin guardarsi negli occhi*. She makes it sound like Latin.

"Embrace," she interrupts. There is a pause.

"Which is it, hug or embrace?"

"Um, both. I don't think they make a distinction." She has always been very adroit with a bilingual dictionary. In the time it takes her to answer, she has already looked up hug on the English side.

"Hug, *abbraccio*. Yeah, they only have one word."

"Oh." Lee sounds totally deflated.

"Lee, I gotta go."

"Can I call you later for the rest of the message?"

"Sure, but why don't you get a dictionary?"

"I have one, but I need you."

She wants Francesca to parse each of her beloved masseur's utterances, frisking the phrases for shades of meaning, hints of undying devotion.

"I'm sure he meant embrace."

"I'll call you later," Lee says, hollowly.

Francesca wants to cry for Lee, who is such a candidate for the healing properties of human touch. Will there ever be enough massages though, to rub away the indignity of her young victimhood?

She calls home. For the past several weeks, only Muth has answered, and only Muth has taken the call. For some inexplicable reason, Francesca doesn't know how to speak to Dad. As if part of his illness is her increasing inability to cope with it. She misses the familiar Belgian-tinged King's English: "How's my favorite youngest dohtah?" And to close, "love you to pieces!" On the fourth ring, he answers.

"Hi Dad! It's Cesca!"

"Yes, hello?"

"Dad? It's Francesca!"

"What can I do for you?"

"Umm, I'm not really—I'm just calling to...say hi."

"Hi." He sounds distracted, even irritable.

"How's everything."

"I wouldn't know."

"Oh. Ummmm...is Muth there?"

"Who?"

"Is your wife there?"

"Not that I am aware. What is it you want?" She wants her father back.

"Oh, nothing, really. I'll call back, O.K.? O.K. Listen, it was great to talk to you, Dad!"

"Not at all."

"I'll talk to you soon!"

"Right. Bye."

"Bye Dad."

Who was that?

These days she is alternately moody, snappy, and weepy. In addition, not to blame any of this on the moon, but let's just say she is a couple of weeks away from ovulation. When Alec asks her before her first cup of coffee, to please turn his jeans inside out when she dries them, she just loses it. Of COURSE she turns them inside out. And she then turns them right side–in before he finds them neatly folded on the crease, on his side of the bed, which, incidentally, she makes every morning while he showers, now that the case of the blonde hair has been cracked. The jeans are ready to be put away, and no thanks to the wearer and soiler of said jeans. If they are at all wrinkly, it is because he has shoved them off the bed onto the floor at bedtime. She throws the green sponge at him—the one that is supposed to be used for floors only, but which she snatches up anyway, it is dry, and hurls at her husband. He prescribes professional help and goes to work. Like they can afford professional help. Later, he emails her directions to an Alzheimer's support group that meets Thursdays at 7:30 at a local medical clinic. By now, she has collected herself, and the sponge, and can be found on all fours poking into linty corners around the fridge and stove, totally lost in the task, except for the stomach-churning thoughts about Dad that gallop through her head.

Chapter 32

A conference call with the Three Graces.

"OK, is everyone sitting down?" asks Lee, bursting with excitement. This can't be about the Italian masseur, because he wrote her to say that *una bella ragazza* half Lee's age accompanied him to Sardinia and they are officially *amori*.

"Go ahead," they cry. Francesca is leaning, not sitting, for there is no chair within reach of this phone attached to the wall.

"I have the biggest news of my life," Lee intones, dead serious.

"You met someone!" Mac screams.

"Yeah, right. Just listen." Francesca can't imagine what is coming. She resolves not to breathe a word about Dad on this call. She has had her share of air time about the decline and fall of Dad's memory. This one's for Lee.

"I sent <u>Love is a Verb</u> to a publisher in Wisconsin, called Brandywine? They publish romance novels and chick lit and stuff for women? Anyway, they want to publish it!!"

"Oh my GOD!!" Mac and Francesca scream.

"WAIT!! There's MORE!" Lee screams over them. "They're giving me an advance and it's a THREE BOOK DEAL!"

"Nooooo!" Mac howls.

Now Francesca is crying. These are tears without so much as a droplet of envy. If Lisa can't have a happily ever after with her Prince Charming, at least she can have one with her goofy love stories.

"Oh, Lee!" Mac is talking a mile a minute about how Lee has already written at least five in the series? Which means more advances, royalties, book signings…Francesca is trying to talk over Mac.

"Lee, use this money for a good therapist." Mac stops Lee dead in her tracks. You can almost hear the screech of tires.

"She's right, Lee. Get a shrink immediately. Do not pass go. Honey, this is your big chance to slay your demons once and for all."

"I was going to use the advance for an Armani suit. I've always wanted to pay full price."

"Sorry, not yet. Therapy first."

"Yup, therapy first."

"You guys!"

"Heal thyself, Lee."

"You got stuff."

"Wow, calling you two is worse than calling my mother. All she wanted to know was, if no one buys the books, do I get to keep the advance."

"Yeah, well, tell 'em you spent it all on therapy," instructs Mac.

"We're so proud of you Lisa-P."

"Thanks, you two. You're my sisters."

"We're your sisters and we know what's best."

Summer in Palo Alto is as perfect as winter was, for different reasons. They have lovely hot days, but NO humidity. It simply never, ever rains in the summer. It is some kind of unwritten law. No gathering clouds in the mid-afternoon, no thunder storms just when you have lit the barbeque, no sweat between your thighs as you sit outside in the late afternoon sun, sipping a cocktail before another meal taken out on the DECK, where there are literally no mosquitoes. Francesca sees so much of her kids this summer, she is starting to feel like she really knows these people. Back in New York, she often woke up on a Saturday morning with a slight stomach ache, the kind of butterflies invading her insides that she had known in her early work life. The feeling of stirring panic persisted on weekends when she was faced with the prospect of a long, empty day, and three children with three very different sets of desires and all of them more or less in direct conflict with the others. She would get out of bed as if in a bad dream, not quite able to harness the will to make her legs carry her into battle, her mind muddled with apprehension over how to gain and maintain the upper hand. Here in Palo Alto, they have come up with a daily routine that works for all of them incredibly well. For one thing, the older two are on the swim team at the public pool, and while they practice in the afternoon, she puts Kat down for a nap, and actually gets some gardening time, no interruptions. She discovered a strip of fertile ground on the south side of the garage and is raising tomatoes and zucchini. She and the kids ride their bikes almost everywhere. They eat lots and lots of fruit, they have lemonade stands at least once a week, helping themselves to the gargantuan lemons off their elderly neighbor's laden Meyer lemon tree. They go to bed late, and they sleep in, even Kat. Francesca is finally getting the hang of at-home-motherhood. Her dad is the fly in the ointment, but he is so far away that sometimes she forgets how sad she is about all of that.

Lee has been in therapy for a couple of months, and Passion Play is in rewrites. She calls Francesca from Los Angeles, where she is selling advertising for *Chic*. She is so nearby, Francesca wants to throw all the kids in the van and drive the eight hours to see her. But they settle for a long, juicy phone call instead.

"How's the therapy going?"

"Oh Franny, I have such a bad case of transference I can barely see straight."

"What do you mean? What are the symptoms?"

"Racing heart, shortness of breath, obsessive thoughts…"

"There must be some drug you can take. I've never heard of this, what did you say it's called?"

"Transference. It's when you're in love with your therapist. It happens all the time apparently."

"Hence the racing heart."

"And the shortness of breath."

"At least you get the obsessive thoughts; that must be fun."

"Oh, don't get me started."

Lee describes him, again. Francesca already knows he is smart, funny and handsome. Today she learns he has a high-pitched giggle, which Lee finds immensely attractive.

"But what do you even know about this guy, I mean really?"

"I know his middle name and I know he likes Jazz because he subscribes to a magazine called Be Bop."

"Oh man, Lee, you've got it bad."

"Tell me about it. I think about him constantly. I imagine him greeting me at the door of the waiting room with his warm, slightly ironic little smile, and as I pass him to walk down the hall to his office, he very gently takes my shoulder, and kind of spins me around, really slowly…"

"Maybe this part should be in slow motion."

"Yes, perfect. And he just looks down into my eyes and I stare into his, he has these beautiful brown eyes and a kind of dorky haircut, but he's got plenty of hair, and it's all curly—he reminds me of Gary Levy, a boy I liked in fifth grade. Anyway, he gathers me in his arms, and I slip my arms under his blazer—he wears really good quality lightweight wool blazers, and we stand in the corridor and just start slow dancing right there in the hall." There's a long pause.

"That's it?"

"Uh huh."

"You slow dance fully clothed?"

"Mm hmm. And then he kisses me tenderly on the forehead and we go into his office and he sits next to me on the couch and holds my hand, and puts his other arm around my shoulders, and I snuggle up close and tell him about my week."

"Wow." It doesn't compare to Francesca's fantasy about a handsome doctor who makes the first move, but don't forget Lee was sexually abused by an adolescent cousin who was probably pretty lacking in bedside manner.

"I haven't felt like this ever."

"Tell him!"

"I don't have to. He knows. He just takes it in his stride. It is so sweet."

"You know you're not supposed to get involved with your therapist, right?"

"I know that. It's just that, I know this will sound so cliché, but I kind of feel like I'm an exception."

"You are exceptional."

"No, I mean if he falls in love with me, warts and all," and here's where Francesca laughs until she chokes.

"—you know," Lee continues, "all my hang-ups..."

"Yeah, O.K. all your hang-ups."

"It's just that I feel like we were meant to meet, even if it had to be on opposite sides of the analyst couch. You can't help how fate throws you together, can you?"

"No, but he could lose his license."

"Only if I tell on him."

"You could end up shooting him, or his wife."

"Only if he's married."

"Is he?"

"I don't know yet. I'm working on a way to find that out."

"Try asking him."

"Oh God, I couldn't. Besides, what makes you the big expert all of sudden, Mrs. Alec-and-I-don't-have-time-for-couples-therapy?"

"Are you kidding me? Just because you don't pay me two hundred dollars an hour doesn't mean I don't know how you think. Which reminds me, you owe me five hundred thousand dollars for ten years of psychotherapy, no interest."

"Can I pay with a credit card?"

"Just be careful, sweetie. You're still kinda fragile."

"I know." She sounds exhausted.

"Oh, Lee, I'd marry you in an instant if I were him!"

"You would?"

"Absolutely. I'd slow dance fully clothed with you anytime."

Chapter 33

*T*hursday night, 7:30 p.m., Redwoods Medical Clinic. The room is lit like a stadium. She moves across the carpet of this movie set living room and chooses from the brown plaid tweed seating. On the two-seater couch is one XXL sized balding man who takes up more than half the couch and half again. A nubbly brown cube next to him holds an old lady the shape of an apostrophe. She lifts her head with effort, and manages only to turn it narrowly to gaze at Francesca from a flounder's angle. Across from them, on the three-seater, a couple shares the middle cushion. Francesca chooses the side next to the petite wife. She feels overheated and self-conscious. She crowds in next to a tabletop lamp, atop a side table that is level with the couch back so she can rest her elbow while she airs out one arm pit. It is clear that these five people know each other. She hears snatches of chit chat about a weekend away, book recommendations: the conversation of the well-acquainted.

"Hi."

She assumes their leader has just spoken to her. She is holding a matchbook, which probably puts her in charge. So that's it? Her official welcome from the Alzheimer's Support Network of

Northern Santa Clara County? Hi? The 60-ish, dyed-red haired, dough-faced, lumpy woman reaches under the coffee table to the shelf beneath and brings up a stout candle whose vanilla scent Francesca can smell from where she sits. Plucking her red turtle-neck in an ineffectual effort to cover up her wattles, the woman with the matches lights the candle and takes in a deep breath, closing her pouchy eyes. Francesca doesn't know whether she is supposed to do this too, so she checks the others. No one is meditating but the lady with the matches.

Conversation dies down—the whispered snatches of dialogue disappear into the vanilla-scented atmosphere.

"Good evening everyone and thanks for joining me tonight. I'm Judy, your volunteer moderator this evening. We are a community of ordinary people who come into contact with Alzheimer's Disease and those afflicted with it. We are caretakers, family members, and friends of people with Alzheimer's. We know first-hand about the progression of the disease, and we can share our burden here in safety. We support each other, listen lovingly to our stories, and with God's help, we can get through this... anyway, that's what we do!" She obviously hasn't worked out the last part of her intro.

Should Judy say God? Francesca supposes it's OK, since it is inscribed on the coin of the realm and of course He's featured in the Pledge of Allegiance...which reminds her to ask the kids if they say the pledge, and if they say *under God*. The separation of church and state is a smart policy, even for a cradle Episcopalian who keeps God close, like a lucky rabbit's foot. Francesca prayed constantly in school and she still nearly failed math. God doesn't belong in school. He belongs at church and in the bedroom, at night, when the day is done and all the mistakes have been made. And apparently he also belongs at support groups and preschool Spanish classes.

They start by going around and stating their names and their affiliation with Alzheimer's. Francesca's affiliation would be wide-eyed onlooker. She lives 3,000 miles away from Al Zeimer, yet she can feel him stalking her shadow. Just when it is nearly her turn to introduce herself, the door bangs open. What looks like a life-sized marionette jiggles in. She is tall, rail-thin, clad in five different bright colors and hung with silver jewelry. Her spiky short hair is maroon. That, and the Indian print scarf draped around her collarbone suggest that she is European.

"Wot traffick toonatt!"

Anna is Swiss. Her mother, in advanced stages of Alzheimer's, has lived with Anna and her family in Menlo Park ever since Anna's father died three years ago in Zurich. Anna's kids are ten and twelve and they manage to work around their batty *Grossmutti*. During the week, Anna works at home as a free-lance graphic designer. She hires a nurse for eight-hour shifts, and does the rest of the care herself.

"My mudder cries troo de door that she is all alone. I know dis isn't troo becoz de nurse is right dere making her her lunch! It's so hard to verk sometimes. But verking is a lot better than taking care of my mom. I go from de frying pan to de fire!"

Through her thick Swiss accent, Anna speaks confidently, melodically. Listening to this sad story, coming from this colorfully clad gypsy on the other end of her couch, Francesca forgets for a moment that any of it is troo.

Later, they are all riveted by the story of Karen, the petite wife Leslie's mother-in-law; Howard's mother.

"Every night she says 'See? LOOK! The world has gone dark!'" Leslie slows her sobbing and, after swallowing some fresh air, speaks more deliberately. She sits up straighter.

"It would be almost funny, you know, someone not getting it about sunset, if only she wasn't so terrified of the dark. We draw the curtains, but she gets up to peek out all the time."

"And each time it's like it's the first time." Howard fusses with his wife's bracelet and looks up for a moment to check the middle distance for something, then back to the bracelet.

"My husband came out one morning with his shirt on like pants." Judy the moderator exhales dramatically. Francesca assumed she would just pass around tissues and blow out the candle, but she is suffering too.

"You can't leave him alone in the kitchen even for a second. I have baby gates up all over the place now."

Francesca is embarrassed at how well her dad is doing. He dresses and shaves himself. Takes four-mile walks on his own. Drives to the post office. He keeps score in table tennis. But he has lost the song in his voice. He sounds short-tempered when they speak on the phone, as if any minute he will hang up on her in a fit of pique. Granted, he hasn't, but lately, it feels like he might. Does this count? And when the next hole in the silence is demanding to be filled, and it would make sense in the proceedings for that to be by the one person in the room who hasn't yet shared, Francesca finds herself tentatively raising her hand, before she remembers that no one else did that. Judy calls on her and she just starts moving her tongue. What comes out is her childhood in New Haven, how Muth was such a force of nature, and Dad was always the steadying influence. She loves Muth, not because she is particularly lovable, but because she demands their affection and they give it to her. But Dad is—was— her rock. She has always depended on him for the sustaining warmth of a low fire...and now the fire is going out.

Howard chimes in from his perch. "I was always so worried about whether or not my mom was getting worse, I lost a lot of quality time. I say enjoy him as much as you can now. Give him calls and just talk to him."

"I taught Frank to hit the button on the answering machine when he answered the phone, and it would record his conversations with our daughter," Judy the moderator adds. "That way, I still got to hear her news, without having to get it from Frank. Tell your mother to put a big red sticker on the record button."

Francesca wants to put a big red sticker on this whole meeting. She scribbles down tricks and tips to share with Muth. She'll let her know all the ways in which she and Dad are so much better off… Judy gives her a phone list two pages long. "Unfortunately," Judy sighs, "this is a growing business," and she hugs Francesca goodbye, until next week.

At least she is feeling much more relaxed about Dad, until her busy little mind latches on to something Judy had said in passing. *Alzheimer's is a disease of the brain. Everybody just thinks of it as a memory disease.* The memory is the first to go, but reason, planning, joy, tranquility: they will go too. If they don't "get nicked" first, as Donald the plus-sized man says, everything else will ultimately follow until they forget how to swallow, or breathe.

Muth calls. She has a frantic quality to her voice these days, as if someone is pointing a gun to her head. She mentions auditions for the musical, Annie. She wants the part of Miss Hannigan.

"Of course it's one of the great contemporary character parts, and since there's not too much dancing, except for the torch song, I don't think Vivian Pinkes has a prayer this time. With all her tap, she had me beat for the—

"Are you sure about this, Muth?"

"Oh definitely! I mean she hasn't got much of a voice, though she CAN dance, and I think that goes a long way with Tommy. Never second-guess a director, dahling, that is, if you want to keep working!" She has on her Katharine Hepburn voice again. Funny how much she can make herself sound like a career actor.

"I was thinking more about Dad...do you really think you should be in a play right now?"

"Oh, he's fine. As long as I give him his dinner, he can watch T.V. or read till I get back."

"It's just that he does seem to be getting more confused..."

"Not at all! He's doing great." Francesca knows when to quit. She decides to move on to the topic of kids because that is the safest subject. She digs out her shiniest gems for Muth to squirrel away—Daniel scoring a goal with the back of his head while tying his shoe, unaware that the game was even in play; Libby's Immigrant Story presentation where she chose to showcase herself, a recent immigrant to California. Her daughter the newest immigrant, flying Business Class on her father's Magic Miles.

"If you really think I shouldn't..." Muth has circled back to the truth.

"It's just that he seems a little lost when I call..."

"Oh no, <u>he</u> thinks he's fine!" She forces a laugh. Francesca snorts rhythmically in an effort to laugh along with her, but it really isn't funny. The phone slips around in her hot hand. There is a pause.

"He doesn't remember Kendra." Now Muth is very serious, because it is inconceivable that Dad doesn't remember Kendra Hook, the friend that brought them together in 1952. Over the next forty years, every time they were in London, and that was at least once a year, they would have dinner with her and see a show. She eventually died of stomach cancer. Like the Alzheimer's it all came upon them so suddenly. One minute they were taking in the new David Hare drama and the next thing they knew Kendra was dying of stomach cancer in her pretty little flat in Pimlico. They didn't even know where to send condolence notes. She was cremated by a brother who flew in from Australia and took care of the whole procedure one Saturday morning while they were all fast asleep in New England.

And now Dad doesn't remember Kendra.

"At all?" She can't think of anything else to say.

"At all."

"What exactly did he say?"

"We were talking about our trip this fall. I said I wished Kendra were still around because there's a new Maggie Smith play and she always loved Maggie Smith. He said, Kendra who?"

"What did you say?"

"I said Kendra Hook, our old friend from London." Beleaguered Muth. She sounds as if she isn't even sure anymore if there ever was a Kendra Hook. If a tree falls in the woods, but you don't remember it happening, did it?

"Yipes."

"It's so SAD." She thinks her mother might be about to cry, which would be the second time in her life that she knows of. The last time was when their de-clawed cat escaped from the house, and... well, never came back. Muth was the one who spearheaded the de-clawing because of the furniture, and it nearly killed her when Marmalade didn't come home.

"I'm so sorry, Muth."

"Me too."

Francesca has never sat on the phone in silence with Muth. It is a dark, heavy silence. So heavy they can't even lift it. Finally, Muth says,

"I feel like this is my fault."

"How could it possibly?"

"Oh, I don't know. Remember the musical with the mute king, and the overbearing queen?"

"Once Upon a Mattress?"

"That's it. What if I did this to Daddy?"

"Muth, that's just crazy."

"I never made him remember anyone's name. Maybe if I had made him try harder…"

"Muth, there are a lot of things you might not have done just right. But saving Dad from Alzheimer's is not one of them."

"I guess I better give Miss Hannigan to Vivian Pinkes." She hasn't even tried out for it yet, and she is already handing over the part to the understudy.

"Maybe just until we know more about his prognosis. You'll never retire from the theater, Muth. Your fans wouldn't allow it."

"OK, well, I better go." Go where? Back to the other room where her husband doesn't even remember how they met?

Dad's 74 year-old baby sister Sheila calls Francesca to see how Dad is doing. She doesn't want to be a bother by calling them directly. The high-definition transatlantic phone line is so clear, she luxuriates in Aunty Sheila's charming English accent. She sounds a lot like the Queen. Her broad a's and lovely r's make Francesca forget how she talks herself. At one point she says *mind you*, which she never says.

Francesca tells Sheila about Dad not remembering Kendra Hook. Sheila understands how serious the situation is. She looked after her mother in a nearby nursing home in Hertfordshire for seven years. Francesca has always been so far away from that branch of the family that she barely even knew that grandmother. There are some family members, the ones who were rooted and reared in Brussels, for example, who only speak halting English. Her uncle's wife, who is Italian, for example. She can hardly form a sentence. Their kids are even worse. To be fair, she can't always understand her English cousins when they say things like *do you want to spend a penny?* which means do you have to go to the bathroom? Or, *said the actress to the bishop*, which follows an off-color comment.

Sheila is such a love; she knows just what to say. There is nothing to say, of course, except, *oh dear.* And *Yes, yes.* Francesca could spend all morning listening to that soothing sing-song.

The following week, Muth calls and says in a stage whisper, "He doesn't know who the president is." She sounds like she's radioing from the front.

"I guess that could be a good thing!" This time Francesca tries to sound hale and hearty. She can't imagine what it must be like for her mother, their family home invaded by this sinister memory-eating monster. They have never really experienced something that just keeps getting worse. Oh, maybe Muth's varicose veins, but she had those stripped in the mid-seventies.

Three days later Muth calls, and she sounds delirious.

"Have you heard from Pat yet?"

"No, what about?" What could possibly have happened to Pat that would transform her worried old mother into a breathless schoolgirl?

"She just found out about a doctor in St. Paul who is developing a drug that will stop Alzheimer's in its tracks!! It might even reverse it. He is looking for early-stage cases for a human trial so we're flying out to St. Paul to see him this weekend."

Francesca start to say, "It's all so sudden..." but she only gets as far as

"It's—"

"It's the Holy Spirit." Muth says in her holy voice, the one she can't help using when she mentions her favorite member of the Trinity. The "o" in Holy seems to whoosh forth, on the wing of a prayer, on the winds of the Midwestern plains where

Muth was raised. She is brimming with faithful conviction on the telephone line.

"It's a miracle," she intones.

According to Dr. Harold Gentry, the current trial for a brand new medicine that could slow, or halt the disease, is one of the most popular trials available. Whatever Pat said to this guy, and one shouldn't ever underestimate her powers of persuasion, he has put Dad on the list of Trial 1 participants; people who are in the early stages of the disease, and have a greater chance of responding to the drug. It is apparently a derivative of an anti-inflammatory, a fairly innocuous chemical combination that might just have the stuff to take Al Zeimer down.

According to Dr. Helen Schucman, a psychologist who, in 1975 apparently channeled Jesus' teachings into a big fat book called the Course in Miracles, a ragged tome her sister Pat lugged around for years after her conversion, miracles are simply an expression of love. As Pat would explain it, you can find miracles wherever you find love in action. You can be talking about a parent/teacher conference you had with some old battle ax who has informed you that your kid has ADHD and Pat will point out how fear is the opposite of love and the miracle is waiting to happen. Or, you might describe a ding in your car door that you don't know how you got, but you think was delivered by a beat-up old truck parked next to you at a seedy Christmas tree farm in Hoboken and Pat will remind you that fear is the opposite of love and the miracle is waiting to happen. Of course Pat has come a long way from reading, re-reading and re-reading aloud The Course in Miracles. Nowadays, she lives and breathes the Course in Miracles every time she shows up in a courtroom.

Pat finding Dr. Gentry is a miracle of sorts, because the reviled Mr. Zeimer is out of the closet once and for all. Released from the contract of silence, they speak openly and with great enthusiasm of Dad's disease. They discuss with Dad the chances of this trial improving his memory, whereas before, they simply talked about the weather and asked to speak to Muth. When Dad answers the phone now, he is bombarded by friendly fire. He seems to take it all in his stride.

Their naked optimism is especially annoying to people like Alec, who have checked around and have found no scientific basis for the use of anti-inflammatory drugs in curing Alzheimer's. But that is missing the point. Dr. Gentry has given the family something to shoot for, and that is what they all need right now. He has not promised a cure, nobody could, but he thinks this drug could stall progression and as Muth says,

"I couldn't live with myself if I didn't at least try it."

The flip side of miracles is, if you don't catch them when they roar through, you're out of luck, though (small comfort) you would never know, unless you knew you let one go. They can't let this miracle get away.

Big brother Henry jokes on the phone with Francesca about how Dad will come out of this thing spouting Pythagoras' theorem and other complex facts as the operation reverses the symptoms of Dad's condition. Or he will suddenly remember the names of their little friends from grade school. Even without Alzheimer's, this would be asking for more than Dad could deliver, because he has never had much of a memory. And although she may joke around with Henry, Francesca firmly believes the trial is their only hope. Like an exorbitant game of *Mother May I*, Al Zeimer will have to go five giant steps backwards.

Pat doesn't joke at all. She views this whole ordeal as an inevitable harbinger of the horrible aging process and ultimate demise of their parents. She is the prophet in the wilderness, crying out for salvation, yet clinging to her faltering faith that miracles can intervene.

Six weeks later, after each of the three children has weighed in on the trial, and the consensus is a resounding *who knows?* Dad is in St. Paul being assigned to either the test group, the ones receiving the meds, or the placebo group, those who get no drug whatsoever. Then, they record the results and her dad is either on the winning team or the losing team, though it is unclear which team is which.

Dr. Gentry is amazed at Dad's overall physical health for a man his age. The doctor is also excited to have a patient in such early stages of the disease. He is used to working with much more desperate situations. Again, she is lulled into a sense of superiority, that Dad still dresses himself and still qualifies for a Stage 1 trial. What she doesn't dare imagine is what he will be like in a couple of years if this doesn't work, which it may not. Especially if he is in the placebo group.

Their parents move in with Pat. Her sister is at her most effective in times of crisis. She has books for Muth, and treats for Dad, and videos, photo albums, even a puzzle set up for them. Dad requires very little. Three meals, a little conversation, and lots of sleep. Because of his youthful constitution, he handles the drugs well (either that, or it's the placebo again) and Pat can go back to work knowing he is OK. It will be months before they know if the trial helped. It has certainly helped all of them, as they cheer Dad on from the sidelines.

Chapter 34

*E*veryone at Francesca's house is maturing, except maybe Alec. He gets grumpier and shorter tempered with every passing week. It is as if he emptied his reservoir of tenderness when they found out about Dad. Then, he would sit and hold her hand late at night as she babbled incoherently about Dad not knowing their kids one day, and what if he becomes violent? Many Alzheimer's patients do. And Alec would stroke her hand and tell her he would be there for her, no matter what. It was incredibly sweet. She hadn't felt that connected to Jiggy since the babies were crowning. Because once they actually popped out, she was extremely preoccupied and he pretty much left her to it.

Now he snaps at them, he has been known to throw things against walls in a fury, he even once grabbed Daniel by the collar, just like in the old cops and robbers movies. Francesca slapped him in the subsequent hushed exchange in the bedroom. She has never slapped anyone. It was incredibly satisfying. In fact, if there were Oscars for slaps, she would be nominated. It was clean, loud and totally unexpected, even by her. They were both a little stunned, but she thinks she made her point.

It turns out, Alec is not able to get R&D to commit to a final prototype and they're burning through the company's cash. When she mentions the situation to her big brother Henry, he says it's exactly the same scenario for him when proposed dental work goes way over budget and he ends up being the bad guy. One patient actually turned down a root canal because Henry had originally hoped to avoid that procedure, but the tooth was too far gone. Ultimately, the guy ended up losing part of his jaw when the bone got infected.

At least Dad is coping well with the experiment. Francesca personally thinks he is in the test group, because these days, he seems more present than he has been. Muth says, *if he stays like this, I can handle this.*

Then the floor falls out from under the Carlton family.

Chapter 35

She gets the Three Graces on a conference call. No speakerphone.

"OK, I need pinky promises here."

They all tap their receivers with their pinkies, or whatever hard object to signify a pinky. They have been tapping receivers since they first met, when they were catching each other up on the office gossip at *21*.

"Alec has a major problem. It's actually more our problem at this point. OK, let's see, I'm going to start with the drives home with the bleach blonde."

"Uh oh," says Mac.

"It's not what you think, just listen." No one makes a sound, so obedient are her two best friends in moments of crisis.

"When Alec was in the final round for this job, there was an internal candidate. It was this blonde woman who had been the number two person in the finance department and she really wanted the CFO job but Alec had more experience, because sometimes start-up companies use their investment banker as CFO when they are still building a management team. And so he had done quite a bit of CFO stuff already, plus he has all the banking contacts, so basically, he blew her out of the water…"

"And she stayed on?" Lee asks this with a note of dread.

"Uh huh. He didn't tell me much about any of this, mostly because he has been so busy, you have no idea, and besides, I don't think he realized the danger he was in."

"You would have."

"Of course I would have. My God, if I had only known…well anyway, she has been sitting back in her little corner, spinning, spinning, spinning her web and Alec has been droning along doing his work, keeping the whole company afloat financially while the cash slowly gets spent and the research people keep asking for more, and time is running out and the banks are calling and the investors are getting anxious and poor Alec just keeps holding it all together…" Her throat starts to tighten as she imagines her hard-working husband just doing his best for the company, for the family, and meanwhile this scorned, pissed psychic vampire just waits for her moment to strike. Now she is gulping for breath so she can keep going.

"Get some water." Mac orders.

"Yeah, take a deep breath, sweetheart."

"It's OK. I'm OK." She hiccups. "Anyway, so this woman, her name is Gillian Castle, so Gillian has been plotting her revenge for like a year, including getting rides with Alec when she misses the last train, and using the time to pick his brains, and according to Alec, she would even have the nerve to quote him verbatim in front of the CEO, and make it look like she thought of it."

"That, that—"

"Dirty rat."

"So anyway, Alec stopped giving her rides, because she drove him crazy with all her questions, and so he would just make excuses about stuff he had to do after work, that kind of thing."

"Good. He got smart."

"Not smart enough."

"Oh God, this is so painful." Mac again.

"Anyway, I guess he thought he had all of that under control, which is when she figures she is finally ready to make her move. She tells Alec that she has lined up a journalist who wants to do a puff piece on the company because Alec had gotten together a group of colleagues to help build some low-income housing one Saturday last month...and so anyway, she arranges the meeting with this business writer guy from the big San Jose paper, which everyone in Silicon Valley reads, and Alec, who doesn't have time for pretty much anything these days that isn't about raising more cash to pay the bills, while they wait for R&D who are madly getting their product ready for FDA trials, anyway, he goes ahead and takes the meeting, because it will run in the Business section, and the company can always use some goodwill..."

"Sure."

"And Gillian makes a lunch reservation for him at the same restaurant as the CEO, who is having lunch with an investor, and those two wave to each other over their menus...so Alec has his lunch and they talk about the community building project, and other stuff about community relations, and Alec tells the journalist what a caring, good company MNS is, and how different from most high-powered CEOs Randy Cramner is, and all that kind of thing, and they wrap it up early and Alec goes back to work and that's the end of it."

"Yeah?"

"The next day, yesterday, the article appears on the front page of the business section."

"And?"

"Well you know how the product they're working on, the one that was going to make them all this money, make US all this money, is a material for genetically engineering bone?"

"Yeah, vaguely."

"Well, there's basically a top secret ingredient. It's some special plastic, I don't know…anyway, the journalist writes a piece about the company, all right, but not about the building project in East San Jose. Instead, it's all about their research, and how they're behind schedule, and he actually NAMES the secret ingredient in their biodegradable polymer, which is what they were banking on as the one totally solid edge they had over their competitors."

"But how could he have known…?"

"This is the killer. The journalist described the polymer compound as the Miracle-Gro of human biology. That's the phrase that Alec used in a recent meeting with the CEO, and guess who else was in the meeting."

"She leaked it."

"Right. He thought of the Miracle-Gro analogy on the spot in that meeting. It's the only time he used it, though, because after the meeting, an engineer from R&D, the one who went to Stanford? He told him it wasn't accurate, and that it wasn't a good analogy."

"And the CEO thinks he leaked it."

"Exactly."

"Because he saw Alec with the journalist at the restaurant."

"And meanwhile Alec knows SHE leaked it."

"Right again."

"So can't he tell the CEO that she leaked it?"

"He tried. Randy told him to get the hell out and not even to bother to clean out his desk."

"But why would Alec tell a journalist the secret ingredient? Has the guy thought about THAT?"

"He said that Alec had about as much media savvy as a summer intern."

"Ooooh, that's low." They are deadly quiet.

"So that's it?" ventures Mac.

"That's it."

"Poof?" confirms Lee.

"Poof."

Another silence. You can almost hear the sound of thousand-dollar bills flapping their wings in V-formation over West Central Park.

"No four bedroom with views of the park, that's for sure." Francesca's eyes start to well up. "Oh, and guess who gets to be interim CFO."

"The blonde?" In unison.

"So what are we going to do about this?" asks Mac, spoiling for revenge.

"What we?"

"Franny, it's time to pull out the big guns. You remember how we bagged Alec. Gillian Castle won't even know what hit her."

"Oh goody!" squeals Lee.

"I'm thinking of something like a public humiliation of her very own… give her a taste of her own medicine…big, bold, and anonymous…maybe I fly out with Hugh, pose as a journalist from the big city…"

"Mac? You know what? I'm kinda done with playing God."

"We're not playing <u>God</u>! We're more like, um, karma conduits."

"No, honey, none of that. I need to take care of Alec."

"Well, OK, but if you change your mind, we're ready to spring into action, right Lee?"

"Just say the word!"

"Thanks, guys. For now, I better go check on my old man. Who's getting older by the minute."

Chapter 36

*S*he uses her Alzheimer's support group to share about their financial setback, for she considers these fellow sufferers to be some of the best friends she has on the Peninsula. They have heard her moan, sob and squeal with laughter. Now she cries and then she laughs or holds her head in her hands, describing the latest perplexing development. And once she is done telling her tale of woe, the Greek tragedy that stars Alec as the suicidal hero, she is done. Officially. It's as if telling the story in that circle, with all those wise, sad people, has allowed her to leave it in the circle, like the ash of a roaring campfire. She doesn't, it occurs to her, care anymore. She doesn't care if Alec never exercises another stock option. She had always wanted big things to happen to her, and they happened all right, and she really doesn't want any more big things ever again. Alec can get a job at the post office for all she cares, and she can write her little articles, and the kids can come home after school and do their chores, and tell her about their day, and then Daddy will get home before dinner, and they can cook together, and clean it up together, and take a walk and everybody can do their homework while Alec and she pay the bills in installments if that's what it comes to. She's done.

As she is leaving the meeting, arm in arm with an older gentleman who moved here from Austin to be near the kids, whose wife is catatonic, she realizes that she has a lot to be grateful for. She determines to enjoy whatever Dad's got left.

Then a thought hits her like a car crossing over the median into her lane. Her parents need to come out here. She needs to find that couple on the next street who are going on sabbatical and line up a house swap. She is the only one of the kids not working right now. She can be a support to Muth, they can have a year of temperate weather, spend time with the grandchildren, enjoy the best of what is yet to come.

For once, one of her brilliant ideas actually pans out. The Metloffs, the academic and his wife who are doing a year at Yale in the fall, have not yet found suitable housing in New Haven. They want what her parents have; a home near the campus, a car to get them around, and no pets. If they swapped, they would of course get twice the house her parents would, given the housing market in Palo Alto. But it's not about the house so much as the chance to be together before things deteriorate any further. Now to convince her parents of this idea, which was, of course, Muth's but that was when she didn't actually have to do it.

"Hi Dad."

"Who's that?"

"It's your favorite youngest daughter."

"And how is my favorite youngest daughter?"

"I'm fine. How are you?"

"I can't hear out of my left ear these days, but I am listening with the right one."

"Well that's smart of you."

"Eh?"

"I said—" he chortles, and she realizes he is pulling her leg.

"Is Muth around?"

"No, she's out. A meeting I think. Or her swim class, is it? Can't recall."

"Did she leave you a note?"

"Might have done. Let me check." He is having a good day. She can't stand the thought of him alone in the house, having a good day without Muth to notice. They are fewer and farther between.

"Here it is! She's at the dentist, just as I thought."

"OK. Do me a favor, Dad, and write on that note that I called. Do you have a pen?"

"Yes, there's one here somewhere. So how's the job?" He has forgotten that she doesn't have a job.

"It's very challenging, but you know me, I love a challenge."

"That's my girl."

"Write Muth a note that Francesca called, O.K. Dad?"

"Is that your name?" He is only joshing now, she can tell.

"Ha ha."

"Nice to talk to you!"

"Write it down, Dad!"

"Right-o. Love you."

"Love you to pieces."

Muth doesn't call back because Dad forgets to write the note. Francesca speaks to her after he has gone to bed.

"You can move in late August, and we'll all be together till the following June—?"

"I don't know about all of this, hon. We're so stuck in our ways here. I am on a million committees, plus there's the capital campaign at church…"

"Muth, Dad needs you."

"Oh, he's better than ever. I write him his instructions and he does what he's told."

"Well, I need you." There, she has finally said it. No more standing on her own two feet. She wants her Mommy. Not the *grande dame* with a gift for accents and impeccable stage presence. Not the serial committee chair. Her *mother*.

"Piffle."

"I need you, Muth. I need you here." Her eyes start to drown.

"You THINK you need me but you don't."

"No, Muth. You think I don't, but I do." Muth hesitates.

"Well in that case, we'll just have to come, won't we?"

"Not if you don't want to."

"I want my husband back, but that's out of the question. The trial didn't work. He's not getting any better." A minute ago he was better than ever. Francesca is glad she pushed.

"Just come. We'll make it nice." She doesn't sound very convincing, but she just knows this is the right thing to do. "I'll find you tons of non-profits to help."

"Don't you dare. I'm traveling incognito. I need a break."

"Sounds good to me."

And before you know it, they are rolling out the red carpet in front of the Metloffs' deluxe tissue box with the real atrium and a hot tub.

Hugh calls.

"Um, I have some news, Cess. Mac is taking a break for a while."

Francesca assumes he means from marriage, but then he goes on. "I took her to a rehab facility this morning. Early this morning. Lee helped me. We did a mini-intervention; I kind of threw it together at the last minute…"

"—Oh. I…uh…God, Hugh, I am so sorry. I wish I—I mean…" She has no idea what she means.

"Believe me, you wouldn't have wanted to be here. It was pretty ugly. But it's a very well-regarded program: four weeks inpatient, no calls home for the first week, then we can visit in two weeks… like I said, I kinda threw it together…she drove with the kids, see. Really out of it."

"Oh no." She is taking this in very slowly.

"You can email her, if you want, starting next week. I am sure she will want to hear from you…"

"So…this is about her drinking?"

"And pills."

How did she miss seeing this coming? Their life in New York as The Three Graces flashes before her. Mac throwing up outside of that dance club they used to go to in the Village, Mac and her to-go cups, Mac singing Broadway Hits at the top of her lungs on cold walks from the subway late at night, Mac's mango martoonies…

"Why didn't I see this coming, Hugh?"

"I know. I guess you just don't see what you don't want to see, but things have kind of gotten out of control around here. Let's just say all the wheels have fallen off the wagon."

"Is there anything I can do?"

"Just be there for her. Right now she's pretty pissed at me. And at Lee."

It's just as well no one invited Francesca to the intervention. She winds things up with Hugh so she can call Lee.

"I was going to tell you after your parents got settled."

"You can't just press pause, Lee. This is Mac we're talking about here."

"I know, but you've been so distracted."

"You don't have to spare me, O.K.?"

"O.K., I'm sorry."

"So, she isn't taking it too well?"

"No. She is furious with us. And since we're not supposed to contact her for another three days, I guess she's going to stay furious."

"So what do we do?" Lee is quiet. Sirens wail in the background.

"Aren't we supposed to pray?"

Francesca had forgotten about God. She does that now and again, just like she forgets about Fireball Wedding, the turtle. *Oh! I forgot I had you!* Luckily, Lee the lapsed Catholic remembered for the two of them.

"Now?" Francesca asks hesitantly.

"O.K."

Lee expects Francesca to do this because she is the one that goes to church. Francesca puts the phone under her chin and clasps her hands together.

"Lord, take care of Mac this month, and make her feel loved, and not afraid. Or if she is afraid, which I know I would be, comfort her and heal her." She tries to imagine what Father Mark would say and continues: "Keep her in the palm of your hand, oh Lord, and surround her in your heavenly grace. Have her know the abundance of your love, in Jesus' name we pray. Amen."

"Amen. Wow."

"I've never really done that before, extemporaneously, I mean."

"You made all that up on the spot?"

"Not the heavenly grace stuff. I borrowed that part."

"It was beautiful."

"Let's hope it works."

The next afternoon she finds a message from Mac on the voicemail.

"Call me on my cell!" an urgent whisper. Mac picks up on the first ring.

"I smuggled it in. We're not supposed to communicate with the outside world for 72 hours but you aren't the outside world."

"I'm right there with you, Mackey. How are you doing?"

"I'm going crazy in here. Come get me, Franny."

"I wish I could, Mackey baby. Hugh said—"

"Don't even say his name, I mean it."

"Oh, hon."

"He is a write-off. And Lee can go to Hell with him, frankly."

"Mac, You're not feel—"

"You should have heard 'em. *We have run out of options! You're a danger to yourself and others!*"

"Then they fucking send me to some nuthouse without warning my kids."

"Oh, but I know they really did want you to have a chance to—"

"Then send me to the Bahamas for Chrissake. Traitors."

"You haven't been doing too well, though, kiddo."

"Oh, so, do YOU think I should be in here?"

"Oh, Mac."

"Well, do you?"

"I know I want you to be safe. And to know you're loved. I know I wouldn't mind going somewhere where I didn't have to cook for a month..."

"So you agree with them. I'm just an old drunk." Before too much silence offsets that pronouncement, Francesca offers,

"You're not old."

"Ha. Ha. I can't talk long."

"I know. O.K." She doesn't know what to say to her best friend. This is a first.

"When I get out of here, and I will get out of here, Fran, I'm moving far away. I'm coming to California."

"You know your family needs you too much for that, babe."

"Oh don't worry, I'll bring the kids with me."

"Well, you're always welcome, but at the rate we're going, we may be back sooner than we thought. Then we can—."

"Start all over? That's what Hugh and Lee said, those sneaky bastards."

"More...um, pick up where we left off." She was actually going to say start over.

"Do me a favor?"

"Anything."

"Tell Lee I don't really think she's banging Hugh."

"She knows that."

"Because I think he's a sick closeted gay man."

"Oh, Mac."

"I'll call you soon. Gotta go." And she's gone.

Big stuff just keeps happening.

Chapter 37

*A*t Cartwheels, they are learning *De Colores*, a very well known Mexican folklore song. Well-known except by Francesca, her thirty students, and the Tuesday teaching teams. The mothers are the real pupils. She teaches as much to them as she does to the kids they share that day. Learning, let alone teaching *De Colores* is a tough assignment: there are four stanzas to memorize, and all of it in Spanish, plus a new tune to learn, but it's a challenge she feels compelled to take on. Earlier in the year, Tina Ramirez, one of the Mexican American moms at Cartwheels, asked her if she knew *De Colores*. She, of course, did not, but she realized at that moment that the last three songs they had sung in class, she had made up herself. She does a color song that goes through the colors of the rainbow in the order of the spectrum: *red, orange, yellow, green, blue and purple. Where are black and grey? They are not in the rainbow!* It loses a lot in translation. She wrote one about flying through space counting stars, to go with a Space Day theme. And then there's the birthday song which her neighbor's gardener taught her, which isn't original, nor is it of the great musical tradition of Indo-Hispanic culture, especially considering the tune for *Que los Cumplas Feliz* is *Happy Birthday to You*.

Tina brought in a songbook with *De Colores* in it, and a dad brought in a CD with it sung in English. They use the background accompaniment to stay on key and on task. At this point, a month away from the end of the school year, not one kid can sing a single line. She calls the singing teacher, Teacher Beth, at home, and asks her if she could work with the kids on *De Colores* now and again, and Beth rises to the occasion. Basically, they are doing a whole study unit on *De Colores*. Teacher Beth copies down the words on a poster board, plus sweet illustrations that prompt the kids, so even though the children can't read, they can follow along, and their mommies can too, if they are paying attention.

They are planning to sing *De Colores* on the last day of school, and since it is about colors of the rainbow, and since it is traditionally sung holding hands and swaying (per the blurb in the folkloric music book she got from Tina), they plan to gather in the play yard right before lunch, both classes plus sibs and parents, all of them wearing t-shirts in the different colors of the rainbow, and they're going to sing their song loud and long, swaying and holding hands.

While the kids form a huge blob shape holding hands on the story carpet at the end of Spanish, trying to see the illustrated board she has propped up on a bookshelf, attempting to associate those pictures with the words in Spanish, keeping time, staying in tune...while all of this is going on at Cartwheels Co-op Preschool, half a mile away, Alec literally hides under the covers. Her monthly cleaning person ("whether it needs it or not!" hoots Muth) is vacuuming right outside the locked door with strict instructions to leave their bedroom alone this month.

When she bursts through the door, she has exactly twenty-five minutes to polish an article on communicating with Alzheimer's patients before collecting Daniel from school and making them lunch and that's just the beginning. Alec is asleep. Or he is faking.

Either way, he is not fit for the civilized world yet and she will indulge him for a day or two more before he needs to suit up.

The next night, after their offspring are down for the night, Alec confesses that they have far bigger financial worries than she had realized. This takes great courage, though it should be noted he waits until she has turned out the light to tell her. He has been putting it off but has finally gathered up the nerve to let her know that on the way to fabulous wealth, Alec made the one single most idiotic move of his career. He put a huge chunk of their savings into MNS shares, and another substantial sum he loaned to his childhood friend who sank it all into a prototype for a three-wheeled, four-seater bicycle for environmentally-conscious families. That money is several prototypes away from being theirs again.

"Well, get the money out of MNS. You don't work there anymore."

"It's not that simple."

"Why? They can buy you out at the same price you paid."

"They could if they had the money, which they don't. I was going to have to raise another round right before all of this happened. With the secret ingredient out of the bag, no one will touch them now."

They are what they call in Finance 101 illiquid. Because of the current state of chaos at MNS, they are, in fact, frozen solid.

Their meager savings are keeping the wolf from the door, and for now, they can pay the rent. All around them houses are going for ten times their value (it's the land people are buying, though 'land' is an overstatement; even 'lot' is too grandiose—patch?): they could not easily find something cheaper than the tissue box anyway. And you can forget about moving back to New York.

Francesca does a thorough inventory of stuff—kids' shoes, jeans that fit right, cosmetics, and she sees that for right now, today, they have everything they need. Tomorrow too, but she is only going to worry about today. They still have their Cost Club membership for several months. She can get a lot of pasta there for cheap. In her thorough going-over, she has filled two boxes to take to Goodwill.

When you ring their doorbell, because the house is so poorly insulated, you can hear the Carltons clatter up to the door. You can practically even hear them breathing as they look through the peephole. As a safety measure, the kids came up with a rule that they have to sneak up on the front door if the bell rings unexpectedly. When it rings after school one afternoon, the three kids all race together to get it, but silently, on tiptoes, like cartoon Indians. It's Grandma Faye at the door. She enters the house beaming like Chris Kringle, with a large basket over her arm, not unlike the one Little Red Riding Hood took to her Grandma's, complete with checkered cloth. Francesca invites her in and shoos everyone out of the main room. The older two take Katharine's hands in theirs and they disappear off down the hall, looking like three little lost children in a storybook fable. Alec is napping. Faye has heard through the Cartwheels grapevine that Alec has lost his job.

She produces an envelope from her worn imitation-leather purse. She hands it to Francesca as she explains that a fund was established in her honor for her 75th birthday called the Grandma Faye Emergency Fund, to be used at the head of school's discretion for families in need. She says there is more where that came from. Francesca stares at the old-lady handwriting on the envelope as it shimmers through her tears. *Francesca and Alec.* Faye gently steers her to the couch and lowers her, gathering Francesca in her arms as she positions herself next to her. She takes her head against her abundant chest and strokes her hair while Francesca sobs.

Later in the week Francesca gets a call from the director of Adult Education for the City of Palo Alto. He offers her four classes of beginning languages: Spanish, French (two sections) and Italian. The Italian is the biggest joke, since she learned most of it in the two months they spent as chambermaids in the Dolomites in her "gap year" as Dad called the year between high school and college when all three kids either worked, traveled, or both. But if she just crams a new chapter each week, and studies vocabulary the night before her class, she is confident she can sound like a de Medici. At her Alzheimer's group, her online newsletter has morphed into a website. They had wanted her to chronicle their discussions, which are honest and meaty, but they can also be punchy and lighthearted and no she is somehow supposed to capture this on a website for other people to learn from. And hopefully others will contribute to it because with these new teaching jobs, she won't have a lot of writing time these days.

Her part-time employment qualifies her for health benefits, even dental. They get a new dentist and this time, Katharine will join them. No more teeth tickling, no more Disney films on the ceiling. The party's over.

One chilly night in early June, six days since the bottom fell out of their lives, she has tucked her last kid in, and they have all shouted goodnight to Alec, who is in a fetal position in their bed. These days, Daniel winds up his prayers with a newly extended closing request:

"And please get Daddy his job back because all he does is lie there." The doorbell rings. She flicks off Daniel's light, cracks her knee on his dresser drawer as she hurries to turn on his night light—she has done this in the wrong order again—and heads for the front door. It is Troy, looking more than ever like a balding mad scientist. He is wild-eyed and breathless.

"Is Alec home?"

"Hello Troy."

"Hi. Is he...?"

"Um, he is kind of busy right now..." Troy pushes past her and heads for the couch, where he lands with a wheeze. She scurries to the back bedroom to see if Alec is still alive.

"It's Troy."

"What does he want?"

"You."

"Why?"

"Ask <u>him</u>. I don't seem to make an impression." Alec sighs dramatically and throws off the quilt. He is dressed in sweat pants and his Wharton t-shirt. He looks like a big baby, scuffing out of the room in his socks with his baggy butt and pillow hair. She decides to stay right where she is, contemplating crawling into the warm spot Alec has left behind. Libby calls from her bed.

"Who is it, Mom?"

"Daddy's colleague from work," she whisper-yells back.

From Daniel's room she hears, "Daddy doesn't have a work!"

"Shhhh!"

Silence. She closes the bedroom door, which muffles the conversation in the living room, but she can tell from Troy's animated voice that there is real news. Her curiosity gets the better of her and she brings a book out to the couch, as if this were the only place she can go to read. The men ignore her completely.

The way he is pacing around the table, Troy looks like he needs the bathroom, and Alec looks like a kid watching cartoons, mouth agape. It seems the 'secret formula' that made it into the public domain is not actually the REAL secret formula at all. But only Troy knows this. When Troy joined the firm, a year or so before Alec, he came with certain proprietary information that qualified him for a higher percentage of the takings if that strand of research played out successfully. He stood to make a tidy percentage of the profits, that is until the Vice President of Research & Development was hired, a job Troy had managed in the early days before they ramped up. His new boss came along with his own research agenda, Troy's molecules were shelved in favor of his boss' and the resulting polymer is what got leaked to the business press.

"You know I didn't leak it, don't you?" Alec's blue eyes get a little bluer, and a little moister.

"Of course you didn't." Troy doesn't even look up from his notes.

"Hey, that's right!" his eyes shining happily now, "You were the one who told me not to call it Miracle-Gro, remember? When we were talking in the hall after the meeting with Randy?"

"Makes it sound like it works, which it won't. Or at least there are still too many unknowns. My molecular structure is proven. And tested in a simulated environment the closest ever to a living organism." He goes on to explain how he has been embedding his precious polymer in beef roasts and putting them in the oven on the lowest setting.

They sit at that table for four more hours. She feeds them dinner, sodas, coffee and snickerdoodles left over from Grandma Faye's basket. She goes to bed. She gets up at 1:00 in the morning to go to the bathroom, and they are still there. When she wakes up at 3:24, for no apparent reason, she is still alone in bed. When she gets up with the kids at 6:30, Alec is passed out on the couch in his underwear with papers and spreadsheets all around him, as on a park bench, but at least there's a pulse. He doesn't even stir amidst the family rituals of cereal munching, homework hunting and dawdling before the shouting and slams.

Alec sleeps through it all. Meanwhile in New York, Luxemburg and Tokyo, his associates, former colleagues and drinking buddies assemble three million dollars worth of capital for Troy and Alec to use to launch Lemur Industries when Alec finally wakes up after lunch.

Chapter 38

N ow that Alec has found his voice and seems to be more or less able to function again, despite the fact that he has no office, no back up, not even a business card, it is time they had a little chat.

"Jiggy?"

"Yes?" It's dark and late. This is when they communicate most clearly—when they can't see each other.

"You know, you would have to do a lot worse than get shafted by a vengeful colleague for me to lose faith in you. You know that, don't you?"

"I could still lose it all. We're trying something pretty radical here."

"I know that." She doesn't really know anything anymore, but she does know that she loves this man who nearly lost his mind when they were going under.

"All I wanted was to get you that apartment with a view of the park, Pash. I couldn't face you after what happened."

"It's when you needed me most, though."

"You're right."

"And we're still not out of the woods."

"That's for sure."

"I don't want an apartment overlooking Central Park if it means losing you again, Jig. We need you too much, and I don't mean as the breadwinner either. We need you here to complete us."

"Well why didn't you say so sooner?"

"Seeing you balled up in bed all those days in a row made me realize how much I need you."

"I just want to make you happy."

"You make me happy when you look my way. The rest is cream."

"Do I make you happy when I do this?" He leans over and kisses her like Henry Fonda kissed Barbara Stanwyck in *The Lady Eve.*

Kat may not have got her lemur, not even a stuffed one, but Alec has given them Lemur Industries and that is at least something. Hopefully, it will pay for three sets of college fees without too many loans attached, and if Kat goes the zoology route, she might get to have her lemur that way. By then, she won't want a lemur anymore, of course. Francesca will probably still want things for her that she no longer wants. Just like the apartment in New York was really all about wanting what everyone else had, just like Kat's talking lemur, and Alec's pot of gold at the end of the initial public offering, these are all cheap substitutes for the big jackpot, which is being together with the sun on their faces and the wind at their backs. With one arm slung over Alec's hip, she drifts off to sleep as he explains the Lemur business plan one more time.

❧ ❧ ❧

She wakes up with that thrilled feeling you get when something great is going to happen but you are not yet awake enough to remember what. Today they actually take possession of *Senior Life*, a move that should quadruple the subscriber base of *Mindful*, the website that ate Al Zeimer. Alec arranged the deal. After eight years of chronicling the highs and lows of dementia and the attendant scientific advances as described by researchers and medical professionals around the world, Francesca insisted that the only way she was going to grow their circulation any more was with zero additional expenditure of energy. After all, she has two teenagers and worse still, one preteen who demand a lot of her attention. This has left her with really only one option: mergers and acquisitions. She prefers acquisitions because publishing is a cash-intensive business and this allows her to plow her earnings back into the enterprise. The advertisers are getting a great deal until she works out new rates, because even though Mindful has only been getting a few thousand hits a week, that will change significantly with the acquisition of *Senior Life*.

She is truly an editor-in-chief now, as most of the articles she prints have originated in the field. She has a top-drawer list of celebrity Alzheimer's sufferers on her board of contributors, though more often, their spouses and loved ones. She doesn't name-drop, but let's just say if a first name jumps out at you, your first guess is probably right. She publishes testimonials at every stage of the Alzheimer's journey: first-hand, heartbreaking accounts of intelligent, successful people losing their marbles. No one ever gets better in these stories. There is really only one ending, but they don't write about the endings, they write about the journey. Her contributors often find humor in the rubble, and those are the stories she likes best. There's the man who thinks he is courting his wife of 54 years; he acts like a bashful schoolboy around her. One afflicted wife thinks she lives in a castle in Yugoslavia. Another man watches westerns all day and night, because he grew up in the back lots of the moving picture industry, when Los Angeles was still the desert. His father kept horses that were used in the early westerns and he and his brother were in charge of exercising and stabling. He just can't remember what happened five minutes ago.

Muth describes a recent dinner conversation with Dad at their table for two in the opulent dining room of *Mayfield Gardens: Aging with Dignity*. (*And a great deal of assistance.*) It is still a fairly new facility—Muth and Dad are in the Founders Club and have an engraved nameplate on the door of their deluxe 450 square foot dwelling indicating as much. It costs nearly ten thousand dollars a month for the privilege of aging with dignity the Mayfield way, but they both have long-term care insurance, so it's practically free. Dad sits companionably on the two-seater with her (they gave Francesca their three-seater, which she gladly accepted), half-listening, half wondering what Francesca is doing there, and where she came from (she lives two miles away, but it might as well be on Mars). Muth recounts him asking her, not for the first time, what his three kids do for a living. She doggedly went through the role call, trotting out a well-rehearsed litany of jobs and titles. She closed with "so does that answer your question?" to which he answered,

"I don't remember. What was my question?"

"You asked me what our kids did."

"Oh? And what do they do?" When she reaches the punch line, she is shrieking with delight. Dad looks bemused.

"Don't worry," gasps Muth. "We're laughing with you, not at you!"

"But I'm not laughing," he responds, bemused. This sets her off again. If this is aging with dignity, you'd hate to see the alternative.

Dad still loves his walks, though now he needs a chaperone, and Muth is not strong enough. After Kat leaves for school, Francesca takes him for a walk along the baylands, across the highway from their house. She hooks arms with him, and steers him out of the parking lot onto the weathered boardwalk that winds through the marshlands along the San Francisco Bay. The salt air blowing off the water carries an exotic perfume of rotting organic matter and the stench off the city dump, which today is downwind from them. They can see what looks like a toy bulldozer from this distance, bumping up the mountain of stinky garbage, barely affecting the profile of their fair city's monument to waste.

"We take the kids out here on our bikes sometimes."

It doesn't smell like this, though. She gives Dad's arm a squeeze, wishing away the foul odor.

"How are the children?"

"Oh, they're just great."

"They enjoying school?"

"Very much. Daniel will be in high school next year, and Elizabeth goes off to college in the fall. Kat is in her last year of elementary school." She uses their names liberally.

"That's wonderful. And what are you doing these days to keep yourself occupied?" Another stock question, but he always really wants to know the answer.

"I publish a magazine."

"That's sounds very interesting. What sort of magazine?"

"It's a family magazine." A big, sloppy, loving family. A family that loves so fiercely, and cares so much, and verges most of the time on a state of total collapse.

"I don't know a thing about publishing magazines."

"Neither did I, but I figured it out."

"That's my girl."

She realizes she is walking too fast. Dad is skittering to keep up, the way she used to do on their Sunday family walks, when one of his strides took three of hers. He always kept his hands clasped behind his back, his fingers wiggling invitingly for any little hand that wanted to catch hold. Now he clasps his hands together across his middle, seatbelt style, pinning her arm against his ribcage.

"When were you last in Brussels?" Here it comes.

"Let's see, I was there in my gap year. I saw Jean-Pierre and Annette, and they drove me all around. We even drove past Avenue de la Tenderie..."

"Avenue de la Tenderie..."

"Where we lived when I was five. When you were working for Monsieur Blaton. Remember him?"

"Vaguely. When you were five?"

"Yes. You had a job there for a year. Then we came home."

They walk on.

"It's amazing how one single day can change everything. How ones whole life can change in just one day. Extraordinary."

"You mean the day the Germans came."

"I went to bed, and woke up to the news that we had to be out within the hour!"

"France fell, too, didn't it?"

"Yes. May 10. We ended up on a destroyer to Dover. Of course you were only small." He means his sister. She tries something new this time.

"I was very scared. But you made me feel safe. You took very good care of me."

"It was a scary time for all of us. Even Daddy wasn't himself."

"You are a very dear big brother. And a wonderful father and grandfather, too."

"We left everything behind. I honestly thought we'd never be back."

"And you did make it back. Right after college, your first job was in Brussels. And of course you met Muth in Brussels."

"Did I? I'd forgotten. That's old age for you!"

He is on what Muth refers to as the treadmill.

"When were you last in Brussels?" It will be Brussels all afternoon if she plays along.

"Oh, it's been a while." An egret flaps across the periphery. It lands gracelessly on a patch of island in the center of a shallow pond.

"Look at the egret, Dad!" she whispers, as if he were a preschooler. The egret strikes a dramatic hunting pose; it is stock still, waiting for the tiny movements of a snack. Dad and she stop. The wind has changed directions and she smells nothing but fish and mud. They watch the busy pond life for a while, pointing out different birds, a fish that comes up for a bug, and three ducks, impersonating decoys.

Muth is home resting. Ever since she was diagnosed with bone marrow cancer six months ago (*Dear Kids, Slight technical hitch…*), she has opted out of more and more activities, while Dad, oblivious to her diagnosis from one moment to the next, gamely comes out with Francesca whenever she invites him. At several predictable intervals, he'll ask oh-so-casually where "the better half" is. She imagines herself one day saying *she's not coming back*, or worse still, *you'll see her later* when she actually means *in Heaven*.

This is chemo week, which Muth takes orally, in the comfort of their "box of walls" as she describes their diminutive new home. Her blood levels look promising, and she has no discernible pain, apart from the familiar aches of arthritis. They say with multiple myeloma, the pain at the end can be intense: after all, with over 200 bones in the human body, that's a lot of marrow. But they prescribe pain patches, and then when things get really unbearable, she'll have a morphine drip.

"I've always wondered what it would be like to be a drug addict!" Muth declares.

When she is not resting, Muth confines her volunteer activities to her immediate surroundings, organizing a weekly bridge game for Mayfield residents who are on average over 90 and on average, totally senile. She bids for every player, and plays their cards, and they have a lovely time. Muth also runs the chair-aerobics class. She leads the movements, shouts encouragement, sings, you name it. It is the most popular sport at Mayfield Gardens. She keeps joking with the general manager of the place that she should be on his payroll. She certainly has a knack for bringing out the best in people who are on a steady decline. One evening, Alice, a new resident, someone who had been brought there against her wishes but who needs a lot of assistance, threw a tantrum at bedtime, insisting that she go home. A big, burly caregiver stepped in and offered to take her down the hall. Muth saw the panic in the old lady's eyes as this great hulking stranger started to approach her. Muth had to act fast, so she ran ahead of him, hooked arms with Alice and steered her to her own front door.

"We're going to have some hot milk before bed!" she announced. "Please tell Nina to come find Alice at my place."

Meanwhile, Dad has no recollection that his wife has cancer. Every time it comes up, you see the shock in his eyes. Francesca can't bear to see him confronting that reality as if for the first time, over and over, so she tries not to mention it. But she has to admit, in other ways, Dad makes a great confessor. She can tell him anything at all, and in the moment, he follows her perfectly, reacts appropriately, offers his advice, and then promptly forgets the entire conversation.

"Dad, I have a little problem."

"What's that?"

"I think I'm attracted to Daniel's rock climbing coach."

"Oh?"

"He's about twenty years younger, and very good looking, and extremely fit." Alec has a little paunch from all the lunches out, a job requirement. She still finds him incredibly attractive, but mostly from behind. The old guy at the climbing gym (30 is very old there) stepped out of a Ralph Lauren ad, with his ripped polo shirt and bike shorts. Her mouth waters when she sees him. She has never experienced anything like it. Maybe she's just perimeno-pausal. It's very disconcerting, but then again, she doesn't seem to mind the discomfort. She stops short of describing the guy's profile when he is wearing the climbing harness because that would be taking advantage of an old man.

"When I drop Daniel off at the gym, I get all weak at the knees and I completely lose my composure. Plus, I think he actually likes me."

"Sounds like you need a new coach."

"You think?"

"Well, you certainly don't need a new husband, my dear. And the children are probably very satisfied with your current arrangement."

"It's just that—"

"If I were you, I would take up a new hobby." It is amazing to her how much of one conversation he will retain, before the erase function takes over. Other times, he just spouts the usual banalities and she isn't sure if he is following anything.

Such is life! he'll say, or *No rest for the wicked!*

Elspeth, née Elizabeth and known by many as several other derivative names, including Ellie, is draped over the couch in the front room when Francesca returns from the press conference announcing the acquisition. Having got into Sarah Lawrence early decision, their firstborn has been able to coast a little bit this spring. While Ellie unwinds, Francesca winds up, grabbing hold of the weeks until they will put her baby on a plane and send her across the country for her college experience. Thank God Hugh is still in New York, so Ellie has somewhere to go for Thanksgiving. In all her free time, Ellie has been adding to her clothing label, Miss Fit, with all kinds of interesting apparel. It is not obvious where the limbs belong in her creations but hey, Francesca doesn't have to wear them. She couldn't wear them, in point of fact. They are designed for young ladies with no body fat, like Ellie. Strategically placed cut outs, with or without mesh, give away too much information about the person under the surface.

Ellie teases Daniel about coming to high school in the fall, how she has set the bar pretty high for him with her B+ average. They all laugh because Daniel has been taking high school courses for two years now. This year he is taking chemistry, physics and pre-calculus. He still prefers home to school, but the toys have changed. He does a brisk dog-walking business for people who work outside of the home, and has saved up enough for a high-grade amplifier. Daniel hopes to be a bass player in a rock band next year, and every year after that if possible.

For her final social studies project of the fifth grade year, Katharine has had to choose and present a personal hero. All spring, she has been working on a multimedia production about Bonpapa. She is producing a video with an original musical soundtrack performed by her brother's band (that way, there are no copyright infringements; she thinks of everything, which will make her a great writer/director/producer one day). She has also put together a short book, complete with original source materials scanned in, which she is having printed and bound. She has been spending hours at the Media Center editing the 'rushes' of long interviews with Bonpapa. She has action footage of him doing his puzzles, playing fetch with Navy, the 'house dog' at Mayfield Gardens, and playing table tennis with Francesca.

He may be completely unmoored from life as he once knew it, but when Dad is playing table tennis, you would never know he was in his ninth year of Alzheimer's. He is still very light on his feet and can get most shots she sends his way. He keeps score perfectly, even knowing when to switch servers. He congratulates her on good shots, and moans at near misses, and at the end of every game he says,

"I think we have time for one more, don't you?"

In their table tennis match yesterday, he took her 21-17, 21-19 and 21-14 (she was losing heart here) before she beat him 21-18. They play in the carpeted, wallpapered multipurpose room, decorated in the style of New Orleans Bordello, according to Muth. After the match, they moved all the Louis Quinze reproduction chairs back in their rows in time for the special screening tonight of *My Hero*, by Katharine Carlton. They have reserved the big table in the dining room for all of them beforehand, but first, they must get all dolled up in gowns and boas for the world premiere.

When they pull up to Mayfield Gardens, the place is lit up like the Queen Mary II. No matter what time of day or night, *the stationary cruise ship with one final port of call* (Muth again) is always blazing with light. This is for the Sundowners, people in advanced stages of dementia who get nervous when it gets dark, and whose whopping monthly fees amply cover the electricity bills. The Sundowners mostly live on the third floor, in the Alzheimer's Wing, where Dad will go next, if Muth 'goes' first. But frankly, there are plenty of people who don't live on the third floor who are glad for the light. In fact, of all the residents at Mayfield Gardens, Muth seems to be the only one who has all her faculties. Fortunately, she is willing to share.

During dinner, they can't help but overhear snippets of loopy conversations at nearby tables.

"You know why they call women broads?" yells Eddie, who is seated with three little old ladies at a linen-swaddled table for four.

"Why?" queries Gloria, his dinner companion.

"Because their hips are broad so they can carry babies. Broad as compared to men, I mean."

"Oh."

Roberta pipes up.

"I bet I'm older than you."

"I'm 87," volunteers Eddie.

"I'm 96."

"That's old."

At another table, an older gentleman has taken out his wallet. You see this a lot. Bonpapa often asks if they have settled the bill when they start to get up from a meal there. The old man fishes in his wallet and pulls out a card. He asks no one in particular what year it is.

"2007," answers a caregiver, another new one, in passing.

"Good. I can still drive for two more years." Twenty minutes later, he goes through the whole procedure again. And then a third time.

They are all in a festive mood. For Francesca, it's partly due to the fact that at this point, they figure Dad must have been in Dr. Gentry's test group because he is definitely holding his own. He has very little anxiety, no hostility, and for now, anyway, he hasn't started making passes at any of the female caregivers.

Alec makes a toast at dinner:

"To Katharine, our baby. You have been very busy this semester. I think I've seen you more on your bike than off it these days!!" Everyone laughs, including Bonpapa. "And it's paying off with lots of great hands-on experience for a future career in film. Plus, I think you'd agree that it's given you a chance to get to know your grandfather better. He certainly has interesting stories to tell."

"We love you!" yells Ellie.

They all raise their glasses, and Bonpapa says,

"Hear, hear!" and his grandchildren chime in, but for all he knows, they're toasting the Queen.

Upstairs, they sit in the two rows of chairs in front of the large-screen TV. Kat fades the lights and the soundtrack swells.

Francesca looks over at Dad, to make sure he can see, and that he's paying attention, but Kat hisses,

"Mom, watch!"

She nearly misses the title, *My Mom is My Hero*. She catches Kat's glance, even in the semi-darkness.

"Me?!" She whispers.

"Shh," answers Kat sternly.

Francesca sits back and takes in a slide show like none other. Accompanied by Daniel's acoustic guitar, black and white stills of her as a baby flash by. Here she is in color, standing with Pat and Henry in front of various family backdrops; Christmas trees, a new car, the Dodge Dart, their bicycles...all the way through to her in high school, playing soccer, pictures of her with all the family when they were taking their last family trips. There are even a couple of shots of her with Mac and Lee. In all of the pictures, she is smiling like a drunken fool. Next, video clips of her bringing in glowing birthday cakes, her pulling kids out of swimming lanes at the end of a race...her washing the car with all three kids helping...her at the pancake supper at church wearing a feather headdress and a matching feather mask announcing the raffle winners...all these stolen moments of her...what would you call it? Impersonating a mom? No, she thinks this video proves once and for all that she is the real thing. Of course she is also a daughter, a wife, and a friend, but she thinks the footage Kat has so lovingly edited makes a pretty strong case for her growing commitment to motherhood.

Kat never knew Francesca when she worked 'out of the home' as the captains of cottage industry describe it. To Kat, she is the mom who was always there when she got back from pretty much anywhere. She sat with her when she had her snack, and they would "work" together in the dining room/cum living room/cum world headquarters of *Mindful*. There she is, playing table tennis with Dad. Kat fooled her into thinking this was all about him! And now Dad in his wing-back chair is talking to the camera.

"She was a very energetic little person. She would run around in her...her...um...her...uh..."

"Trundle bundle!" yells Muth, off-camera. A trundle bundle is what they used to call a zip-up sleeping bag with arms. One of her earliest memories is going down the stairs with her feet tucked in the corners,

"...like the Gingerbread Man!" hoots Dad.

"I recall us getting word in the middle of our lessons, that this little object had appeared! We went straight from school to the hospital!" Now he's talking about his sister Sheila. He chuckles as Kat cuts to Muth.

"Francesca has shown me how to be a better mother." She pauses for dramatic effect. "A little late!" she barks. Then she adds as an afterthought, "I wish I could have met her sooner."

Lee is a voiceover that Kat recorded off their voicemail box. The visuals are a weeping willow beside a running stream—it may be at the ranch where she and her new husband settled a few years ago—these days you can send video over the Internet.

"Kat, honey, it's Auntie Lee. It sounds like a charming idea. There is only one problem. Franny can't be your hero because she is <u>my</u> hero. But I guess I will have to share."

Her daughter snuck around town, interviewing people from Cartwheels, from school and church, all behind her back and she has edited these sound bytes into one long paean to motherhood. Grandma Faye says,

"She knew how to build loving community. It's nothing we taught her. In fact, she taught all of us."

She hears her sister Pat next.

"The thing about Francesca is no matter how much you want to envy her, you can't, because she is too darn generous. Always has been. OK, maybe not always. I remember wanting to borrow her typewriter in high school—she had bought one with her own money—but she informed me that I might curse it. She said *this typewriter is meant for great things.* And she was right. She has done great things with her life." Francesca honestly doesn't remember saying that, but she would have only been in eighth grade at the time. Sounds a lot like Ellie.

Finally, a silhouette of Alec against a brick wall reads a poem that starts by saying how he literally staggered when he saw her, and goes on about her shapely legs and long hair (she wore it up 98% of the time) but he saves the best for last:

Oh sure, you're still stunning, bewitching and gorgeous,
But I love your get-up-and-go.
And how you are raising our kids reinforces
What drew me to you long ago:

A principled, passionate, pincher of pennies,
You're whimsical, wacky and wild.

You operate out of a deep empathy
In how you relate to each child.

No matter how storm-tossed we've been in this ocean
Of love, we have held our position.
Your steady gaze fixed on that distant horizon
Has seen us through every condition.
With you by my side, I can conquer the planet
That's easy, with you in my life
As long as you're near me, and helping me plan it
My one inspiration, my wife.

Swelling strings in the background. All for her.

Kat, at last. In her bedroom, the camera on a tripod. No soundtrack. You can hear her wall clock ticking.

"This is my tribute to you, Mom. It is a collage of all the things about you that make you my hero. When you're not driving us kids around, you're helping out at school, or church, or you're visiting Gummy and Bonpapa, or you're publishing your magazine. You use car rides to stay up to date, you help out whenever it's needed, which is all the time. You take care of your parents because they took care of you. And everyone who reads your magazine knows how much you care about their situation. But mostly, I just like having you around. You make me feel special. You're special. You're my hero."

The film ends with a long shot of seventy-five or more kids in t-shirts in all the colors of the rainbow, standing on the grassy knoll outside the big classroom at Cartwheels holding hands, swaying all in the same direction, and singing *De Colores*. She had asked Kat to film them this year, because they keep forgetting to, and it is such a festive tradition. Kat never did show it to her. There is

Francesca in the center of the circle, standing on a step stool waving her arms and singing lustily. Fade to white. The credits roll. Kat's name appears in every category, except for the people who played themselves.

I'm a hero!

"How did you track down Mac?" She asks Kat late that night, after everyone has gone to bed and they are alone, in the dark, having a last de-brief.

"Easy. I can tell when you are talking to her and once I grabbed your cell phone and took down the number you had just been speaking to. When I reached her, I vowed I wouldn't reveal her whereabouts. But how did you know we were in touch?"

"That poem from Daddy. He didn't write that. There's only one person who could have."

"Not a tall," says Mac when Francesca thanks her for her husband's love poem. Mac is quite well known these days, if a total recluse. Her musical, *Hats Off*, is a household word. That's uncommon for original shows. Most times the retreads make it big. But if you think about it, Mac is a kind of retread, in the sense that she has a lot of miles under her, but the road hasn't always been smooth, so she needed to rig up a tougher outer layer. After several relapses, which she likes to call "little slips," one divorce and a near miss with a much younger performance artist, she has finally settled down at a Zen monastery where they keep a watchful eye on their craziest houseguest.

"How much of that stuff did he actually tell you to include?" Francesca asks, suspiciously.

"Oh, how you met and how beautiful you are, etcetera, etcetera, etcetera." What that says to Francesca is she just got a love poem from her best friend. Her other best friend is on her ranch in Montana, where ten acres will cost you about a month's residuals on a bestselling romance series. Her husband of a few years used to ride a white horse around their property, taking the analogy of Prince Charming to absurd levels. But what do you expect from a shrink? Or former shrink. He closed his practice down before they got married. He wanted everything to be legit. Now he writes motivational books and lectures around the country. Lee is no longer married to him though, because she gradually discovered he didn't want to marry her, he wanted to brand her. They say not to marry your shrink for a reason. She is dating a real cowboy now, who knows how to treat a lady.

Her *other* best friend leans back in his swivel chair and asks her to drop whatever she is doing and come play tennis with him. He is in between projects right now, and that makes him antsy. After MNS collapsed, Lemur Industries limped along for a while until Troy sold his secret recipe to a Swedish biotech conglomerate and Alec began consulting start-ups in second-round financing phases. He has had to turn down work, so in demand is he, but the work is closer to home, and a lot of what he does he can do from their home office, and that gives Francesca a lot of flexibility. The kids love having him around, too. They wouldn't trade the current arrangement for anything.

FIN

For more information about the author and her published work,
visit joanbigwood.wordpress.com

26274787R00195

Made in the USA
Charleston, SC
31 January 2014